THE WATERING PLACE OF
GOOD PEACE

GEOFFREY JENKINS was born in Port Elizabeth, South Africa and educated in the Transvaal, where he wrote his first book – a local history – at the age of seventeen. After leaving school he worked as a sub-editor in Rhodesia, later becoming a newspaperman in both Britain and South Africa.

His first novel, *A Twist of Sand*, was published in 1959 and immediately became a bestseller; it was later filmed. Since then he has written eight more successful novels which sold over five million copies in twenty-three different languages.

Geoffrey Jenkins and his wife Eve Palmer – also an author – live near Pretoria.

GEOFFREY JENKINS

The Watering Place of Good Peace

FONTANA/Collins

First published in 1960 by William Collins Sons & Co Ltd
First published in this revised edition in Fontana Books 1974
Sixth Impression November 1980

© Geoffrey Jenkins, 1960 and 1974

Made and printed in Great Britain by
William Collins Sons & Co Ltd, Glasgow

AUTHOR'S FOREWORD

The publication of *The Watering Place of Good Peace* in Fontana coincides with the installation this year at a South African resort of the world's first effective electrical anti-shark barrier. The apparatus, which comprises a 600-metre long cable weighing fourteen tons, represents the culmination of fifteen years of experimentation by the Shark Research Group of the Council for Scientific and Industr al Research. My novel originally appeared when these experiments were in their infancy, but the basic principles which I described then remain valid today.

Pretoria, 1974

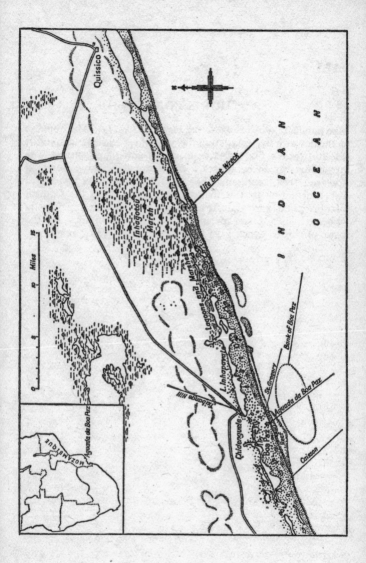

PART ONE

SOUTH AND EAST AFRICA
1960

I willed him to his death over the positive electrode.

But he was reluctant to die, or just plain stupid. He moved away, staring at me. His eyes remained calm, empty almost of all thought, as he watched my calculated attempts to send him to a writhing, twisting death. He turned away slightly as if to avoid the compulsion in my eyes, but suddenly swivelled round and came across within a few inches of my face. I could see the drops of moisture on the ends of his moustache and the slight flicker of a pulse at his throat. His skin was murky and blotched but he showed no signs at all that he was being affected. We gazed at one another in detached hatred.

Move across three feet to that copper electrode! I pressurized him. Move over!

As if to oblige, he did move a little towards it. Then he stopped and his face came close to mine again. If I could smell his breath, it would stink, I thought.

My glance went down to the copper cable strung across the floor. There were the two electrodes, copper-pink in the diffused light like a woman's nipples. Just touch them! I murmured. Just touch them! You don't know which is positive and which is negative, but I do.

All he did was to tilt his head slightly down. He moved away again – a foot farther away from death. I could feel the muscles and nerves in my shoulders as I tried to will him back.

I turned away to step up the current and found that my hands were sweaty. With them like that I could very well electrocute myself and leave my victim unscathed. I had gradated the power regulating switch from zero amperes in tens upwards, but he didn't seem to feel it. I'd pulled down the heavy venetian blinds to keep out the late glare of the afternoon sun, and since they'd all gone and only the security guard remained at the high fence, the place was quiet except for the hum of current.

500! I stabbed the switch over. For a moment I had taken my eyes off him. Hurriedly I swung round and nearly fell off the high stool in my eagerness to see the way he died. The oscilloscope screen flickered a new pattern in the half-dark as the current pulse leapt. 500 amps! He moved uneasily and again I turned to stare at his eyes. You must die! I told him, but with misgiving now. You fool, I reminded myself, getting a grip of my tensed nerves. He can't hear you anyway behind that transparent screen.

You don't speak English, you bastard, I said to myself. But electricity knows no language and I'm going to kill you. Move over, damn you, and show me I am right!

I thought I had him.

He had moved over until he was only six inches away. But from the negative electrode. You won't find release in that one, I chided him. That one hurts. It is sharp and stabbing: the current pulls your guts in like a birth-contraction. Try the positive! It's soothing and easy, a warm nipple of death.

But he stayed, within six inches of death, and gazed at me with calm, unperturbed, almost lidless eyes.

Another ten amps? How much longer could I stand the strain? The room was hot with the heat of late summer and I was sweating from tension and from everything that I had stored up and kept in check all these years. You can't live as *I* have had to live without it tearing you to pieces.

Ten amps! The hell! I said to myself. I'll make it a hundred at a time and then I'll at least know between what ranges it will destroy a victim of the same weight and size. Size and mass were vital. It wasn't just a case of finding a victim.

I think my hand acted in advance of my reasoning. I jerked the switch up another 100 amps. The oscilloscope reflected a new pattern of light, brighter now, for the room was darker and the eighteen-inch screen looked unnaturally bright. Its reflection gave the only light through the thick screen and the electrodes had become duller, more coppery. It's not an easy thing to kill, I told myself, aware of my shaky hands. I thrust a cigarette between my lips and lit it unsteadily. He moved away from the lighted match as if he were afraid I would torture him with it.

The extra 100 amps had done nothing to him, despite what the dancing pulses on the oscilloscope screen read. It was incredible that it was not enough – not enough even to produce some sort of reaction. He can't get away from me, I thought grimly. Not bottled up in a cage ten feet by eight by six. But he had some sort of immunity to electrical shocks which I had left out of my calculations. My finger strayed to the switch again. I'd give him the whole 3,000 which the special electronic machinery was capable of delivering. That would end him! Then, impatient at my own impatience, I thrust the thought away. It must be *how* he died, as well as *if*. If? Perhaps it was because my whole nervous system was shot to hell with the strain that everything that had gone before suddenly came looming over me like a tidal wave. I felt a surge of nausea.

I decided to give the business of killing a rest for a moment and collect myself.

I switched off the current from the condensers where it discharged into the electrodes. I had made my own electronic equipment with killing in view. I had taken the current from the mains, stepped it up, rectified it, and fed it into the condensers. It was the discharge from them that was to deal the lethal blow. As I flicked the switch, the bright oscilloscope pattern fell away. I was alone in the big laboratory, alone with my victim, who now crouched away in the corner almost out of my sight.

I stumbled over to the venetian blind and pulled up the slats. The laboratory seemed to have soaked up all the day's heat. Deliberately, I tried to draw some comfort and mental balance from the everyday scene outside. Away to my right they had already put on the red lights on the radio mast to warn low-flying aircraft. I opened the window to let the cooling air in, and felt once more the soothing benison of a Transvaal Highveld sunset, an exhilarating freshness after a day of stifling heat. As a Northern European, I have always felt this more than most.

I looked out: in this quiet, beautiful setting on the eastern outskirts of Pretoria among thorn-tree-clad hills, was the headquarters of the Council for Scientific and Industrial Research – millions of pounds' worth of laboratory buildings into which was packed all the top scientific knowledge and equipment in South Africa.

I sucked in the cigarette smoke, revelling in the peace of the laboratory setting; I could see the sidelights of cars as late office-workers went home to the suburb which adjoins the site. Gradually, as I stood there, my jumping nerves began to calm.

I lit another cigarette. For a few moments I was safe, the tension was behind me. Some last rays of sun were licking at the stately Union Buildings, turning them a lovely rose. You never saw those colours in the Hebrides, I thought, nor the hard blue of the South African sky. In those high latitude Northern islands the sky always seems washed out: above Stornoway the trees – the only ones in the Outer Hebrides, I think – cling with a fierce will for life to the desolate hillsides. The Hebrides had never meant anything in my life, I decided, thinking back to that grey little town among the grey, icy seas of 58 degrees north.

'Black mud,' my grandmother had said there once, in her soft, stylised English, all shot through with Gaelic twists like the fleck in Harris tweed. 'Black mud.' Uttered like that, it was an evil incantation. The words fitted her: I never saw her in anything but black. She had stabbed a finger at the trawlers going out past the breakwater into the Minch for the night's catch.

'Black mud and the sea. That's the curse that's on the Ogilvies. Your name is the same as his – Ian. Ian Ogilvie!' The frail old body shook with hatred. 'He's been dead over a hundred years, but I still say I hope he rots!' She stared at me with the unwavering malice of the aged. 'No one ever dared after him to call an Ogilvie by the name Ian until you came along. And you'll go away one day like he did. Black mud!'

Damn the old harridan, railing against something which was as crazy as she was. Black mud! What the hell did it mean anyway? When she said it, it made little impression except that I thought her even madder than before. But over the years the puzzle had gnawed at me, especially in the long months I had lain at death's door. I remember screaming the same senseless words when they brought me out of the water, over and over, into a long repetitive keen, although my reason told me there was no mud – certainly not in five fathoms. They told me there was no mud on me, but I couldn't help myself. I just went on screaming the words until oblivion overtook me.

Why should the damned thing suddenly crop up again at this juncture, just when I needed all my powers of concentration? It was still quite clear in my mind, fresh as the washed out day on which she said it. I found myself fumbling for another cigarette. I'd also stripped my tie off: it made it cooler against the heat. My mouth suddenly felt as dry as ashes. Raw brandy was what I really needed.

I stayed, balancing myself at the window. It was a long while later when I turned away and by now it was quite dark outside.

I drew the venetian blind tight and switched on a small light above the bench. My victim seemed to be exactly where I had left him.

The big fish in the transparent Perspex tank was not just a fish to me. He symbolized the secret I had lived with for so long. He was the focus of all the years of stored-up hatred which had made me what I was. His death would be an expiation – to some extent – of all that, but it would only be the first of many killings. Perhaps in some mysterious way it would also expiate black mud – whatever that might mean. My hands were steady now. To keep them so I decided to go over each connection, each piece of electrical gear which I had pieced together painstakingly into this strange electronic machine. I wondered what the Director would say if he saw this collection of state material to which I had not the slightest right.

I checked the leads where they entered the tank at the bottom. They seemed fine. I obviously couldn't do more with the copper wire and electrodes which I had strung across the inch of mud at the bottom of the tank. He was a mudfish, or barbel, and he had to have his mud. Black mud! I cursed softly and dismissed my grandmother's phrase with the voice of reason. It was brown mud, anyway, which I'd brought from a little dam nearby.

I check-snapped the gradated switch. My kill-lust had returned. I can't think of you impersonally, I told the fish. You've got to die so that I can see how others like you will die.

I checked minutely through every other piece of equipment. Nothing must be left to chance.

This is it, I finally told myself. I straddled the high stool awkwardly, knocking against the wooden bench. The current pulses would be one millisecond long and they would snake from electrode to electrode at a repetition rate of five a second. I'd start where I left off earlier.

I switched on. 700 amps! The discharge from the condensers showed on the oscilloscope screen, a repetitive rapier of light. The fish stirred uneasily. I resisted the temptation to plunge my hand into the tank. It was he, not I, who was to be the victim.

800! Was I mistaken, or had he given a start? I felt the sweat down the back of my shirt, past my buttocks and on to the seat.

900!

The ends of my legs tingled. It was as if someone was also pressing a tight band round my head.

1000! I could feel my shattered nerve-ends jumping. I felt like a pilot going through the sound barrier in an old 'plane. I resisted another impulse to plunge my hand into the water. What in the name of Faraday and all the electrical saints was making him immune to the current? I tried once more to will him towards the positive electrode.

1000! And he had never even moved.

The iron band felt tighter round my head. The brown mud seemed to be turning black. He was close now, as if under a magnifying glass. I poured hate on his blotched gills as I jammed on peak current amplitude of 3000 amps.

The fish lunged towards me. I screamed . . .

I had never heard my first scream ten years before. It was one of those screams which pure terror must make supersonic. I told the onlookers later about that first scream and they said I'd imagined it. If they had heard, they said, they might have saved me. During the attack I don't think I made a sound. It was only later in my state of shock that I kept repeating my grandmother's phrase. I can only remember two distinct tastes of salt in my mouth, one of blood, the other of seawater.

The bay of Espirito Santo, or Lourenço Marques, is one of the finest along the whole coast of South Eastern Africa.

It is over twenty miles across and slightly more from north to south. At its seaward extremity is Inhaca Island. On a clear day, the low line of the island is visible from the town of Lourenço Marques itself. Inhaca is more than just an island: it is a pleasure spot, as is Lourenço Marques, transformed by the Portuguese from the once inhospital, malaria-stricken focal point of three great rivers into Southern Africa's leading resort. Here one may drink the green wines of northern Portugal, unblemished after their long sea voyage from Europe, eat the tangy cheeses of Madeira, and hear the *fado* in a setting almost as good as the wineshops of Lisbon itself. On Inhaca Island the Portuguese have built a night-club. A ferry takes revellers across the bay in the evening and returns only the next morning. Inhaca also offers some of the best fishing along the coast.

I was still in evening dress, although it was Sunday morning, and Stewart and the two girls were waiting for the boat. We had been night-clubbing all Saturday night; the wine had been good, the piri-piri prawns better, and the sun, rising with nothing but Indian Ocean between Inhaca and Australia 3000 miles to the east, was as fresh as a trade wind. There was an hour to wait for the boat to start and Stewart and I decided on a swim. We stripped behind some low bushes on the sandy dunes and used a small boat to get well clear of the island's sandbanks.

I never saw Stewart disappear. If I had, I might have made an attempt to reach the boat. I first spotted the shark which took him when he came at me, mouth agape. He made his first run swiftly past me and just brushed by my side. His skin was not rough as I thought a shark's would be, but soft like chamois leather. It was that almost affectionate, soft brush that started my soundless scream. Later I learned that the shark waits for the first panic noises from a fish before he strikes. As he had with me. I saw him wheel in the clear water and then he came at me upwards at a slight angle. I knew what was going to happen but I could not move.

He took off my right leg so cleanly that later the surgeon didn't even have to trim it. There was no feeling at all.

But he fluffed his second attack – and that hurt. Perhaps he was still chewing because he shot on like a torpedo for about fifty yards before making the same spectacular wheel for the run in on my left leg. I waited, frozen. Time stood still, then he gathered my remaining leg just above the knee. It did not come away clean. It sounded like the crunch of a breaking prawn shell like those we had eaten the night before. He tugged at the still unsevered muscles. A pain lanced through my groin. I think that was the only physical agony I felt.

Then he was gone. I was left floundering with the double salt taste of blood and seawater in my mouth.

I mustn't spoil June's lovely evening dress, I thought, when the girls dragged me into a boat they had cast off when Stewart was attacked. Turquoise doesn't go with scarlet, I added dazedly, with still no sense of pain. Sobbing hysterically, June dragged me over the gunwale. I sat upright in half an inch of bilge water. I could still feel my toes, although they were now inside the shark's stomach. I looked down at the right stump, cleanly severed. I moved the left into view. June vomited. The untidy tendons and blood vessels, split longitudinally, looked like a crude anatomical sketch.

I eyed my naked, shattered torso. I still feel a man, I thought. The ragged tangle of tendons and ripped blood vessels twitched, as if of their own volition. In that moment I needed a woman.

I started to scream, wildly, out of control: Black mud! Black mud! Black mud! Over and over and over again, black mud!

Back at the night-club where they carried me they tried to tell me – and I kept on saying that I knew – that there was no mud on Inhaca. Sand, yes, but there was no sand on my stumps. The pilot of the light 'plane which made Sunday pleasure flights to the island kept repeating that too as he raced to get me to hospital before I bled to death.

Black mud! I kept whispering, weakly now, to the ambulance driver who met the 'plane at the airport. Then the sterile corridors of the hospital of Miguel Bombarda . . . oblivion.

I was jerked back to reality in my laboratory at the C.S.I.R. by a light in my eyes. For a moment I thought it was the Portuguese doctor come to examine me during a respite from pain-drenched coma. But in fact I was lying on the laboratory floor where I had fallen off my stool in re-living the agony of the shark attack. Everything was wet. The Perspex tank lay split open on the floor and the mudfish kicked on the floor against me. I crushed one of my somewhat buckled artificial limbs against his head and ground the life out of him as a sort of reflex backlash from the event ten years before. I guessed I must have had a momentary blackout as the result of reaction.

'What is going on here?'

It was the quiet, level voice of the Director which finally dispelled my nightmare.

'Take that torch out of my eyes,' I snapped.

The beam swivelled away from my sweating face on to the mess in which I lay, and then on to the oscilloscope. That meant only one thing to his trained mind. I might talk my way out of a lot of other things, but he knew I was checking, calculating, measuring. There'd be no way of bluffing him that it was all part of some harmless little out-of-hours scientific frolic.

The beam followed the leads to the condensers, and then went on to the copper electrodes. At first I thought he mightn't spot them but he did. Then the light travelled back to me, sitting like a Buddha deprived of his godhood. There was some blood on my shirt from the fish and I was wet and smelled of fish and fishy mud.

The Director was standing well away from me and the mess of mudfish, blood and water. Now he took a step forward.

'Be careful, sir!' I said urgently. 'This whole floor may be alive.'

'At least one thing is alive, that I see,' he retorted. 'There seems more evidence of violent homicide than of planned electrocution.'

'I . . .' I began.

'Where is the switch?' he asked.

'There are two,' I replied. 'I put fuses in the circuit just in case . . .'

'Just in case – what?' he demanded.

They say that a policeman gets his best answers when a murderer is still under the first shock of his crime. How could I explain my secret in a few words, even if I wanted to? Who would understand the driving need to settle the score?

'Just in case they blew.'

'A moment ago, Ogilvie, I would have thought you were qualifying for a mental home. Your answer reassures me.'

'That reassures me too,' I said with the air of cultivated flippancy which had stood me in good stead against all the pity for a legless man. Pity such a nice man is wasted, they would say but of course, if you'd been through the same sort of thing, you wouldn't look the same either, would you?

The Director followed the cables back into the darkness and I heard the click of switches.

He said, 'I wouldn't offer you a hand, except that you'll probably slip on that fish you've been so unkind to.' I knew what he was thinking. You'll only get resentment from a helpless cripple if you attempt to be kind to him. Play the man.

'I know enough Afrikaans to remember your saying, "I admire a man who can stand up for himself",' I replied. I gave him a glance of appreciation.

'It's a long time since I got down to a Rugby scrum but here goes,' he went on easily. He'd make a fine orthopaedic doctor, I thought. He came behind me and transferred the torch to his other hand. As he heaved me up its light showed a man standing at the door.

I saw Doctor John Barrow for the first time.

CHAPTER TWO

I am not sure whether I saw Barrow first or the bitch.

The animal gave to the man, at a time when my over-wrought nerves were capable of seeing anything, an air of sinister hideousness which auraed them both all the time I knew them.

My reason told me that no creature could have legs like that. It flashed through my brain, now clear with the clarity of purgation, that it must be an angle of the light, or the angle at which the Director was helping me up. They stretched down like a pair of stilts. It seemed the height of a small donkey. The light drew into bright relief the exquisite pelt, like a fox's. It had a sharp pointed face like a fox, but the beautiful streamlined body of a whippet. I started at the grossly elongated legs and slipped heavily on the bone of my own right leg.

The creature never seemed to move, so swift was its strike, and in flash I was half-kneeling in front of this unreal animal. It gave a soft growl with an oddly high note to it. It was probably smelling the blood. Or perhaps, with such legs, it simply was overcome at seeing another living being without them. Its silver mane was dulled by the half-yellow torch beam, but even so, it was lovely enough. The luminous great eyes revealed that it was a night hunter, a solitary creature from some primitive place; those dramatic legs had evolved only as part of a pattern of survival.

'Shine that torch in her eyes,' ordered the man at the door. His voice had a fogged quality about it.

The light dazzled the creature, which turned aside. The man said something in a foreign language and, in two steps, it was back at his side. The luminous eyes watched my every move.

The Director hauled me up unceremoniously on to a stool. He was panting with the effort.

'Lights – we want lights,' he said, and moved away.

There seemed to be some sort of sleight of hand about

the man and his animal, both so silent and so swift, at the door. I blinked now in the strong light. Over the animal's eyes was a soft linen mask, like racehorse blinkers, with celluloid eye-holes.

He burst out laughing when he saw my look of incredulity. The fox-like beast looked more beautiful and sinister than ever and the eyeshield added to the impression.

'You're not still in your coma,' he said in that clouded voice. He smiled and showed large teeth in front.

'I had an oculist prescribe these especially for her in Rio,' he went on conversationally. He brought the Director into the social circle with a gesture. I could see he was shaken at what he saw of me. The mess of the floor looked even worse and the strange animal was craning forward to sniff at the bloody remains of the mudfish.

'He said it was unethical for him to prescribe for an animal. He eventually agreed when I pointed out that no vet had ever been called on to do anything similar. And probably won't be again.'

We might have been discussing a visit to a chemist for a pair of Polaroid glasses. The gambit at least gave me time to recover my breath, both physically and mentally. I didn't care for the look on the Director's face.

'Those aren't legs it's got,' I grinned weakly.

It's easy to wound a man without limbs. 'Nor are yours.' he said deliberately. He came across with a cigarette carton held open.

'You bloody bastard,' I said. I struck the carton aside.

If he hadn't grabbed the creature by its thick mane and snapped something sharply in the same foreign tongue, there would never have been any trouble, and no one would ever have heard of the Watering Place of Good Peace.

I think the Director felt he'd had enough of me for the night. He said coldly, in his slight Afrikaans accent with its Harvard overlay: 'May I introduce Doctor John Barrow, the distinguished physical scientist?'

So I'd all but assaulted one of the Director's top-brass colleagues as well.

The Director turned to me. 'Mr Ian Ogilvie, one of our most promising men.' He glanced round the wreckage in spite of himself. It's as good a write-off as any, I thought.

He must have seen the half-sneer on Barrow's face, for he added unnecessarily; 'Mr Ogilvie has carried out some very promising research into electronics and acoustics.'

Barrow waved his hand round the mess.

'Is this electronics or acoustics, Mr Ogilvie?'

'I also specialize in fisheries research,' I sneered back. That's what Barrow did to me even at that early stage. 'That one didn't get away.'

'I must apologize,' said Barrow with a foreign sort of social air which I couldn't place, 'you haven't met Rina.' He said something to the bitch. With a peculiar stiff motion, like one of those huge waders you see in the malarial lagoons in Mozambique where the great South African rivers dissipate into swamps and mudflats, it extended one of the stilt-like paws.

'That's her only gesture towards human society, which she also despises,' said Barrow. There was a peculiar inflexion about the 'also'.

'The special goggles are because she has always hunted at night and artificial light hurts her eyes. I assure you that torch did more just now to stop her than a gun. She's probably still half-blind from it.'

I leaned down to take the extended paw, which was strong and thin.

'Don't touch her,' Barrow said sharply. 'She's doing that on sufferance.'

'I've never seen anything like her before . . .' I began.

'Of course you haven't, Mr Ogilvie,' he said impatiently. 'I would say that of your thirty years you spent most in two places – in a laboratory or in hospital.' He went over and recovered the cigarette carton, just to show me he wasn't letting me get away with it. 'This is one of the rarest, the mose savage, and the most beautiful of all animals. Rina is a pure South American maned wolf. She'll keep up with a South African cheetah at full speed and she's twice as beautiful.' He spoke again to the bitch which nudged him affectionately.

'You can see for yourself, she looks like a fox but in fact she's a wolf. The male has a longer mane. In South America they call her kind the "fox-on-stilts". I am not usually fond of popular or newspaper catch-phrases but it fits her beautifully.'

The Director interrupted our interlude on natural history:

'I was bringing Dr Barrow here tonight to collect some isotopes which we have specially manufactured to his specification,' he said. 'They're isotopes we've made in the cyclotron which Dr Barrow intends to use in some of his own trace element experiments. Dr Barrow is from Mozambique. They're in my office in a lead container. It's too heavy for just one of us to carry. I also want to speak to you,' – I didn't like the way he said it – 'so we must either carry on our conference here, or in my own office.'

'You mean you want to talk but you don't want to have to humiliate yourself and Dr Barrow by carrying me to your office?'

'Ogilvie!' snapped the Director. Harvard became swallowed up in the Afrikaans accent. The mister was also missing. He spoke half to me and half to Barrow.

'One makes considerable allowances for a man . . . ah . . .'

'Say it,' I plunged on heedlessly. 'For a cripple . . .'

There was genuine pain in his face when he went on and I hated myself for my words.

'It was on my recommendation that you were taken on in this establishment,' he said and I could see his anger mounting. 'But when ah . . . ah . . . disability is made the excuse for downright impertinence and rudeness, then . . .'

Barrow looked at me distastefully. He had made it quite clear from the first moment what he had thought of me.

'Send him to a psychologist,' he said incisively. 'Give him the treatment. He's just compensating. They'll sweat it out of him.'

I think it was Barrow's presumption about my behaviour that needled the Director as much as my own remarks.

He looked at me levelly. 'Can you give some very satisfactory explanation of what you were doing here, in a government laboratory, with government material, in the middle of the night . . . ?'

'It's not the middle of the night,' I retorted. I could see the Director's resentment mount still higher. 'It is now after half past nine . . .' Pity those fuses blew, I thought in a moment of self-pity. It could have been suicide with a difference.

The Director's cold voice cut through my thoughts.

'What were you doing, Ogilvie?'

'I was trying to kill a fish with an electric current,' I replied lamely.

He took my point like counsel in a murder case. He followed it up equally smoothly.

'Then with your extensive knowledge of electronics, why did you not do what any schoolboy would have done under the circumstances – simply connect up a positive and a negative to the fish's nose and tail and turn on the switch?'

Barrow was smiling at my discomfiture. If I hadn't been so bloody-minded, the Director and I could have had all this out between ourselves. I had sampled his great kindness: now it was boomeranging on me.

'I . . .' I began, but I couldn't go on.

The Director cast his eye over the electrodes, the oscilloscope, the condensers, the wiring and general set-up. I wished he had left Barrow out of it then.

'Dr Barrow, what do you consider this equipment would be worth – just at a guess?'

He was not at a loss although his figure was about fifty per cent higher than it should have been.

'Five, six hundred pounds.'

'I would have said so myself,' agreed the Director.

'What were you trying to do, Ogilvie?'

'I was trying to kill a fish by using the principle of a pulsating electrical field.'

'A pulsating electrical field?' The Director looked incredulous. 'You don't have to have a pulsating electrical field to kill one harmless mudfish.'

'I didn't kill him.'

'Oh yes, you did,' laughed Barrow mirthlessly. 'Yes, you did, Ogilvie. You killed him with a pulsating left stump.'

I felt like knocking his teeth down his throat – if I'd had legs to reach him.

Despite his anger the Director was still prepared to hear me out.

'Killing the fish might have been the secondary purpose of what you were doing, but what was the primary purpose?' he persisted.

I knew he was trying to help me if he could. He'd made it possible, on his own special recommendation, to get me the job and a contract, despite the fact that my qualifications weren't all that good. I wasn't bilingual for a start, one of the pre-requisites for a permanent appointment on any state or semi-state body.

'Start from the beginning,' he urged. Rina gave a little jump as Barrow pinched her ear. If they terminate my contract, what shall I do? The thought hit me like a blow. Stumble round begging electrical jobs? I must keep a close tongue in my head.

'Well,' I said slowly, 'I built this tank out of Perspex. I had to have a clear tank so that I could see exactly what was going on, how the fish reacted to given amounts of current. I took notes as I went along. I got mudfish because I wanted a particular weight of fish which, if I succeeded, could be used as a multiple. In other words, this fish weighed seven pounds. The crucial weight is 420 pounds.'

The Director and Barrow goth stared at me.

'Why 420 pounds?' the Director asked.

How could I tell them that the monster they caught at Inhaca two days afterwards with fragments of my bathing trunks in his stomach weighed 420 pounds?

I shook my head and looked away. The fox-wolf offered me no compassion from behind her goggles.

'It's too long to explain that part of it. But I wanted a seven-pound mudfish. It also had to have its mud – as you see.' I pointed at the sopping floor.

'When and how did all this happen?' went on the Director. 'Not, I take it, during normal working hours?'

'No,' I said. I grinned, imagining the comments this would have brought from my colleagues. They, who knocked off at 4.30 in the afternoon, did not wait to see me bring it across from the pond in the Botanical Gardens . . .

'I netted this brute,' I said gesturing again at the mess on the floor.

The Director smiled.

'This is not the Hebrides, you know, Ogilvie. Netting of

fish is strictly illegal in the Transvaal.'

I smiled back. 'I didn't net only one fish, sir, but a couple of score, until I had my seven-pounder. I then hid him in the pond at the Botanical Gardens over there –' I gestured towards the darkness to the left of the radio mast. 'His final journey was made in a big Thermos flask, plus mud.'

Black mud! I remembered again.

'One cannot class lack of resourcefulness among your qualities,' said the Director.

'I graded the switch from 100 to 3000 amps,' I went on. 'That was to have been the peak. There were short pulses of current one millisecond long. I noted his reaction at every rise of 100. It was nil . . .'

'I'm not an electronics expert, but what is the purpose of all this elaborate paraphernalia?' asked the Director.

'It was in order to create an electrical field, which could be regulated either to kill a fish or merely to shock him. Hence the gradations. It didn't work.'

'Did you test it thoroughly?' the Director went on. He seemed to be interested, despite himself.

'Yes,' I replied. 'He wouldn't even move over to the positive electrode.'

'What do you mean?' he asked.

I explained: 'The negative electrode, if it was having any effect, would produce a sharp, painful reaction, a sort of stabbing I think. Therefore the fish would move over to the positive. The more amperage that went through the negative, the closer he'd be forced to the positive. The positive meant death. He'd be electrocuted. That's the theory, anyway. It simply didn't work.'

'How much amperage did you give him finally?'

I winced at my action in retrospect.

'The whole 3000.'

'And he never moved?'

'No,' I lied, for they must never know. 'No, he never moved.'

I'd been so engrossed in the telling of it that I'd forgotten Barrow. My mind was running ahead, trying to sort out the scientific reason for my failure.

Barrow cut in, as if he were part of the interrogation and had the right to put a question.

'So, when it didn't work, you sat down and drummed your heels and went into a screaming tantrum, eh Ogilvie? The new science!'

He was right. I turned uncomfortably to the Director, who had been nicely side-tracked up to then. Had my offence remained unformulated, it might have been easy enough for the Director to condone it, but Barrow had put it in a way which made me nothing less than a dangerous neurotic in charge of equipment which could easily be lethal.

'I don't know what Dr Barrow's position is in relation to the organization,' I said, hoping the Director would react as if his own authority was being impinged upon, 'but I feel I could better put my case to you alone.'

I was wrong. The Director's brows came together.

'I feel that a third impersonal opinion could be of great value in this rather unusual circumstance,' he said distantly. 'It may also help me to a decision which might be onerous if I had to make it myself.'

That was the writing on the wall. There was now a judge and an assessor. I could see that Barrow didn't mind passing judgment on me. I expect he would have anyway, without the Director's invitation. He was clever enough to let the Director do the talking at this stage.

'I feel that you have been evasive and misleading up to now, Ogilvie, but you still have the opportunity to state your side of the case. What are you up to with this electrical gear?'

The grotesque bitch gazed at me unwaveringly from behind her goggles. Like a woman, she was beautiful – and dangerous. Barrow, the judge, had his executioner at hand if he wanted her.

'I was simply trying to kill the fish with a pulsating current and see how much it would stand before it crumpled up,' I repeated.

The Director looked at me judicially.

'How old are you, Ogilvie?'

'Thirty-seven.'

'You're not a South African, are you, but English?'

'Scottish,' I retorted.

Barrow added, 'They're so damned proud of it, these Scots, aren't they?'

'How long since you came to us?'

'You gave me the job about two years ago. I'll never forget your kindness.'

'How long was that after the . . . ah . . . accident?'

I felt my inside turn. Barrow stroked the beautiful silver head.

'A fast car, a pretty girl, and half a dozen drinks, I suppose.'

I rounded on him.

'I was swimming off Inhaca Island in the bay of Lourenço Marques,' I said tersely. 'A shark took off both my legs. My companion was lucky. It killed him.'

'I see,' said Barrow. What he saw, I don't know.

'The rest of my biography is short and sweet, if you want to hear it,' I said. 'Was training in electronics when war came. Active service, Royal Navy. Bored to tears for five and a half years. Voted Socialist. Immigrated – nice country, South Africa. Odds and ends of private electrical research jobs. Went swimming. No legs. Now subsisting on state pity.' I knew as I said the last that I was finished as far as the Director was concerned. He had always made it seem as though I was doing a normal job in a normal way – as indeed I was. I also knew it was useless trying to hide my real motive any longer.

'If you really want to know,' I said harshly. 'I was experimenting with this damned fish in order to find a way to kill sharks. I *want* to kill sharks . . .'

'For what they did to you?' asked Barrow.

'For what they did to me,' I said. 'For what they did to me,' I repeated.

The Director gave me one last chance. 'You mean, you are trying to develop some method of making bathing-places safe by using some kind of electrical barrier?'

I threw it away. 'The hell with that,' I snapped. 'I don't give a damn how many bathers are eaten by sharks. I just want to kill them. I want to have a way of killing hundreds of sharks. I want to see them laid out dead by the score. Just for what they did to me.'

The Director sighed and turned to Barrow expressively. 'A revenge motive of this kind can't do yourself or anyone else any good, Ogilvie. You've ruined hundreds of pounds' worth of equipment because of some wildcat idea. I rather

agree with Dr Barrow that your best course would be to
seek some kind of medical help. I thought this kind of work
would be rehabilitative in itself, but I see it was nothing more
than a means to provide expensive gear for erasing a personal,
psychological scar. I think you had better seek medical
advice.'

Black thoughts blanketed my mind.

'Did you hear what I said, Ogilvie?' he said, not unkindly.
'I am going to my office to get something to show you
which arrived from my opposite number in Australia today.
Perhaps it will help you to a better understanding of yourself
and your problems.'

He went. I glanced uncaringly at Barrow and saw, to my
astonishment, that his eyes were alive with interest. His whole
attitude seemed to have undergone a radical alteration.

'Do you really mean to say that this method of yours
could create a safe enclosed place where sharks couldn't get
in?'

'I told you,' I said, 'I don't give a tinker's damn whether
all the sharks in South African waters eat all the bathers in
South Africa . . .'

His former air of impatient intolerance was gone: he was
pulling up the long silky hair of his creature like a barrier
of electrodes.

'Don't be so bloody sorry for yourself all the time,' he
said and then, without even pausing: 'Why didn't it work on
this mudfish?'

'The theory was dead right but there's some factor I can't
have taken into account. No fish would stand up to that
amount of current.'

Barrow dropped on his knees among the mess, heedless of
what the blood and water was doing to his suit. He pulled
out a small pocket knife, the sort of thing a smoker uses for
his pipe, and slashed along the length of the mudfish. He
looked up and grinned at me, sitting perched on my stool
above him. I almost liked him for a moment.

'How much mud would a mudfish catch, if a mudfish
could catch mud?'

'What the hell are you talking about?'

He didn't get up.

'There's one of your unknowns,' he said, grinning with

enthusiasm. 'Look, this thing has got a sort of protective layer of mud adhering to its skin . . .'

'What?' I exclaimed. I snatched the dead fish from his hand. The cut he had made showed it to be true. What a fool I was! I could have wept with frustration.

His iron hand closed over mine, reaching for his knife to make another check.

'I wouldn't do that,' said Barrow. 'Look at the door.'

The beautiful creature was poised, ready to jump me.

'She is South American and in South America when anyone reaches for another man's knife, it means only one thing. If you'd got hold of that knife, I don't think the future would have needed to concern you over-much.'

I drew my hand back. The tension died out of her. She lowered herself almost clumsily on her long haunches. I saw the electrodes, then, too.

'Christ!' I exclaimed in disgust. 'What a blind idiot I've been! I deserve this, after putting up a black like that.' It gave me the measure of Barrow's brain. 'Look, I strung the electrodes through all that mud – a whole inch of it which I brought specially so my fish would feel at home – and then I expected to kill him!'

Barrow was grinning like a schoolboy, with the knife and fish in his hand. I couldn't believe the change that had come over him in a few minutes.

'Could a shark have any sort of similar resistance?' he demanded. We were like two kids.

'Might be,' I said. 'It certainly opens up a whole new field –'

Barrow interrupted me, glancing towards the door where the Director had disappeared. 'Ogilvie, if your theories are correct and you find a means to break down a shark's – shall we say, inherent resistance – could one erect a kind of electronic barrier inside which no shark could live, but a human being – say a skin-diver – could?'

His eagerness was catching.

'I don't see why not,' I said. 'Provided the sharks had a lesser resistance than humans to an electrical charge. It would require quite a bit of testing . . .'

'Do you think it would work?' he repeated.

'Yes, provided . . .'

'For God's sake stop saying "provided". Time is short. Yes or no?'

'Yes . . .'

He smiled. 'So in theory again, supposing we have a small enclosed bay, or a section of sea, surrounded by electrodes, you think you could keep sharks out and let human beings swim inside?'

'With the pulsating current, yes,' I said, wondering where all this was leading.

The Director opened the door. He had a thick typed report in his hand. He flicked over the pages. He failed to notice anything between Barrow and myself.

'I think you should take this into account and make it plain to your medical adviser,' he said. He turned almost to the end. Most things of value seem to be at the end of scientific reports.

'"The Committee",' he quoted – 'that is, an Australian committee of scientists which was set up specially to investigate the problem of keeping sharks away from bathing-beaches, for you know there are as many sharks in their seas as there are off South Africa – "wishes to state that it has tried out 16 different methods of rendering bathing-beaches safe from attack from sharks. These include all the known chemical repellents, as well as some specially evolved for the tests, but although the latter proved temporarily effective (in some instances up to about four hours) the committee is of the unanimous opinion that as yet no foolproof method has been evolved to combat the menace of sharks . . ."'

I interjected: 'There's nothing specific there about electricity.'

'There is,' said the Director. 'There's a whole lot about it. He went on quoting: '"The committee conducted an extensive series of tests with an eye to using electricity as a barrier in itself, or by means of creating an electrical field, similar to those used for the detection of submarines during the past war, but none of these were found to hold out much promise. It is felt that the physical problems alone involved in creating such an anti-shark barrier are insuperable, having particular regard to the nature of the seas and surf on Australian beaches. The loss of expensive equipment in the event of a storm would also place this method beyond the reach of the ordinary local authorities responsible for the beaches." Do you want me to go on, Ogilvie?'

I shook my head. Then Barrow shocked me.

'I think that clearly puts paid to this young man's rather futile attempts to do underhand what a responsible scientific committee spent several years, with plenty of funds and equipment available, trying to do without success. If I were in your position, Mr Director, I should continue to urge him to seek medical advice.'

I looked at him in amazement. I simply couldn't believe that this was the man, who a moment ago, was down on his knees grovelling and grinning at his discovery.

'You can't grab my ideas like that, you bastard! You think you can milk my brain and get away with it!'

Barrow looked across at the Director and shrugged. There was a look of almost professional concern on his face.

'I want your protection for my ideas.' I told the Director. 'This man is trying to steal them. I . . .'

There was another exchange of glances between them.

'Somehow or other, Barrow,' I went on. 'I'm going to get even with you for this.'

He turned to the Director. 'There seems to be a very considerable measure of persecution mania present,' he said. 'Plus this extraordinary revenge motive. Revenge against sharks . . . get even with me . . . a perfect stranger whom he's never seen until a little while ago! I leave the matter in your competent hands, Mr Director,' he said urbanely. 'Shall we carry the isotopes together?'

The Director nodded. They went.

Well, that is the end of me, I thought. Any minute now they'll lock me up. The whole world stank like the smell of the fish and mud. I was seized roughly by the shoulder. It was Barrow.

'Go away, haven't you done enough already?'

'How much are you earning here?'

'What's it got to do with you?'

'Answer, you fool! Cut out your self-pity. How much?

'£120 a month. Thanks to you, I haven't got it any more.'

'If I give you £200, plus everything all found, will you come and work for me?'

'What?' I ejaculated. 'Why?'

'Will you? Yes?'

'I've got no choice, thanks to you.'

'Thanks to me, you now have a good job and your sole function will be to develop an electrical shark-proof barrier,' he replied. 'It doesn't matter if you burn up a piddling five hundred pounds' worth of equipment. You can have all you want. Right? Not a word to the Director. As far as you and he are concerned, you're on your way to a psychiatrist. Frankly, I couldn't imagine a man saner.'

I came up for air.

'Where is all this?' I managed to say.

'On the coast of Mozambique, about 200 miles north of Lourenço Marques,' he said. 'My lab's there. I'll explain all that later. Where do you live?'

I gave him the address and he jotted it down rapidly in a pocket-book. 'Good!' he said. 'I'll be round first thing in the morning with a car. We'll have to get your passport, entry permit and so on, but I have friends who will fix it quickly. We'll get those legs straightened out and you'll be mobile. The sooner the better. Right? Now I must get back to the Director – made an excuse about having dropped my pocket-book.'

There was a gentle pressure against my side. It was the strange bitch. I said unthinkingly, 'Dr Barrow, that animal of yours gives me the willies.'

A deep, angry flush came across his face. 'Mr Ogilvie,' he said quietly, 'where you are going is a wild, remote spot, so cut off from everything that I should say it has remained the same for 500 years. It's wild and lush and the sea is always in your ears. In front of the lab is the sea, and at the back a chain of lagoons. It's called Aguada da Boa Paz – the Watering Place of Good Peace. The marshland and lagoons are full of game. Rina loves to hunt, and I turn her loose at night. The natives have a name for her: they call her "the Ghost Walker of Boa Paz".'

CHAPTER THREE

It was breath-taking enough to see a sketch of Drake's astrolabe among demijohns in a Portuguese wine-shop, but I couldn't believe it when I saw the *padraoa* or beacon cross and the old chart as well. The map was finely marked with intersecting lines, like a Consol radio beacon. The astrolabe was set on 25 degrees – it is strange how small things like that can change one's life. If it had been set, say, on 26 degrees, I probably would never have found out the secret of the Watering Place of Good Peace. The *padraoa* – well, that too was just one of these things. She told me later it was quite by chance.

The girl was busy at a fine piece of grained vellum, soft honey in colour which she had fixed with a couple of clothes-pegs in the mouths of two five-litre bottles of *vinho de casa.* She was working by the over-bright acetylene light of the bar, sitting on the sort of small canvas stool fishermen use.

I clumped up behind her. She did not look round.

'What do you think, Jerry?' she said, with laughter in her voice. 'What shall it be – shady sugar loaves? Cockscombs? Or hairy caterpillars? Make something like the appropriate sound in English, and it shall be yours, just for the asking.'

'I'd plump for hairy caterpillars any day,' I said, 'although I haven't a clue what the quiz is about. Nor, I gather, has Jerry, whoever Jerry might be.'

She swung round with the long mapping quill in her hand and knocked over some of the little bottles of coloured ink which were on a Casal Garcia box by her side. I waited while she picked them up. She was obviously even more surprised that I had made no attempt to help her. People find out that you are legless quickly enough. There's no need to make it an opening gambit.

She scrutinized me and cleaned the quill absently on the knee of her tight-fitting American jeans.

'That's taking a completely unfair advantage,' she smiled. 'Besides, I don't think hairy caterpillars are a very good choice. They don't match the marsh and swamp lines, which are three vertical with one horizontal underneath. The whole thing would be covered in scrappy little lines. And the first principle of drawing a decorative map is that one should be decisive, not messy. What do you think Mercator would have said?'

'I thought he only drew utilitarian maps,' I said. The one she was working on was big, about four feet long and three broad, showing the coast beyond the village where the wine-shop was – the coast of Aguada da Boa Paz.

'He was in the fortunate position to have been a carto-grapher, calligrapher and engraver all rolled into one,' she said. 'His maps were meant to be used and so, tidily, he kept the sea from merging into the land, and the bits and pieces of ornamentation from knocking you punch-drunk – you know, sea monsters, whales and cherub-like things blowing from every corner of the compass.'

I liked her large hazel eyes but there was a sort of olive pallor about her. Probably malaria.

'I still don't know what hairy caterpillars are,' I said.

She smiled and the bright acetylene light – it was an anti-quated looking brass thing which I am sure must have begun life in a fishing-boat in the bay of Espirito Santo – made her hair fairer than it really was.

'Hairy caterpillars is – or should I say are? – just the name map-makers have for drawing contours in relief. I'm trying to decide how to get in all those hills between here and the coast. Like this –' she sketched quickly on her clean knee.

'And shady sugar loaves?'

'The same. Also contours. Like this –' Again she sketched, higher up towards her thigh. This time it was a series of elevations.

'And cockscombs – so,' she did another series of lines. 'But I think they'd look a little harsh for this job. I think it will have to be shady sugar loaves. It's like love – there are only a set number of permutations.'

At that she turned away.

'Jerry!' she called to the back behind the bar. 'Jerry! Some more of your special *agua*!' Her olive pallor was slightly flushed. 'This Chinese stick ink of mine has to be rubbed down to the right consistency and it needs distilled water. Jerry distils it for me – maybe he distils other things too?'

The Portuguese wine-shop, part bar, part restaurant and part pension all rolled into one and pervaded by the characteristic odours of each – wine, garlic and a lingering trace of poor sanitation – had an air of unreality for me. Perhaps it was because of the long, fast motor journey from Pretoria to this remote part of the coast of Portuguese East Africa. It was like being transported from one world into another. One might have been among the Alfama wine-shops of nether Lisbon – except for the wild lagoons and savage crash of the sea a mile or two from the village.

Barrow and I had left Pretoria with almost undue haste. I hadn't even bothered, after the scene in the laboratory, to see the Director again. I had merely written him a short formal letter of farewell. Barrow's actions seemed to be spurred on by a haste as pressing as if I were one of his perishable isotopes in the heavy lead container. His offer seemed genuine, and for the hundreds of miles we raced across the high plateau of the Transvaal, by-passing little towns like Machadadorp in a swoop of speed as the finely-engineered national road curved up and down the high hills, Barrow talked of little else except the scheme. Every time I led him round to the question of why he wanted to have an enclosed, shark-proof area for skin-divers, he fobbed me off by digressing into what were, in fact, absorbing technicalities regarding the experiment on a gigantic field scale. Barrow never seemed to have any doubt that the thing would work. His enthusiasm was catching and my own cautious approach was thawed and broadened by it.

'It's the will,' he said as the car sped down the aloe-lined curves of Schoeman's Kloof, the barrier between the high plateau of the Transvaal and the rich, sub-tropical Lowveld in the east.

'Will, motivation, action, call it what you like,' said Barrow, ignoring the green wonder of the great citrus orchards which line the road for scores of miles, fenced by hedges of scarlet and mauve bougainvillaea. 'It's why I like your electricity idea against these bastards of the sea who have got in the way of what I want – it's dynamic. It's power.'

'Revenge motive,' I said ironically, still not forgetting in

Barrow's present mood what I had seen of the man in the first minutes of the laboratory fiasco.

'Not at all,' he said equably. 'I don't want to kill sharks—not just for the sake of killing them. They're in my way, that's all. You've got a way, I think, to get rid of them.'

'The only sharks I like are dead sharks,' I said.

'You'll have to face up to the idea of seeing, even touching sharks,' he replied. 'I can't have you having an attack of temperament every time you see one. If you do, you're quite useless to me.'

'I won't,' I said quickly, too quickly perhaps, and was glad that Barrow couldn't see the layer of sweat that had broken out over my stumps.

We raced on through the warm air and Barrow demonstrated his driving ability through the last mountain barrier before the road finally descends to the flat land which runs along the southern border of the Kruger National Park to the Lebombo Hills, the natural boundary between South Africa and Portuguese East Africa.

'This country smells like a million brides in the spring with all that orange blossom,' said Barrow, pointing at the trees now heavily laden. 'At night it is simply terrific. Rina couldn't make it out—she'd never smelled anything like that before, eh, my girl?'

The creature, which occupied the whole back seat of the big American car, licked him in affectionate half-sleep.

'Back to your dreams, Rina,' he said to her. 'A real lady of the night, my Rina. You'll see her special room at Aguada da Boa Paz.'

I waited in the car at the hot border post—Komatipoort on the South African side and Ressana Garcia on the Portuguese. Barrow certainly wasted no time. We were cleared in ten minutes, despite the goods we were carrying. When Lourenço Marques came in view eighty miles later, he turned to me.

'Are you tired? Shall we stop? Or a glass of wine and a plate of piri-piri prawns and on our way? We might get near to Boa Paz tonight if we push things.'

I looked at the great bay of Espírito Santo and the dim line, 25 miles across it, of Inhaca Island.

'Prawns and wine,' I said. 'Then let's get the hell out of

here as soon as we can.'

We turned into the tree-lined, four-carriage highway leading to the city. I kept glancing out beyond the ships and quayside to that remote, dim line out to sea.

'Where did they bring you ashore?' asked Barrow with an out-of-character touch of gentleness.

'They didn't, they flew the remains in to the airport – it's up there to the left of the cross-roads where we came in.'

'I thought . . .'

'You don't need to,' I retorted. 'I've told myself a thousand times that I would never see this bloody place again – or that place on the horizon.'

'That where it happened?' he asked. The note was wrong. It was professional compassion. He wanted me mentally fit, fit for the job in hand – his job. The volte-face was too glib. My dislike of the man returned.

'Inhaca Island,' I said. 'You know, like Trinity Church, where I met my doom. But for you, I'd also be living in a top back room.'

'I'm not offering you charity, get that quite clear,' he said. 'You'll get into the sea among sharks and if you don't damn well like it, you can go. Understand? There's going to be no messing around or moping because you just don't feel like sharks on a particular day. You'll feel like them all the time – or else you'll get out.'

Barrow drew in under the big shady trees off the main Avenida de Republica. It was all the same – the endless crowd drinking coffee and beer at the pavement tables, the orphans selling lottery tickets, the South African tourists in short khaki shorts, talking over-loudly. Barrow ordered a litre of Campo de Casa and piri-piri prawns. The bottles came cold, wet with condensation. Never, I thought, has green wine tasted better. The faint sparkle in the wine – something like a Moselle – frosted the outside of our glasses.

'You'll have to meet Jerry at Boa Paz,' he said, with a complete reversion of his earlier attitude. 'Jerry remembers everything. If a man comes by one day and says, "Your *vinho de casa* is magnificent but it should be a little cooler for my palate" and Jerry doesn't clap eyes on him for two years, he'll still remember next time that he likes his wine cooler. It's really quite staggering, his memory. Faces, tastes, likes, dislikes – it's his stock-in-trade. He is our biggest character.'

I awoke at mid-afternoon in a different world. Green wine is not strong stuff, but on top of my tension at seeing again the place where the shark had dismembered me, it knocked me cold. I surfaced in a world of rolling green hillocks, green swamplands and on the right the sea, beating against the dunes a few miles from the main road from Lourenço Marques to Vila de Jaoa Belo, a small town at the mouth of the Limpopo River, about half-way to our destination.

The road proceeded in a long, shallow curve through the swamps, over a series of high causeways and bridges, between two lakes and eventually to our objective, a village named Chidenguele, well after dark. There in the wine-shop the over-bright acetylene light, the girl and her map all helped to create the air of a different world.

After our exchange on mapping, the girl didn't get up but turned round on her canvas stool and eyed me cautiously.

'You're a tourist?'

I shook my head.

'Well, thank heavens for that,' she replied. 'Since you aren't, here's what you might expect at A Tendinha.'

'A Tendinha?'

She indicated our surroundings. 'The Little Pub,' she replied. 'Or Jerry's own extra special.' She grinned and took a phial of red ink. On her left knee she sketched a triangle with an 's' inside it, another triangle with several smaller lines inside, and something like a bird sitting on the bottom of a rocking-chair rocker. She looked at me quizzically. Well, I thought, A Tendinha might be a dump, but it had something which wasn't included in the sketch.

'Your round,' I grinned back. 'No, wait – something out of Michelin guides . . . ?'

'Clever boy,' she grinned. She gestured at the drawings on her leg. 'Red – pleasant places. Triangle, with 's' – monti – and there are ruddy mountains everywhere. That's where you came in. Lago – lakes, that's the other.

We were both laughing like a couple of kids.

'And that's the first cuckoo in spring,' I said, pointing at the bird.

'No,' she said. 'It indicates a quiet and remote site.'

She sketched again rapidly. There was a tiny telephone, a

bath, a bidet, and a shower.

'All this and waterborne too?'

'*Non, non, non*! No telephone – except there.' An instrument for which Bell must have turned in the original patent was fixed above the bar next to a Coca-Cola girl. 'Bath – available but not recommended.' She drew a big black cross through the bidet. 'Alas, this is not Paris. In fact,' she went on, 'A Tendinha has everything, except what is really necessary. And why the hell you should choose it, I wouldn't know.'

Certainly the pub was pleasant enough. The bar was part of the dining-room. There was a stack of wine bottles where she was sketching and their mustiness mingled with the fresh warmth of the white rolls, wrapped in bright clean napkins, in baskets on the tables for dinner.

'I've come to work for Dr Barrow,' I said. 'I'm Ian Ogilvie.'

I may have imagined it but it seemed to me that some of the brightness went out of her smile.

'Yes, we all know Dr Barrow well – he often comes here from St Gregory.'

'St Gregory?' I said. 'Aguada da Boa Paz, you mean.'

She pointed at her map.

'Your geography needs brushing up,' she said. 'Look, Dr Barrow has his headquarters down at St Gregory, which is the old fort they built hundreds of years ago. Aguada da Boa Paz is a sort of composite name for this whole section of coast here. I don't think you can point to one spot and say, that is Aguada da Boa Paz. The village is called Chidenguele.' (She pronounced it almost like Chiddingwell.) 'That's where you are now. You're at least half a dozen miles from Boa Paz, or rather, St Gregory.'

'Then why set the astrolabe on 25 degrees?'

Barrow's voice, fogged with anger, startled us.

He said to her, 'Why do you waste your time drawing this bloody fancy stuff which hasn't any meaning at all?'

She looked taken aback. 'I'll draw what I wish. If you don't like it, I couldn't care less.'

Barrow peered at the map. His anger seemed to grow.

'Rubbish! Rubbish, every line of it! Boa Paz is 24 degrees 53 minutes south.'

The girl was silenced by his vehemence. My first dislike

of Barrow returned.

'This is a pictorial map,' I said. 'What difference does it make whether it is shown 25 degrees or 24 degrees 53 minutes?'

'It's a map, isn't it?' went on Barrow, peering closely at it. 'What's the idea of this?' He jerked his finger at the cross.

'It's the *padraoa*,' retorted the girl. 'You should know.'

'Yes, I know,' he said softly, the fogginess in his voice making it sound strangely sinister. 'Yes, I know, but how do you?'

'They planted the *padraoas* as navigational guides on headlands and things hundreds of years ago, she said. 'They were Portuguese navigation points. A marble pillar in the form of a cross, about the height of a man. White marble . . .'

He looked beside himself.

'Why an astrolabe, why *Drake's* astrolabe?' he went on.

The man's mad, I thought.

'What the hell's wrong with using a symbolic astrolabe and an old cross on a decorative map?' I interrupted. 'What's all the fuss about anyway?'

'Listen, Ogilvie,' he said. 'I'm paying you to do a shark job for me. That's enough. I don't want you snooping around offering me advice. Particularly on subjects which you don't know anything about.'

He seemed to get a grip on himself.

'I'll give you ten pounds for that map,' he said to the girl.

'I wouldn't sell it to you if it were the last thing I had.'

Barrow paused, picked up one of the bottles of ink, and splashed it across the sketch of the astrolabe. He splashed more across the *padraoa*. He then swung on his heel and disappeared through a side door.

She looked at the mess, biting her lip.

I said gently: 'It looked like Perestrello.'

'It *was* Perestrello,' she said. 'Look at those lines.'

'I do not know this Mr Perestrello,' came an oily voice from behind me. 'He is new to Chidenguele, yes?'

I turned to see the fattest man I have ever set eyes on. His unwashed jowls hung in folds, hiding a stained, sweat-soaked shirt. His trousers may have been white once, but now they were an undefined dirty dun colour. They were so distended it looked as if he had elephantiasis. He smelt bad. His breath was ghastly.

'Jerry,' said the girl, almost in tears. 'Jerry, look what he did.'

The eyes looked shifty. 'It is a bastard,' he said. I noticed the use of 'it' instead of 'him'. Never offend a customer. Especially the great Dr Barrow.

He put a huge grimy hand on the girl's shoulder.

'This Perestrello?' he pressed in his greasy voice.

She shook her head. 'A Portuguese navigator who surveyed this coast centuries ago,' she said. 'He did a wonderful job. Drew a wonderful map.'

'So did you,' I said.

'Did, being the operative word.'

'Dr Barrow did this?' asked Jerry. 'Why did you make Dr Barrow cross?'

'Look here,' I said. 'I'm employed by Dr Barrow and he may be a big shot around here, but anyone who does what he does just for the sake of a couple of minutes south latitude is a bastard, in any language. I intend to tell him so.'

'I am Jerry,' he said as if that were sufficient. 'I know Dr Barrow. He is very clever. You must have been very rude.'

'Look . . .' I began.

'Jerry,' said the girl, 'Dr Barrow became very offensive when he saw I had marked Aguada da Boa Paz in as 25 degrees. He insisted it was . . . what?' she turned to me.

'24 degrees 53 minutes,' I said. 'I'm going to ram it down his throat.'

Jerry caught me by the arm.

'Life is funny,' he said, breathing heavily. 'Here I have enough meat on my legs for three men, and you haven't any at all.'

Barrow had told me he never forgot anything. Nor, it seemed, did he miss anything. He waved a placatory hand.

'Dr Barrow is a man all by himself, and strange things happen to a man who thinks so much,' he said suavely. 'Good wine and good food is much better.' He slapped his gross belly. 'It serves me well. Come, I have some special fish from the lagoon and I cook it a special way for Miss Hunter. You will sit at her table and you shall have a bottle of Solar de Minho to calm you.'

'Jerry has an almost female quality of killing the great problems by tending the little needs,' she said. She took his arm affectionately. 'Lead on, Jerry. Good wine, good food, and blast Dr Barrow.'

He led us to a table. 'There will be a full house tonight,' he said. 'They are coming from beyond the village. Plenty people, plenty food, plenty drinking. But first the Solar de Minho.'

He shuffled off, obsequious and over-friendly.

Silence fell between us. It was one of those awkward pauses when one seems unable to trespass beyond the initial stages of a friendship because that simple liberty might wreck the whole thing. That is how I felt. I wanted to say something more about Barrow's loutish act in defacing her exquisite map, but I feared if I did I would be presuming. Jerry returned with his bottle. The tables were starting to fill up.

'*Solar de Minho,*' he rolled it round his greasy tongue. 'A great wine.' He slapped his Falstaff-like middle. 'Look, I have taken on the figure of a barrel from all the good wine I have drunk.

He had just started on the wiring of the cork when eight men walked in. They looked different from the others who had been coming in ones and twos to fill the place.

'Birthday party?' I asked.

'No,' he said. 'They are from the centre up there.' He waved his hand vaguely.

'Centre?' I asked. 'What sort of centre? Are they Portuguese?'

'Ah no,' he said, and I thought for a moment he was nervous behind his oiliness. 'Not Portuguese. But good customers, you understand.'

He was gone before I could ask him further questions. The group were certainly foreigners.

'Who are they?' I asked the girl. 'What's this centre Jerry seems so shy about?'

The big hazel eyes looked at me curiously.

'You're asking a lot of questions.' She raised her glass and almost consciously put her thoughts behind her. 'Pleasant hunting in Chidenguele.'

I lifted mine. 'Or St Gregory. Or Aguada da Boa Paz – I don't know which.'

'It's a sort of U.N.O. tropical health research centre about ten miles from here – more inland,' she explained. 'I really

don't know what it's all about. Dr Barrow seems chummy
with the head of the outfit. He'll probably be along soon. He
usually comes on a Saturday night.'

The hubbub of voices grew. Men were at the bar, at the
tables, Jerry seemed in his element.

The uproar was cut short. There was a roll of chords struck
on strings from the direction of the Bar's side door. Everyone
stopped talking and drinking. Like a celebrity emerging for
his concert, Barrow appeared, striking rapid chords on a
strange instrument. The wolf on its stilt-like legs came behind.

'I'll be damned!' I exclaimed.

I had thought of Barrow as conservative in his clothes, but
there was nothing like that now. He wore a scarlet shirt with
a bright blue handkerchief knotted round it and black jeans.
In his hand he held a remarkable instrument. For want of
a better word I would have called it a guitar but I could
see it had five strings, unlike the usual six of a Portuguese
guitarra. The sound-box was made of some animal's shell.

Jerry had materialized at my side. '*Argita,*' he whispered
as the men shouted and stamped. '*Argita* is a Bolivian guitar.
You know the doctor was in South America. The sound-box
is the shell of an armadillo. You watch how he plays with one
finger. It is masterly. No spangle, just his finger-nails.'

Barrow jumped up on a couple of boxes in front of the
bar, the wolf next to him.

Then the strings began to speak. Jerry told me later the
piece was called a *nocturno*. The men round the bar stood
motionless while the chords rang through the shabby bar.
Then the tempo changed. Jerry whispered, 'It's different now
– *corrindho*. He's dreaming about the almond trees in bloom.
Sometimes he sings, but not always. Listen if he sings.

Perhaps the music made me over-sensitive but I sensed a
meaning behind his words. The chords died away. Men
banged their glasses. The girl was moved. Barrow was enjoying the adulation. The noise died and he seemed about to
begin again.

'*Oba, oba!*' called an ironical voice.

A man in the doorway clapped his hands faintly. It was
the sort of face you could see staring out of a portrait of old
Spain. The thin face and over-red lips under the sharp black
beard didn't belong to the year 1960. It was half grandee,

a quarter monk and a quarter sadist. He smoked a thin cheroot. Barrow didn't seem disconcerted. He waved to the newcomer.

'Dr Pinto,' Jerry told me. 'In charge of the United Nations research group.'

'What did he say?' asked the girl.

'*Oba, oba* – like the English say: jolly good show, encore, bravo.'

The man with the grandee's face moved forward, towards Barrow. It seemed to me that he gave a flick of the cheroot and Barrow relaxed.

Then Barrow began to sing. It was a voice with which to make a fortune, not to waste on a crowd in a second-rate pub miles from anywhere. The fogginess did not spoil its natural deepness and mysterious resonant quality.

The beat quickened.

'*Barco Negro*,' whispered Jerry in my ear. 'The Black Ship. A woman's lover goes away to sea and the other women say he is drowned. Listen. The Black Ship.'

I felt my spine tingle as the husky voice probed its way through the song.

'Listen well,' he muttered. 'Listen well. And now the woman sees a black cross on the rocks. A black cross. On the rocks.'

Barrow started to thump with his thumb on the sound-box. I noticed Dr Pinto's thumb, under the cheroot, signal once, twice, three, four times in time with Barrow's. Five, six.

Jerry interrupted. 'The Black Ship and the Black Cross! The woman thinks she is gone mad. They say he will not come back.'

Barrow's thumb rang against the armadillo shell and there was a pause. Then the quick beat resumed and he sang lightly through the remaining minute of the song. There was a round of applause. Barrow grinned and waved. Then, with a gesture, he struck a chord. He waited for the applause to die. They all thought – and so did I – that he was about to sing again. But with a movement of contempt he turned and spat across the bar at the small statue of St Joseph against the mirror.

One of the Portuguese pulled a knife and rushed at Barrow. It was exactly what he had hoped for by his contempt, his deliberate defiling of the saint precious to all Portuguese homes. Barrow bent down and said something to his pet. She didn't move as the knife came down towards his bent back. Then in a flash Barrow had the hilt of the knife and the man's hand in his. He gave a cry of pain and Barrow forced him back, the arm still stiff. He jerked his head back and spat in his face. Simultaneously Barrow struck him across the eyes with the end of the *guitarra*. He fell to the floor. The bitch leant down and sniffed at his face. Barrow stood back, looking around the crowd, daring them. He stooped and picked up the knife. With a swagger he pushed his way through the silent crowd to Pinto's table and sat down.

'That's your boss,' the girl said. 'Heaven help you.'

I was too shaken to reply immediately, then I said. 'Miss Hunter . . . ?'

'Shirley.'

Then I noticed Barrow ordering his pet outside. The crowd gave way to let her pass.

Jerry appeared. His oily face was grinning through its sweat.

'Lagoon trout, Miss Hunter and Mr Ogilvie,' he said. 'The serving must be quick; Dr Barrow will be wanting his chessmen.'

'Chessmen?'

'Yes.' Perhaps it was the way he said it which gave it an extraordinary meaning, or perhaps it was the tension which seemed to linger in the air after Barrow's song. 'Dr Barrow and Dr Pinto are to play chess together once a week at A Tendinha. The first game is tonight. They are both experts.' He smiled at Shirley.

'Think,' he said, 'the first European man stepped ashore at Boa Paz nearly five hundred years ago. For five hundred years the lagoons have had the most beautiful trout in the world. And until Jerry discovers them, they are neglected. Entirely, utterly.'

I opened my mouth to congratulate him but he went on.

'Both are such experts,' he said, 'that they have arranged to have a new set of chessmen every time they play.'

'Don't be silly, Jerry,' Shirley said. 'What's the point of that?'

'I will show you after that.' He indicated the meal, smiled

and went off. He came back past our table carrying the chessmen. Shirley said, 'They're not chessmen – they're tiny elephants!'

Jerry showed us one. 'Not tiny elephants, but real elephants from the womb,' he said.

Each minute, white thing was complete in detail. The umbilical cord even. A strange feature was that they were not upright but slightly slanting.

Jerry said quickly, 'The side door through the bar. Second door on the left. Go in.'

There we found an old man carving. I had knocked but he had not heard. Even now, no sound reached his dead ears. On the rough table made of old wine cases was a set of little chessmen.

'Look, more embryo elephants,' exclaimed Shirley.

The old man hadn't heard us yet.

I gestured at a shelf.

He must have made a couple of prototypes for the first set,' I said. 'These are like those they're playing with now.'

The tiny embryos were smaller than those he was completing. They were not only larger: each was a little more upright.

'What is all this about?' she asked. 'He just can't go on carving one ivory set after another . . .'

'It's not ivory,' said Jerry, who had materialised next to us. It seemed almost indecent for a man of that bulk to move so silently. 'It's a local soapstone which is very soft. The old man can make a complete set in a week . . .'

'Look Jerry,' I said. 'I don't know what goes on here, but whatever it is, it is giving me the creeps. First, that outburst by Barrow at the map. Then that song and now this crazy chess game. I suppose this set he's making is for a week hence?'

'Yes,' said Jerry. 'I told you. Once a week.'

I picked up one of the embryos. The old man saw us for the first time and smiled.

'Look! It's off-putting because it's too perfect. Why the umbilical cord? Why are they now slanting slightly vertical?'

Jerry shrugged and raised his palms outward. 'So you noticed that too, eh? So the too perfect becomes repulsive? Holy Jesus, then I must be a saint!' He gestured. 'My bed, the loveless bed of a saint, because my body is too lovely for any woman.'

He roared with laughter.

'And in amongst all this, the old deaf man sits carving his beautiful umbilical cords! We are a fine group here, my friend! An old man whose fingers only remain in this world the rest of him has already passed beyond. A fat, stinking hulk of flesh they call Jerry. And a legless man who is sensitive to atmosphere. Only you, Miss Hunter, are normal. Or, I suppose so, yes?'

The light dipped as its acetylene supply faltered and then died.

From beyond the open window came a scream which ended in a gurgle. My arm was taken in a steel grip. It was Jerry. In his other hand was a knife.

'*Septentriones, Meridies, Oriens, Occidens,*' he chanted softly. 'Quiet! Quiet!'

North, south, east, west, he had said in Latin.

'Poor Manuel,' he went on, 'he was probably still stunned from Dr Barrow's blow and didn't see the wolf coming. Aguada da Boa Paz is not a place to go for walks, Mr Ogilvie – especially at night.'

'Barrow – the bastard!'

'Quiet, Mr Ogilvie, very quiet, if you please. Dr Barrow is a very good customer and I would not like him to think that anyone was involving him with that . . .' The knife point indicated the open window and beyond a glimmer of water.

I tried to shake myself free.

'Blast him and his game of chess.'

The oiliness went from Jerry's voice. His grip remained.

'Except, Mr Ogilvie, it isn't chess,' he said.

CHAPTER FOUR

'The shackle!' yelled Shirley. 'The pin in the shackle – knock it out, knock it out!'

I was off balance and the angle of cant was growing as the wire from the winch paid out. In a moment the boat would be on her side on the rocky verge of the lagoon. I missed the blow.

'Hurry!' called Shirley.

The boat was leaning over towards her, waiting to jump aboard when it ran down a kind of launching ramp made of greased poles to the water. I connected with the pin at my second attempt. It shot out. The old boat staggered on the greased poles and shot towards the water. Shirley made a practised leap over the side and grabbed the wheel. We careered straight towards the water, gathering speed at every yard. 'Hold on!' she went on, enjoying the thrill. We hit the water with a wave of spray and came to a slowing halt.

'That slide makes every trip for me,' she said. 'Now get that engine going before we find ourselves in the middle of the lagoon.'

'You'll have to help me up,' I grinned back. 'This old wreck and I have a lot in common – we can't stand upright without help but once we get going . . .'

'Then?' she teased.

'One is apt to get becalmed. It never lasts, you know.'

She bit her lip. 'No,' she said. 'It never lasts. And then one has to be pushed along. Just like that engine.'

I stumbled towards the motor, seeing the way we had come. The old lifeboat started every voyage on the lagoons in a most flamboyant way. From the massive roots of the wild fig trees, a wire from a winch was run through a tackle and spliced on to the end of the heavy chain. At the end of the chain was a pin and shackle. The boat's path down the steep shore into the water was marked by a row of heavily greased poles. The drill was to ease the winch wire a few yards and then, before the old boat toppled on her side, to knock the shackle out. She then shot down the poles into the water.

I reached for the ancient starting-handle when something caught my eye.

'Did she take part in the Battle of Trafalgar?' I asked Shirley.

Her black moment seemed to have gone.

'So you've seen it.'

'I wouldn't have believed it. Kelvin 1904.'

She smiled at my amazement.

'And take a look at this,' I went on. 'Special screw valves in the top of the cylinder head. What on earth – or sea – are those for?'

Shirley joined me. She had changed out of the tight American jeans of the previous night into more serviceable corduroys. Her breasts made a firm line under her white cotton sweater, piped naval-fashion in blue.

'Them were the days before hemispherical combustion heads, hot-spots and the like,' she grinned. 'If it's cold, all you do is pour petrol straight into the cylinder through one of those, screw it tight, swing the handle and hope you don't get your arm broken in the process.'

I looked closer. 'Magneto only.'

'That's right,' she went on, amused and pleased at my admiration for her boat. 'But this wasn't part of the original specification.'

'You mean this old engine is – was – something more modern? What in heaven's name propelled her first – oars?'

'This was one of the first experimental steam lifeboats ever built. Newhaven, 1888. She was an enormous success. This set the design for all subsequent lifeboats round the British Isles.'

I looked at the high, old-fashioned stern and bow.

'It's like putting a jet propulsion in the *Victory*.'

'The hull's still magnificent,' she said. 'There's a double stressed skin of mahogany, and all the rivets are copper. There's not a single galvanised nail or a piece of iron. Not a trace of dry rot anywhere!'

She sat down on the edge of the engine well. She looked very lovely.

'You'd need all that, the way you launch her,' I replied. 'The hull must be like iron to take that punishment.'

'That's the way they did it in those days and she was built for it,' she said.

'I can pronounce Kelvin and Newhaven, but I'm damned if I can get my tongue round the name of this boat.'

'*Txibange?*'

I tried. 'It's like two fenders rubbing together.'

'*Txibange,*' she repeated. The ending was soft and half swallowed, in the Portuguese fashion.

'What does it mean?'

'It's the name of the hill where we were just now,' she replied. 'Txibange. Look, you can see it from almost anywhere in these parts. It's where the soapstone for the chessmen comes from.'

She had shown me, before coming to the boat-house, a superb glimpse of the lagoons, the lush hills, the great marsh to the north-east and the tiny village from the five-hundred-foot summit of Txibange. And, beyond to the east, the line of the sea behind brilliant white dunes.

Barrow had disappeared by the time I got to breakfast. There was only a terse note from him which Jerry handed to me. 'Come to St Gregory and report to me.' Jerry, oily and obsequious, gave no sign of the previous night. After the screams had died away, he had left Shirley and me and the old man alone in the darkness, while he went for a refill for the lamp. On his return he refused to talk about it. Later I kept my bedroom window tight closed. By morning I felt I had a hangover.

'You still here?' asked Shirley when she came to breakfast.

I showed her Barrow's note.

'How does he expect you to get there, anyway?' she asked.

'I wouldn't know even in which direction to start,' I said. 'Or how far it is.'

'There's a sort of track which Dr Barrow takes. It's every bit of eight miles. I know, I'll take you in the *Txibange.*'

'What's that?'

'It's a boat I run. It really belongs to Jerry, but he'd sink it if he got in. It's a much longer way round to St Gregory, but we'll make an expedition and go via the lagoons. It's tricky, but it's worth it. It'll take half the morning. It's probably nearly twenty miles, because you've got to twist and turn. They're not all big lagoons like Inhapavale.'

'Inhapavale? These names are beyond me.'

'That's the big lagoon we saw from the window last night,' she replied. 'Txibange's on its edge. I'll give you a look-see from the top before we start. Then you'll know exactly where you're going.'

'Everything, including the geography, seems a bit bewildering round Aguada da Boa Paz.'

'Chidenguele,' she corrected. 'And no one gives Boa Paz its full title. St Gregory is O.K.'

'Well, I'm glad about that.'

'You're not the only one who's mixed up,' she replied. 'The map-makers are way out in everything. No one rightly knows where Boa Paz is, despite the fact it was the principal Portuguese watering-place on the sea-route to India five hundred years ago.' She dug at the fresh white roll with her knife. 'That's what I was trying to show on my map.'

'The bastard.'

'How did you get mixed up with him?'

'I'm a shark-hater by profession,' I said lightly – and I told her briefly about the Pretoria fiasco.

'How does Barrow expect a man . . .' she hesitated '. . . without any legs to build a shark barrier in the sea? And just where?'

I didn't care for the note of pity.

'Look, Shirley,' I said. 'Just forget about my legs – or lack of legs. I eat, dance, swim and walk like any other man. I even make love, like any other man.'

The smoke wreathed about her. She watched me through the haze. There was a long pause.

'Just where in the sea does Dr Barrow want his anti-shark barrier?' she asked finally.

'He didn't say. I don't know why either. But I'm to have all the equipment I like to play around with.'

'Come, I'll show you what it looks like from the tip of Txibange,' she said. 'We'll be able to see the Baixos da Boa Paz – the Bank of Boa Paz. My bet is that it's somewhere there that Dr Barrow wants his barrier.'

She didn't ask if I could make it to the summit, but obviously it was in her mind. She put her hand on my arm.

'You scared the pants off young Tonio this morning,' she said. 'He told me all about it when he brought my tea. He saw your legs standing by your bed and damned near dropped everything. He didn't know, of course.'

Somehow she'd put things on a normal basis. I hadn't felt so good in years.

We went through the thick sand which was the village main street between a few off-white houses. At the end of the roadway track was a high hill. A giant Indian Cupang tree added another sixty feet to its height and must have been visible for thirty miles out to sea in clear weather.

I was sweating heavily when we reached the summit and sat down on a low stone wall at the base of the huge tree. The lovely lagoon – much more like a Scottish loch to me – lay below us between lush green banks: we could also see the sea breaking against the reefs beyond a lower fringe of lush hills between us and the coast.

'Across the loch there – what's that patch of scarlet?'

'It's a good Portuguese lagoon and has been for five centuries. That's a sort of poppy. It puzzles me, though. All the hillsides between the lagoons and the sea for about twenty miles from here are covered in it. It's not the ordinary European poppy, but a big one about four feet tall, although the flowers look the same. Funny, I've never seen it on this side of the lagoon.'

I continued to stare out across the water, feeling some inexplicable unease.

'What is it?' she asked.

'I don't know – something to do with the poppies, maybe.'

'I expect you haven't got over last night.'

'Perhaps.'

'Why this series of lagoons is not better known I cannot fathom,' she went on. 'We are now about the middle of the chain . . .'

'I don't know the beginning or the end. I was asleep for part of the journey here and I arrived in darkness. You'd better start to orientate me.'

'There's the village called Chidenguele, about eight miles inland from the sea. In between it and the sea are two big lagoons. There's a gap between them which leads into the sea. That's where Aguada da Boa Paz is. On the shore of one lagoon, Inhapavale, which is the bigger of the two, is the fort of St Gregory. It looks one way on to the lagoon and the other way out to sea. Got it?'

'Go on.'

'We are about 180 miles north of Lourenço Marques – in fact, if you look out to sea, you would be staring almost at the southern tip of Madagascar – across the Mozambique Channel which separates Madagascar from Africa. About two-thirds of the way between Lourenço Marques and Boa Paz is the Limpopo River: it flows into the sea at a little town called Jaoa Belo. You passed through there on your way here. Just north of the mouth of the Limpopo there begins a big complex of lagoons only a mile or two, and sometimes less, inland from the sea. They are mostly small ones until you reach Boa Paz. The gap where Boa Paz is lies between the two biggest until you get much farther up the coast. The lagoons are all fresh water, despite being so near the sea. Boa Paz is the only spot where there is a gap in the lagoons to the sea – that is why it was used as a watering-place for old ships. As an anchorage it is dangerous. I can't imagine why the Portuguese didn't water from the mouth of the Limpopo or some other big river. A little way out to sea from where the lagoons break through at Boa Paz is the bank of Boa Paz, which is a strange kind of shoal. I'll take you there.'

I faced towards the sea. 'So, I've got a big lagoon on my left, and a slightly smaller one on my right, and a gap between them which is Boa Paz?' I repeated. 'And on the one side the old fort of St Gregory, which has one foot in the lagoon and the other in the sea of this bank or shoal you talk about? Right?'

'Right.'

'All this and Boa Paz too.'

'If we had Boa Paz too everything would be fine,' she replied. 'Although Boa Paz was the principal Portuguese watering-place on the sea-route to India, no one knows exactly where it is. It might be anywhere within a radius of ten miles.'

'I'd say St Gregory provides the answer,' I said. 'A gap between two lagoons, flowing into the sea, and a fort to protect it.'

'See if you say the same when you see St Gregory,' she replied enigmatically. 'We're on our way there now.'

The old Kelvin tap-tapped its way up the beautiful lagoon

like a blind man in a park on a spring morning. The lifeboat made its way past one big island in the lagoon obscured by reeds: a giant Jabiru wader-bird poked his red and black beak through the undergrowth; one of Jerry's lagoon trout rose lazily and eyed us with no thought of what wine and garlic could make of him. Ahead a sharp cliff seemed to split the lagoon in half.

'Starboard,' said Shirley. 'There's the star attraction round here.' She indicated. It seemed all lush greenness.

'Inhagotou,' said Shirley. 'You pronounce it like a boot sucking out of mud. The haunted marsh. No one has ever been inside. The natives won't go near it.'

'It looks formidable.'

'I hate to think what's inside there – apart from malaria. It's an enormous place. It's got a sort of square section at the bottom about eight miles long and then it shoots off northwards and forms a head just like a dragon. There's a river which comes out from the head like a dragon's tongue and there are swamps, tiny ones, which make the dragon's ears. It's a dragon of a marsh in more ways than one.'

'I realize now why your decorative maps are so good,' I said.

Perhaps I allowed my growing boredom to show because she snapped. 'I'll take you to your bloody St Gregory and your bloody Boa Paz. I hope you find it more interesting.'

She spun the wheel and rammed open the throttle. It was a long twelve miles. She never said a word. I sat behind the old engine, just to be out of the way of her anger. We headed eventually for the narrow gap between two lagoons where the seaward entrance was.

Suddenly the bar and breaking sea was right ahead. Shirley had misjudged the force of the tumble of water. It was too much for the old lifeboat. The bow swung wide and she went over on her side. Shirley, panic-stricken, spun the wheel.

Txibange turned turtle.

I clung on, trapped by the up-thrust of the water, trying to hold my breath. I spotted Shirley caught in the spokes of the wheel.

But *Txibange* was made of stern stuff. I felt her try to right herself with a curious sideways planing movement and then with a heave and water pouring from the self-draining cockpit, *Txibange* turned over again. I lay on the deck. I gulped in air. *Txibange* still cavorted in the breaking water. Shirley hung half in, half out over the rail and was beginning to slide overboard. I ripped my pants down and unhitched my artificial leg using it as a sort of clumsy fishing rod. I thrust the foot into the waistband of the girl's trousers. But the knee bent and wouldn't hook.

Then *Txibange* rolled and the knee snapped shut. I twisted the harness strap of the leg round my wrist, and slowly, uncertain that any moment the knee would snap open again, I hauled the half-drowned figure up the deck. I grabbed her shirt, but the sodden material gave, revealing her breasts. I released my hold on the leg and grabbed her under the arm and at the same time I slipped the leather strap free of the leg and drew it tight round her arm.

She was unconscious.

I had to find something to make the boat fast to but I didn't suppose I would have seen the white of the caisson shaft amid the broken water if it had not been for a black splash of paint on it. My first thought was that it must be a buoy, but the shape was wrong. It seemed to be half submerged and yet, from the way it swung, I could tell it was not fast on the bottom. A trough swept by, showing the shaft set into what looked, for the brief second I saw it, like a bell-shaped steel caisson. By now we had been carried more than a mile out to sea by the current. Such a race could only be round a bank – the mysterious bank which Shirley intended to show me.

I got a line round and through a piece of steel projecting from the caisson. *Txibange* calmed like a runaway horse. She was grinding against the shaft but she was safe for the moment. I reckoned I could get the engine going, given time. Shirley lay strapped by one arm to a stanchion. I balanced on one leg to free her. Her eyes flickered open for a second. Her glance went to her naked breasts and then to me.

'Is this rape?' she murmured and relapsed into unconsciousness.

I half fell into the cockpit. I pummelled away to get the water out of her lungs. Within minutes she stirred and was sick.

She sat up. 'God! What a stupid bloody fool I am! If it

hadn't been for you, I would have thrown away both our lives. To have tried that entrance against the bar! No one but a suicide or a crazy, angry woman would ever have attempted it!' She felt for her cigarettes and threw the sodden pack on the grating. 'Dear God! There's about two fathoms with hard sand underneath, and five and four on either side, with a damn great chain of rocks across the entrance into the bargain. "Entry impracticable for all vessels!" Heavens!'

I managed to get myself into my trousers. I gripped her shoulder to keep me steady in the rolling craft.

'So there's no way out at all?' I asked.

'There is and I know it – that's what makes this damned performance so unforgivable!' she burst out. 'Look! You see the Boa Paz light – no, more to the left.'

The white circular tower of concrete with two windows stood out against the hill, which rose two hundred and fifty feet high. The white was thrown into sharp relief by a swathe of scarlet poppies. Much more striking, however, was the Txibange hill far inland. The giant Cupang tree stood out like a beacon. The ancient seaman who planted it there had known his stuff. It was the best landmark for miles around.

'There's a reef close to where we came out,' said Shirley. 'The correct drill is to turn hard round there and run alongside the walls of St Gregory. You keep going inside the reef for about a mile and a half and then you can slip outside opposite that hill – that one with the two white sandy streaks and the reddish look. It's not as high as the lighthouse hill but you can't miss the gap in the reef.'

I scanned the line of low hills backing the dazzling white shore.

'St Gregory?' I echoed. 'I just don't see it.'

'I told you it was odd,' she said. 'Whoever heard of a fortress guarding an anchorage – one of the most important to the lifeline of Portugal to the East in those days – which doesn't even command the anchorage? And where is the anchorage?'

'Perhaps this is it.' I replied.

She started.

'What are we fast to?' she asked. 'What did you find to

get a rope round on the Baixos da Boa Paz? This is about the most dangerous place on the coast.'

'It's some sort of steel caisson,' I said. 'I didn't stop to examine it.'

She looked more puzzled.

'A caisson? Out here? Impossible!'

'See for yourself.'

She was back in a minute.

'I just don't get it.'

'Nor do I.'

'The whole thing is so wrongwayround, it isn't true,' she said. 'Look, you can see for yourself what I mean. This bank is about eight miles long and forks away to the east. We must be nearly on the south-westerly end. The current tears round it. The bank is a couple of miles across. Out there, do you see anything?'

I looked out to sea but all I could see was still, quiet water.

'Nothing but waves.'

'Exactly,' she replied. 'Now this.'

She turned me round facing down the coast. Companion hills to the lighthouse one gave the coastline more decisiveness than the flat, level north-eastward line near the outfall entrance.

'I . . .' I began. 'Why, damn it, the sea breaks on this side . . . no that's incredible.'

'It *is* incredible,' she said. 'The sea doesn't break on the bank on the seaward side, but waits a couple of miles before it breaks on the landward side. It should be just the other way round. There are rocks and shoals and God knows what, and yet the sea chooses a spot only a mile offshore to break, and yet there are the same obstacles out to sea. There's only a couple of fathoms on this bank and out on the seaward side it is only four and a half feet. And just round the edge of the bank – we're a couple of hundred yards from it – there's thirty fathoms. I almost think there's a gap in the bank somewhere – it drops away from six fathoms to twenty-three and then back again to only one and a half, but I haven't ever had the courage to explore.'

'I'd like to see this buoy we're tied to,' I said.

'A buoy? Don't be silly, Ian. Who'd want to put down buoys in this part of the world? All shipping gives this section of the coast a wide berth right up as far as Cape Correntes. If they're buoys they're certainly not for shipping.'

'Well there's one for you,' I said, pointing at smoke to the east. The ship's upperworks were just visible.

Shirley looked taken aback.

'That's the first ship I've ever seen in these parts,' she exclaimed. 'Whatever she is, she's way off course. I don't know how you managed to get a line round this thing,' she said. The top of the caisson or buoy – whatever it was – was almost submerged.

'Why, look!' she went on. 'It's got a white tarpaulin or something tied round the top.'

It wasn't a tarpaulin, but plastic. It was white, painted the same colour as the main body of the bell-shaped thing underneath. It was about three feet square at the top.

'It's wide enough to admit a man,' I said.

'What makes you think . . . ?'

'I don't know what I've come to, Shirley. Nothing in this place seems to add up. Not even you.'

'Let's get the engine going, shall we? The sea seems easier, and we can skirt round the bank into deep water. Then I'll take you to St Gregory through the gap in the reef.'

We cast off and within yards the caisson was invisible. We ran the length of the bank and then turned in toward the land. I admired her handling of the old craft.

'I don't know how you know your way around in all this broken water,' I said. 'Are you sure we're not in for another buggy ride?'

'I'm not sure how Dr Barrow is going to feel about your arriving mermaid-style.'

We ran close through the gap in the coral reef and I could see the crabs scrambling for their lives at the sound of the Kelvin. *Txibange* swung hard aport and we were in a still, wide channel behind the barrier reef, whose flat top might have been laid with slabs of prepared concrete. Against the land, the water ran deep against the solid rock of the cliff above.

We started to turn to where the steep, grassed slope ran down to the water, broken by trees which overhung the water and gave it a civilized look by contrast with the jungle wildness of everything I had seen so far. Then the engine coughed and died.

Shirley grimaced. 'She must have shipped a drop of water in the carburettor,' she said.

'I'll clear it,' I said and opened the engine box. The engine had been waterproofed meticulously. There was a magneto. Far from being a Kelvin 1907, it was a Bosch 1959. I checked its electrical leads. The trouble certainly wasn't there; every one had been waterproofed. There was no corrosion, no accumulation of half a century's oil and dirt about the engine. Above the casing it looked as oily as Jerry, and as dirty, but underneath it was all as bright as a Le Mans racing car.

I spotted what had caused the engine to peter out. The throttle lead had become stuck. I jiggled it for a moment to get it working. Then I saw something as puzzling as the engine itself. The throttle could not be advanced to the full because a tiny steel bracket with a retaining screw had been fixed across the linkage. The throttle of the engine's power could still be delivered – if one turned back the screw. I eyed the engine speculatively. What lay beneath that shabby old casing with 'Kelvin 1904' so prominently embossed? I was certain it was a powerful motor in prime condition.

I tried the starter. It fired at once.

I said casually to Shirley: 'You keep this engine in good shape.'

'I don't – I can't. I haven't that sort of skill.'

I also wanted to check the exhaust to see that it was clear. Then I saw something else. There was a silencer, but a pipe ran right round it. Attached to the silencer itself were two other loose sections of piping. They would take three minutes to connect up. Then the boat would have an almost completely silent, powerful motor in place of a worn-out rattletrap. A wolf in sheep's clothing.

Above the boat the old walls of St Gregory towered sombrely. I looked up and felt cold.

I resolved to get at Boa Paz's secret.

CHAPTER FIVE

As the lifeboat swung towards the landing-stage of St Gregory, I saw something else which sparked a fresh wave of speculation in my mind. I looked up at the old stone walls, loopholed windows and gun bastions high over my head.

'The whole thing faces the wrong way!' I exclaimed. Those guns should face out to sea, not across the lagoon. You don't build a fort to protect an anchorage and then point the guns away from the sea towards the land. The old Portuguese had nothing to fear from the landward side. If there was danger, it would be from the sea. It's all wrong.'

'I told you St Gregory was all wrong,' she said. She must have seen something in my face.

'Leave it alone, Ian!' she said urgently. 'Leave it alone! Don't go digging even if there are things here which don't add up. Just let it be. I also want to tell you something. You're a different man somehow from the one who set out from A Tendinha this morning. Something's happened to you – I could almost wish it hadn't. I'll swear you even walk differently.'

She tied the boat to a rusty ring in the masonry.

'You'll need a bit of steadying over these cobbles,' she said.

'Thanks, no,' I replied, slipping over the rounded, irregular stones which led to the main entrance. 'I'd rather Barrow saw me under my own steam.'

I went through the gateway to St Gregory. Shirley came only as far as the door. Barrow must have seen – or heard – because he was waiting for me.

'What the hell do you mean by coming to start work at midday?' he demanded.

For a moment I forgot Barrow in surprise at the chair he'd been using. The back, of heavy indigenous ironwood, was supported by two native heads and jutting out from either side at waist level, were two jackal heads. The arms were twice as long as any ordinary chair and extended into finely-worked triangles, open at the centre with carving all round. In the nose of both jackals were rings of finely-carved silver.

'How did you expect me to find my way here – walk?'

'Always the play for sympathy,' he sneered. 'No legs, help me, please give a penny to the poor beggar who has lost his legs.'

I looked at him levelly. It flashed across my mind that perhaps Shirley was right. Perhaps I *was* different.

'I've come to Boa Paz to do a job,' I retorted, 'and I intend doing it. What I need to know right now is exactly what you want done.'

His mood and anger evaporated. He walked to the window. The room might once have been the quarters of the long-dead Portuguese commandant. The low ceiling was white-washed and solid. The doorway had been widened to accommodate a big wooden carved surrounding, the sort of thing one finds in a rich Arab's home in Zanzibar. The desk at which he sat was really just a huge slab of wood, littered with papers, and supported by two old cannon trunnions. A wall was hung with native weapons and a brace of old pistols.

Its most striking feature, however, was next to Barrow's chair. Sunk into the stone floor was a thin pole about six feet high, surmounted by a fish worked in some pale metal with a sheen like silk. It was almost as broad as it was long. Tail and fins swept back as if they had been designed for space travel and, with fine artistry, a long thin sliver of metal ran backwards from the lowest portion of the jaw.

'It is magnificent, is it not?' he said, easily now. 'It was washed up about a year ago, where the reef ends and the channel begins. From some old wreck.'

I ran a hand along the metal. 'It's too new to come from a Portuguese caravel.'

'Yes, of course,' he replied. 'It's much later than that. I'd say about a hundred years, judging from the binnacle which was washed up at the same time.'

'It would be easy enough to find the wreck if she's as close as all that.'

'Do you think I hadn't thought about it? What do you think I want an anti-shark barrier for? The whole place is infested with sharks. No one has ever explored inside the reef or even taken soundings of the bank. It's too dangerous. Now

– let's get down to business.'

He gestured through a doorway behind his desk. I could see the outline of a small laboratory furnace and the smell of hot asbestos penetrated the room. I caught a glimpse of the leather harness used to carry the orange-coloured lead container holding radioactive isotopes.

'Your lab is all ready for you – beyond mine. That is, until we devise something out on the bank itself. Everything in the way of cables, power, oscilloscopes and the rest of it will be here in a couple of days. You've got a completely free hand Ogilvie. I give you six weeks to do the job.'

I stared at him in amazement.

'Six weeks? Don't be absurd. Six months, at the earliest.'

He led me by the shoulder to the window facing the bank where we had nearly come to grief.

'I want an anti-shark barrier built to cover about half a mile square on that bank, in six weeks. Six weeks, do you hear? Either you do or you don't. I'm offering you a £1,000 bonus. But I must have it – soon.'

'Nothing at all is known about the characteristics of the shark,' I began, sounding pedantic. 'The first problem will be to catch a live shark and carry out various tests on it. There is also the question of skin resistance, water resistance, resistance of the cables, mud, sand and so on. I can't build an anti-shark barrier from scratch without any data in six weeks.'

He indicated the ship Shirley and I had spotted out to sea. She was closer now. She had heavy top-hamper and square masts like gantries.

'That's a salvage ship. Mine.'

'What do you intend to salvage?'

'In September 1505,' he replied – 'September 21st to be exact – a Portuguese captain called Pedro Barreto was on his way to India. He'd watered at Boa Paz and his ship was lying out there, just beyond the bank. A gale came up suddenly from the south-east as they do here. The ship was on a lee shore. It was only a matter of time before she was wrecked. In that vessel, Ogilvie, was a complete treasure exchequer for buying spices in the East. I reckon in terms of modern money it was worth half a million sterling – maybe more. In gold. It's out there now. Half a million, Ogilvie!'

'Why wasn't it recovered at the time?' I asked.

'The other ships of the squadron lay offshore, because St Gregory was in the process of being built. They stayed, but Barreto went on to India. He thought they'd chop off his head for the loss of the whole expedition's exchequer. For years the Portuguese tried to recover the gold. They never did. There are records to prove it. Sickness – always sickness. Boat-loads of men drowned – and eaten by sharks. The outlet from the lagoons brings down silt and the small fish sharks love. The Baixos da Boa Paz is the biggest place of sharks on this coast. Look!'

He pointed down to the channel through which Shirley and I had just come.

In its slow-moving, clear water I saw three Blue Pointers. They moved lazily under the battlements of St Gregory. My old horror returned.

I said, 'Thanks for the offer, Dr Barrow, but I don't intend to risk the rest of my chewed-up body just for the sake of netting you a calm half-million. And you have the cheek to offer me a mere £1,000! It would have been fun – but six weeks to play around with a half-baked experiment in the worst shark nursery in Southern Africa! No thanks!'

The Blue Pointer lay in the middle of the channel. The others had gone. He was alone. He was holding himself steady and in the clear water I could see the faint pinky-blue at the base of his dorsal fin and on the sides towards his belly. The eyes, at the back of the sloping, curved snout, were malevolent.

I jerked myself back to what Barrow was saying.

'I thought when I saw you amid the wreckage of your tank that you were the man I wanted,' he said, his voice brittle. 'I was wrong. It was purely dillettantism. An intellectual shark-hate, with some props of scientific rubbish to back it up. You haven't the guts of a mayfly.'

I scarcely heard him or noticed Shirley come in. The Blue Pointer flicked his tail and the muscular contraction ran right up his back. The water was as clear as that. He was like a boxer coming into the ring after the bell. I'd have to go down there and tangle with him. No holds barred.

I found myself wanting something to throw at the shark. Hanging on the wall was an old-fashioned harpoon. I reached for it.

'Ogilvie!' warned Barrow.

I scarcely heard him. I swung myself on to the broad stone of the window-ledge. I took the harpoon and looked at Barrow.

'I take my intellectual pleasures seriously,' I said.

Then I lurched sideways so that I rolled down the steep slope into the water.

The splash as I hit the water startled the shark. I plunged the harpoon into him but his speed tore it out again. He left a red trail behind him, however.

Then he came back at me. He opened his jaws and I thrust the harpoon at him. The blade went deep into his throat and was wrenched out of my hand. There was an upheaval. Then everything became quiet.

I must get the hell out of here, I told myself. All the sharks in the neighbourhood will be here in a minute. I struck out and hauled myself on to the bank as the first great fin came streaking past. Barrow and Shirley were waiting for me.

'I'll get him up to his quarters,' he said.

He swung me up across his shoulders and we re-entered the fort via a small door leading from the roof of the building. We made our way along a whitewashed passage into the first room we came to, which had once been the Portuguese garrison chapel. Shirley found a chair and they seated me in it. The place was bare and the windows were without panes but the centre was taken up by what appeared to be an old-time ship's binnacle. The compass section had disappeared but its socket remained and the wooden pedestal bore stains of long immersion in salt water. Where the original binnacle lights must have been was a strange object about fifteen inches high. It looked like a vase of thick crystal and was shaped something like the final stage of a mini space missile, with a pointed nose and wider base. This base merged into a heavy piece of brass. There seemed to be some sort of mechanism at the base from which a crank projected. The 'vase' contained some thick, viscous liquid like glycerine.

I felt fine. Shirley fussed over me but Barrow saw my interest in the binnacle and said, 'This was washed ashore at the same time as the fish back there in my study. It's definitely not Portuguese and I can't bring myself to break the container to find out what the liquid inside really is. That crank operates some sort of mechanism but it's too rusted up to tell what it is. There's some lettering cut into the brass – the ship's name, perhaps.'

Shirley went and looked and spelt it out for my benefit.

'I-N-C-R-O-Y-A-B-L-E.'

Until then I'd been fine. I blamed a delayed shock reaction for the way I started to shake. Both Barrow and Shirley switched their attention to me but it became so bad that Barrow again picked me up and carried me to a bedroom, still shaking uncontrollably.

Six weeks later was D-day for testing out the shark barrier I had constructed, six hectic weeks into which both Barrow and I had thrown all our energies. The experiment was to take place out to sea on the bank of Boa Paz, centring on an improvised floating workshop consisting of a shack supported by floating 44-gallon steel drums. Inside was a mound of equipment, electrical gear and batteries as well as a diesel generator for feeding current through the barrier cables. The salvage ship, named *Gripper*, stood by. Originally I had used current from her engine-room but had to discard that source because I found it fluctuated too much. Now the diesel was running full belt for the experiment.

Barrow's support for my night-and-day effort had been invaluable. He had a genius for holding a tight overall rein without getting in the way. I had wanted miles of cable for the barrier. It came. I needed two sets of condensers in case one failed. They came. A steel door for the floating workshop: Barrow had them tear out part of the salvage steamer's engine-room. Special trays for carrying equipment, welding cables, and conveying testing instruments; Barrow said crisply that I wasted half a minute every time I walked across the moving floor of my shack. Instead he begged two wheeled surgical tables from Dr Pinto's hospital and had long handles attached to each. I never had to move when working on the complex wiring system. The shack, moored to the *Gripper*, had been my prison day and night. The naked electric lights in the lab were often the only light at night for miles.

Now the diesel pulsed. It was another one of Barrow's examples of go-getting. I wanted direct, high-voltage current.

Within days he had a first-class power unit brought by road from Lourenço Marques and slung aboard my workshop-raft. Now I was ready to put my theories into practice – and see if they really would work.

With H-hour only a little away, I found myself sweating with anxiety as well as the morning heat. The set-up was the same as my Pretoria experiment, only enlarged to field scale. There were the same condensers, the same oscilloscope with its flickering ballet of light, the same gradated switch. Heavy cables, thicker than my fingers, ran in a cluster out one end of the shack, tilting it slightly, despite the counter-balance of the big engine in the other corner. I fiddled with the electronic gear and tightened up, quite unnecessarily, a connection to the cables. I'd slept overnight in the shack after checking and re-checking every item of gear into the early hours. My head throbbed from sleeplessness and the odour of diesel fuel. We'd set the time for mid-morning. Barrow hadn't turned up, nor had Shirley. I'd had nothing to eat. My breakfast consisted of a cup of black coffee.

Now there was a thud against the side. It was Shirley. I hadn't heard *Txibange* above the diesel. I grabbed the painter and made the old lifeboat fast. Shirley looked tense.

She took my hand and jumped aboard. She indicated the empty coffee cup: 'Do you think you could rustle up some for me? I feel I need it.'

'You've nothing to lose on all this,' I said. 'After all, it's my experiment, and if it fails . . .'

'This is mine too, Ian, because I want it for you. For you and what you stand for.'

'We've been through all this a hundred times,' I replied. 'You know the odds are stacked against this experiment. It's all too empirical, too quick, too many loose ends.'

'I know we've been through everything: I know all that,' she replied. 'But . . .'

'But what?'

It was Barrow. He didn't need to be cat-footed. He glanced round as if checking.

Shirley covered up. 'But nothing. It's Ian's day, that's all, and the sooner we get the agony over, the better.'

'Better be,' remarked Barrow.

I said above the diesel, 'Better be damned! Look, this is

one big shot in the dark. What do I know about sharks and their characteristics? I've never had the opportunity of studying one. Time, time, time! Six weeks! God's truth – I needed six months!'

Barrow said, 'We caught you a Blue Pointer in the channel.'

'All I found out about it was that it was dead!'

'We caught six others – remember?'

'All that taught me is that a shark is an extremely delicate creature – and I mean extremely delicate,' I retorted. I gestured at an illustration of a shark on the wall. 'Topography of a shark! I couldn't care bloody less about its dorsal fin, its pectoral fin, its caudal fin, its inter-orbital width, or anything else. What I want to know is, what happens when it undergoes an electric shock? Has it got any sort of mucus covering like my blasted mudfish? I don't know the answers and without them this is so much playing around!'

Shirley finished her coffee. 'After all,' she said as quietly as the diesel would permit, 'That's the way they made the first jet engine, isn't it? Pure trial and error. Nothing to go on.'

'Except hope,' I answered. 'And not so much of it in this case. I don't even know what the seawater resistances are – they probably vary with the salinity. I don't know what bottom there is – whether it is all sand – as I hope. I don't even know . . .'

Barrow interrupted me.

'Have you linked up all five sections of the barrier?'

'Yes. The basis of my theory is that a barrier can be built round an area like this, about half a square mile, by two heavy electrical cables laid parallel to each other on the sea bed. I've made a refinement and laid a third cable, a sort of mobile sweep, which we can trawl across the area in case sharks get trapped inside or are not electrocuted. You know the theory – a shark can be made to swim involuntarily towards the positive electrode if you give him a big enough shot of current. It must be direct current. Short pulses of current create an electrical field between the two cables and will prevent sharks from crossing it. At the same time the water inside will (I hope) be safe for *Gripper's* skin-divers to get down to the treasure ship.'

'It looks like a great big horseshoe with two rails round

it,' said Shirley looking at a diagram of the circuit which Barrow was studying.

'That's as good an analogy as any. A great big horseshoe, with two cables right round it, with the open end of the horseshoe closed by the reef at our backs.'

'How do you know that the shocks intended for the sharks won't kill my divers?' asked Barrow.

'I know nothing, and nobody else does either, about the reaction of sharks to electrical fields,' I said. 'Damn it, that is just what I have been trying to tell you. Everything is hope and guesswork. I haven't had time for reasonable experiments.'

'But your theory's right?' Shirley insisted.

'It's like designing a jet engine for a motor-car. The theory is easy. The practical difficulties are enormous. I do hope, however, that the relatively low potentials involved won't kill the divers. There's only one way to find out – to try. I have a hunch too, that the effect of the electrical shock might be proportional to the length of the shark, that is, the bigger the fish, the smaller the electrical potential required.'

Barrow said, 'That's the sort of deduction I like to hear. Let's get going. Throw that switch.'

'Are you sure there are sharks inside the barrier at the moment?' asked Shirley.

'There's probably half a dozen of them right under this raft at the moment,' he replied. 'Haven't you noticed the sardine shoal today? And if that weren't enough to lure them, there's all the debris coming down from the lagoons for them to feed on.'

I put on the switches leading from the condensers. The oscilloscope began its pattern. The rectified charge of 2,500 amperes waited to dart down into the sea. I decided not to give it the peak amplitude of 3,000 – not just yet, anyway.

Suddenly I felt detached. I had none of the screwed-up tension of my laboratory experiments. I fed the current into the barrier.

Nothing happened.

The oscilloscope told me that short pulses of current one millisecond long, at a rate of five pulses a second, were flowing into the heavy cables. I knew the positive was on the outside of the horseshoe, and the negative on the inside.

The current pulsed – one, two, three, four, five, a second.

I suddenly had a great desire to burst out laughing. Then I turned on the inner, or sweeping, cable. It was as undramatic.

The water over the bank was calm and the waves barely rocked the *Gripper*. The sea had ignored my puny experiment. I sat down on a stool and shrugged.

Barrow eyed me. 'What do you expect – boiling sea, sharks fighting madly against death?' he asked. 'Sunday paper stuff. You've put an electrical barrier into operation, and its value is now to be assessed. It keeps sharks out, or when they cross, it electrocutes them inside. Not so?'

He was right, of course.

'I'm going back to St Gregory in the *Gripper*'s boat,' he went on. 'You'll want to make your observations. Let me know this evening. Give the thing a thorough testing.' He was so calm, so easy, that I could scarcely credit his fret of the previous six weeks.

Shirley and I went out on to the little wooden platform round the floating shack. Barrow cast off. He disappeared in the direction of the fort. We stood a long time, saying nothing. Then she turned to me.

'You're not happy with it, are you Ian?'

'I simply don't know anything more now than I did before I switched it on,' I replied. 'For it to be of any value, I must know. I can't just sit and watch the surface of the sea.'

Suddenly an idea hit me.

'I've got it! Hydrophones – that's what I need. Then I can hear what's going on . . .'

'Why hydrophones?'

'Fish make panic noises when they're chased or caught, and sharks must do the same! If I string half a dozen hydrophones round the barrier, I can hear if the sharks are being affected. I can step up the current or cut it down –'

'Let's make a tour of the barrier in *Txibange*.'

'Good.'

We set off towards the reef. We hadn't gone far when I spotted a Blue Pointer lying stomach upwards on the surface. Shirley threw her arms round me.

'Oh Ian –'

She kissed me. 'Take the wheel while I get into swimming gear.'

While she was changing I saw a Lazy Grey and two more Blue Pointers, belly upwards. I didn't stop. I wanted to get close to the cables on the reef, which partially closed the bank on the seawards, and see what was happening where the electrical field converged.

Shirley rejoined me wearing a bathing costume.

We were within fifty yards of the inner side of the reef when she called out: 'An act of faith, Ian?' and dived into the sea.

'Shirley—' She was swimming strongly towards the reef, which was flat-topped and smooth, about twenty feet wide. She was making for a smooth spot capped with the grass 'lawns' which the mussels keep trimmed. I reached for the gear lever to slow the boat and as I did so my eye caught something in the clear water, close inside the reef.

The masts were gone, but the beautiful hull and powerful quarters were unmistakable. For the first time in a century and a quarter, I had removed the ocean watchdogs from the wrecked clipper.

PART TWO

CHINA AND EAST AFRICA
1838

CHAPTER SIX

Canton Harbour. China. 1838

He'll take the masts right out of her on the next tack,'
observed the wizened little man with the smashed-in face.

The Portuguese sailor shook his head in wonderment.

'There's more north than east in this wind,' he replied.
'She'll go right over on the next tack. Nothing will stand up
to that sort of hammering. She'll capsize right here among
all the shipping.'

The sad eyes of the wizened man became more thoughtful.
He put the telescope to his left eye, as if the brass of the
eyepiece might still bring pain to the shattered right side
under the cheekbone.

'He's right on the limit but he's handling her superbly,'
he said. 'Just look. The helmsman as well as her skipper must
be a genius.'

The Portuguese took the telescope. He snapped it shut with
a slight shudder.

'Superb, I grant you, but madness,' he retorted. 'Only a
Baltimore-built slaver could stand up to that sort of thing.
I'll lay my head on a block that every seam on deck and
below, is spurting water.'

'I expect they have been every mile up the China Sea,'
replied the little man dryly.

The Portuguese gasped. The tall white fabric of the sail
and masts leaned, checked, leaned again, and then righted
itself. She had missed the junk by feet.

There was a faint anxiety about the little man.

'Do you really think he'll capsize, Captain Barros?'

The other shrugged with a Latin gesture.

'How can he not?' he asked. 'Look, Houqua, there are
certain forces which can be taken to the limit, but beyond

that limit other forces come into play: the wind and the sailing ship. You can take a ship to the limit of her sails and her masts. Then the wind gives one little extra puff . . . and . . . pouff! A lovely ship like that one lies in the water with no more use than a racehorse which has failed to take a jump. I say that your Captain Ogilvie cannot get away from those forces. He is heading now for the jump. In a moment he breaks the horse's back. The wind is more north than east, I said. It has that extra half-knot which is more than the limit. And your lovely ship goes over. Nothing can save her.'

'And my lovely cargo of opium goes too,' said Houqua. 'Except . . .'

'Except what?' asked the Portuguese roughly.

'Except,' replied the tiny Chinese. 'This man Ogilvie may have something up his sleeve. He is a very daring sailor, they tell me. In fact, if he were not, I would not be entrusting a cargo of 500 chests of opium worth £60,000 to that little ship of his.'

Barros frowned. 'That's a lot of opium, Houqua,' he said.

The faint smile was lost in the shattered cavity under the broken cheekbone.

'This is not London,' he replied. 'This is Canton, and the year is 1838. I have none of the scruples about opium that your London reformers have. To me opium is a marketable, highly profitable commodity. No moral issues. I have made Canton the centre of the market for the drug in the Far East. I need opium for my business. And my business demands its transportation rapidly. That is why I charter a man like Ogilvie. He'll take any risk to make a mile or two on a day's run. As he is doing now. I am interested to see how he pulls himself out of what you as a skilled sailor regard as an impossible situation.'

The thickset Portuguese frowned.

'I am a pilot by profession, not a racing yachtsman,' he said. 'All I can say is that I have sailed with many fine skippers and think I know about every dodge. But the cards are stacked against that ship and Ogilvie.'

Houqua stared down the Pearl River, his eyes thoughtful. The flags over the thirteen European factories – including the famous East India Company – stood out straight across the river. From his austere office Houqua commanded a great

view of the Pearl River towards the clipper anchorage at
Whampoa, although at this distance he could only see the
top of the big pagoda on Hanan Island, at the north end of
the anchorage. Ogilvie's little topsail schooner came tearing
through the cluster of small craft and junks which littered
the water fronting on Canton and its suburbs. Braced up
sharp, she flung water up under her three jibs; the steep rake
of her masts told her ancestry at once to the sailor's eye:
fast, low rakish. That could only mean Baltimore-built for
slaving or privateering. Since the latter was long past in 1838,
it meant she had been a slaver.

The schooner bored in towards French Folly, at the
Southern end of the old city.

'If she doesn't go about, she'll be ashore in a moment,'
said Barros.

Houqua replied. 'Perhaps from my point of view it would
be better to have a cargo of opium stranded than a cargo
of opium sunk.'

'He's going about!' exclaimed the Portuguese excitedly.
'He can't do it! He can't do it!'

Some movement of the lovely fabric, some shadow moving
on the sails, had told him what Ogilvie was attempting.

'Holy Mother of God!' exclaimed Barros.

She started to go about but as she did so, a flicker of
white canvas burst from under the long bowsprit, now starting
to turn almost on its own axis as the bow swung round
towards the opposite side of the river. Then it billowed, like
the first curve of a woman's breast in adolescence, then filled
and leaned proudly forward. The sail, hard as a board, bit
as the fool-wind of the three jibs above spilled into it. It
forced the lovely head down into the water and held it hard
as she went about. It held it down still as the extra half-knot
of wind came from the north. The schooner jumped like a
mad thing as the long booms and spars came round, but the
helmsman held her. She leaned over on the opposite tack
towards the big island across the river, over the limit and
yet within it, balancing herself between destruction and breath-
taking perfection. The small boats scattered away under the
creaming forefoot.

Barros was sweating.

'Holy Mother of God!' he repeated. 'I've never seen a sail

like that before. Under the bowsprit!'

The wizened Chinese was smiling now.

'I think you will agree, Captain Barros, that Ogilvie is a very remarkable skipper.'

Barros watched the ship tearing across the crowded anchorage.

'That, Houqua, was genius. I've never seen a sail like that. Did you see what he did as she hung in stays . . .'

'Let us not get technical, shall we, Captain Barros?' said the tired voice. 'All I know is that I have a man who did something which proves to me he is the man I want for the job. How he did it doesn't really concern me.'

'But . . .' said Barros. 'Look, look now again!'

The big triangular sails dropped with precision. The square spars swung on the raked foremast, back into the wind. She checked like a reined horse. She lost way. There was a splash under her bows as the anchor went down. At the same moment, the two square sails were clewed up, the sailors on the yards being invisible from the two watching men.

'Man-o'-war drill too,' said Barros.

'Do you realize, Captain,' asked Houqua, 'that Ogilvie could be tortured to death for bringing his ship up here? No European has ever brought, or is allowed to bring, a ship to this zone. They must anchor down the river at Whampoa. The Emperor says so.'

'The Emperor in these parts is Houqua,' said Barros. 'I suppose, Houqua, you must be the richest man in the world. You could buy out His Celestial Highness and not notice it, and yet you live in a place like a monastery and work in an office like a cell. You don't even have a fancy desk.'

The Chinese fiddled with the rope of stones which hung round his neck.

'My merchant colleagues of the Co-Hong believe in having a good meal and a good wine: they dress their women up with jewels and there's not one of the thirteen of them hasn't had all the women he ever wants,' replied Houqua quietly. 'To me it's worth 100,000 dollars. There was a time about twenty years ago when I felt the compulsive need for money, what it could do and what it couldn't do. It's like life itself, is money: one passes from one extremity to the other, and my great wealth has brought me – willingly because it is naturally – only a desire for austerity. I have demonstrated to myself that money is nothing.'

'That's a neat philosophy which only a man as rich as you can afford,' replied Barros. 'And yet you'd not begrudge paying out the best part of 10,000 dollars to square the local mandarin because Ogilvie brought his ship up here to be under your very nose. It's still good business, in any language – 60,000 in sterling on your doorstep with only 10,000 dollars on the debit side.'

Houqua nodded towards the schooner.

'Ogilvie is making sure that I take delivery of the opium, even under my own nose. Look, they are loading the twelve-pounder amidships, and that broadside of four-pounders would be quite enough to keep any pirates at bay.'

Barros looked at the ship. The gun crews were standing ready at the trunnions and a rammer was being pulled from the ugly muzzle of the long-tom between the raked masts.

'Ogilvie knows that gunpowder is the best insurance on the Pearl River,' nodded Houqua. 'Any river pirate or any mandarin between Canton and Hong Kong, or anywhere along the coasts for that matter, would cheerfully cut his throat and all his crew's for a third of what he's got below.'

A boat dropped into the water and came swiftly across the anchorage towards the office.

Houqua seated himself behind the small desk when Ogilvie came in. The newcomer cast one penetrating glance at Barros and said in a husky voice, clouded with shouting orders to topsail hands: 'Thirty-eight days from the Sandheads, Houqua, and she's leaking like a bitch in heat. Fifteen hours from Lintin Island, with the wind right in her teeth. That's eighty miles. She's making more water than the pumps can cope with.'

The tiny little man behind the desk said nothing. His face seemed dominated by its large nose, slightly askew to the right, and even the high collar, like a latter-day marine's, did not fill the scrawny neck. The wispy beard lost itself, like his smile, in the scarred cavity under his cheekbone. He fiddled with the necklace of priceless stone, but Ogilvie could not see his fingers, which were lost inside the silk cuff, folded back almost to the middle of his forearm.

Barros gave a low whistle.

'Thirty-eight days from Calcutta to Canton against the monsoon! Impossible!'

'Listen,' snapped the schooner captain. 'For six weeks I've scarcely had a couple of hours' sleep. I've driven that ship right out of the water and when I make a record passage, I don't like my word doubted. I don't know who the bloody hell you are, nor do I care. I cut clean through the Natunas and Paracels. The wind was good. My first mate's still constipated from shock.'

Houqua looked at the eyes, hooded like his own, not with world-weariness and asceticism, but with fatigue and some inner, frantic drive. He noticed the white lines of evaporated salt on the high, turned-up collar of the jacket of pale green Hebridean tweed and in the two buttonholes on the high lapels. He frowned a little at the careless way the home-knitted cravat was tied round the half-shaven throat: he dwelt thoughtfully on the wide, cruel mouth and dominant nose. He's not thirty, Houqua told himself, but he's almost bald from driving himself the way he drives his ships. He hadn't even bothered to brush down the hair over the temples which spurted sideways above the black decisive eyebrows. He was swaying on his feet with tiredness, and yet Houqua knew that for a bonus of 1000 dollars he'd drive the tiny *Poppy* down the river again – or down the China Sea, half waterlogged as she was.

'You don't cut through the Natunas and Paracels as if – as if you were cutting bread,' exclaimed the Portuguese. 'I don't believe you could take a ship through them – why they're the foulest reefs and the biggest ship graveyards in the China Sea.'

Houqua looked with inward misgiving at the two men he had chosen to sail together. Within minutes of meeting one another a flashpoint of temperaments had been reached. That was in a calm office too, not a ship's deck in a heaving sea, with all its tensions.

Ogilvie wheeled on the Portuguese.

'I came through the Malacca Straits,' he retorted. 'I cleared Singapore just twenty days ago. I was off the Anamba Islands a few days later, right close in, looking for a breath of air. It was practically dead calm. Then I got a long slant and I hung on it through the Natunas. I then beat to windward, tack and tack. *Poppy* was magnificent. I worked the light airs all the way along the Cochin China coast. Then I got another lucky slant. I could either cut through the Paracels or lose a week on the passage. I chose the Paracels.' He grinned, a professional grin of pride with no warmth behind it.

'I took her through with even the crew's washing hung out,' he went on. 'Stunsails, ringtails, watersails – the lot. *Poppy* lay over twelve degrees. Thank God she's flush-decked. She'd normally draw ten feet but the opium is light and she was riding high. Murray pissed himself sick as we shipped over the coral and the niggerheads.'

Houqua watched the cruel mouth and thought that Ogilvie must have enjoyed his mate's terror. 'When I take a look at her bottom next, I'll bet I find oysters sticking to it.'

The Portuguese wouldn't leave it alone.

'Singapore's 1,400 miles and there are 700 miles of current against you. I don't see how . . .'

'You and Murray the mate,' replied Ogilvie. 'You haven't the guts of a sampan cleaner.'

Barros flushed. But he kept the needle going.

'The Paracels are about eighty miles across,' he said. 'That's a day's sailing against the current. I don't see . . .'

'That's the second time you've said that,' went on Ogilvie. 'Fair enough, it's eighty miles. I conned her through from the foremast. At eight to ten knots. Sometimes I couldn't see when the jib-o'-jib got in my way. But she went well.'

'The whole place is a deathtrap,' said Barros. 'There's not a chart to tell you even when it starts and finishes . . .'

'If you need an Admiralty chart every time you venture your delicate toes out of an unknown port into an unknown sea, then God help you and anyone who sails with you,' replied Ogilvie.

'The opium captains all have their own maps of the China Sea,' intervened Houqua. 'But I'd say Captain Ogilvie's knowledge is best. Any and every short cut, eh Captain? What was that man-of-war you raced from Singapore?'

Ogilvie shrugged. 'He hadn't a clue. Stuck to Admiralty maps like your friend here. I had been lying at Whampoa twelve days before he showed up from Singapore.'

Barros flushed again.

'I am a professional pilot, Captain Ogilvie. Although I do

not know the China Sea, in my own waters there is no one the equal of Jaoa Barros.'

'If it's not the China Sea or the Bay of Bengal, then I'm not interested,' said Ogilvie.

'I think, Captain Ogilvie, you may be, after we have had a little talk,' said Houqua.

Something in the tone of his voice diverted the Scot's attention away from Barros. Houqua waved his cuff towards a chair; his hand did not show.

He watched Ogilvie's heavy slump into the chair. He's dead on his feet, he thought. The staccato sentences, the raw edge to everything – that was the price of his triumphal cut through the Paracels with every sail drawing, something not even the most daring opium skipper had tried before. Houqua had heard of the drowned cross-trees sticking out of the coral, of the reefs and the pirates' flower-decked shrine made of English brass and Burma teak from the lean ships which carried the priceless drug. A pipe of opium wouldn't do him any harm at the moment, thought Houqua.

The Portuguese still wouldn't leave him alone.

'This jib-o'-jib – is that the sail you used just now, under the bowsprit?' He turned the 'under' into a reproach. Houqua feared another outburst.

Oddly enough, Ogilvie laughed.

'I've got the finest sailmaker at sea,' he replied. 'He's a genius is James Green. Comes not far from my home in the Hebrides. He's a thinking man, is Jamie. Thinks the shape of sails have something to do with their power. Flat curves draw better than full on a wind – he's got a word for it, something like dynamics of the air, or some such. There are all sorts of fancy clews and sheets for the *Poppy*'s sails. On any wind Jamie Green gets half a knot more out of the *Poppy* than anyone else could.'

'But *under* the bowsprit,' repeated Barros.

The cruel mouth eased a little.

'I called it a Jamie Green after him,' he said. '*Poppy* was built in Baltimore – you can see the sharp bow even at this distance. So I raked the spars back even farther than is usual. God, the weather helm of that little bitch! So Jamie Green thought out the idea of putting a jib-topsail up on the foretop-gallant stay, and another under the bowsprit. He cut it like a foretop-gallant stunsail. It's a wonder on a wind. But your crew has to be really smart to handle it when you're tacking. So it's called a Jamie Green.'

'When sailors get together, it is like this game called golf I hear they play in your country, Captain Ogilvie,' Houqua chided them. 'There's simply no end to saying how you did or didn't get one small ball into one small hole with one small stick.' But his eyes were unsmiling at the schooner captain.

'As a weighted assessment, Captain Ogilvie, would you consider this sailmaker of yours with the advanced ideas worth – how much on any day's run?'

Ogilvie's tiredness did not cloud his appreciation of the question.

'Running free, thirty to forty miles: maybe half that beating to windward.'

'A gratuitous gift for any ship,' murmured the Chinese. 'So from Calcutta your Jamie Green was worth from a thousand to fifteen hundred miles to you?'

'Yes, if you put it that way. I hadn't given it a thought in those terms. Of course, there's one hell of a current for anything up to eight hundred miles up the China Sea.'

Houqua said: 'How long, Captain Ogilvie, do you think it would take you to get to Mauritius?'

Ogilvie was sitting more upright now in his chair. The sagged slump of weariness was less noticeable.

'Given fair winds – and of course, the monsoon in my favour?'

'Yes.'

Ogilvie's eyes strayed towards the little schooner at anchor in the river. It was a lover's look: he would hand her out a beating but she'd revel in every moment of it. His eyes went over the delicate fabric, the assessing eye of the lover before his passion sweeps him off his feet. That passion would be the thrust of the monsoon, the adventure of the uncharted reefs, the great days of free running with all sail set, the spurt of the sea across a lee deck half awash.

'Five weeks.'

'Five weeks!' broke in Barros. 'Rubbish! Never! Why,

the *Medusa* holds the record, since way back in 1804! Your little ship would never stand up against a 32-gun frigate's time.'

'Why should I listen to a damn dago telling me about the Royal Navy? You'll be quoting Nelson at me next.'

Barros cut in. 'I'm called Jaoa Barros but that's the Portuguese form of John Barrow. That's what I was christened, anyway. And I'll quote Nelson at you, whether you like it or not: the *Medusa* carried Nelson's flag when he attacked the Boulogne flotilla in 1801. Fastest ship ever afloat. Even your opium clipper wouldn't stand up to her. She . . .'

'Rubbish!' said Ogilvie. 'The *Poppy*'s forerunners sailed rings round the Royal Navy. Ran in and out of the American ports during the blockade just as they wished. She's Baltimore-designed, and you know what that means.'

Houqua's voice became edged.

'Gentlemen, I didn't ask you here to argue about the merits and demerits of ships and their designs. You say five weeks, Captain Ogilvie, given a reasonable wind?'

The sailor nodded.

'And from there to the African coast?'

'Depends where.'

'Say directly opposite Madagascar.'

'Another ten days. I don't know much about those waters, or the currents.'

'That's why I have asked Captain Barros – or Barrow – which do you prefer?'

'Barrow, since the company is English.'

'Scarcely – a Chinese, a Scot and a Portuguese. But let it pass. Barrow, then.'

Houqua fiddled in a drawer. He pulled out a rolled piece of silk and spread it in front of him. The movements were deliberate, with a meaning and purpose which had Ogilvie upright in his chair, his fatigue gone. Barrow was staring too, at the square of silk.

Like the *deus ex machina* of the Greek chorus, he strung up the tension. He rang a little bell on his desk.

'Ask Idrisi to come in,' he told the servant.

The Arab came. Ogilvie waited, taut as a backstay in a south-east trade. The three men waited for Houqua to begin.

'This,' he said quietly, 'came into my possession. Let us

not ask how. Rich men gather things, you know. It is a map drawn a long time ago by a namesake of our Arab friend here, Idrisi. It is a map of the Portuguese coast of Africa opposite Madagascar. It is in detail. Idrisi was a brilliant geographer, and there's been no map-maker like him of this part of Africa since. In fact, you won't find a map like this anywhere in the world. It shows the coast from the north of the Limpopo to Cape Correntes. It is, I think, only a section of what must have been a complete detailed chart of the East African coast. The rest is gone, but this is all I want.'

Houqua turned to Idrisi: 'You know the island of Ouro?'

'We pilots do not go south of Cape Correntes,' he replied. 'The sea is evil south of Correntes. I have heard of the island of Ouro. It is evil.'

'Perhaps then, Captain Barrow, you will be able to help us.'

'I have never head of Ouro.'

'Perhaps you know it by its Portuguese name,' said the Chinese softly.

'Aguada da Boa Paz.'

The Portuguese gave a throwaway gesture.

'The Watering Place of Good Peace! We abandoned it hundreds of years ago. The island of the strange sickness. Everyone died. The sailors also had a rude name for it— they swore they were impotent after visiting Aguada da Boa Paz.'

Houqua smiled.

'Perhaps that is why I never have had any desire for women. You see, I lived there. There is a race of small negroes, small like myself. Only we called it the Isle of Poppies.'

Ogilvie slumped back in his chair.

'Look, Houqua, I came here to deliver opium. I have. Not to listen to a lot of bull about evil islands and little negroes. It's a dream from an opium-den. I don't want any dreams. I just want to sleep. To me evil is a barometer at 28.30 in a typhoon. It's evil, but I understand it. To me a lee shore is evil. I know what it is. To me . . .'

The Arab eyed his slumped figure. Houqua noticed the affinity between the two men as clearly as the antagonism between Ogilvie and Barrow.

'Cape Correntes and southward are evil, Captain Ogilvie,' he said in a quiet voice. 'For centuries we Arab sailors have known about Correntes. The waves chop back from Correntes. There are strange currents, tidal waves from nowhere. The compass lies like a woman in love. They are tangible things, and yet I say they are evil. I have never been to Aguada da Boa Paz . . .'

'I say it is evil, an unknown evil. That is why the Portuguese abandoned the island,' Barrow asserted.

'And I say, gentlemen, that Aguada da Boa Paz is evil,' Houqua interrupted. 'I know. I have lived there.'

With a conjuror's gesture, he shot his hands from out of the enveloping cuffs. He turned the hands round and the three men recoiled.

Only the thumbs and forefingers of each hand remained. The palms were solid scar tissue.

He ran his hand up under the shattered cheekbone.

'The little men on Aguada da Boa Paz did this to me,' he went on. 'Even if your strange sickness had not taken away my male powers, Captain Barrow, do you think that any woman would have ever looked at me? Even those whom I bought would go and be sick outside after I had paid them. I am the richest man in the world, gentlemen. Aguada da Boa Paz will make me richer still.'

'How did they do that to your hands?' asked Ogilvie.

'They didn't; I did,' replied the Chinese. 'You see, they only chopped off my fingers. But for ten years I cut the flesh off my hands. Look . . .' He held out his hands palm upwards '. . . I haven't got any fingerprints.'

His voice became incisive.

'But, as Captain Ogilvie says, let us talk about evils which are tangible. Like opium.'

'But your hands . . .' said Barrow.

'It is part of the opium story,' said Houqua. He got up and unlocked a cabinet and brought out a number of bundles wrapped in dried leaves as well as some withered pods.

'Cannon-shot opium. From Malwa. The best in India,' said Ogilvie.

'You should know, Captain,' said Houqua. 'Your holds are full of it at the moment. Yes, that is the best opium in the world, from India. There is also the Patna and Benares opium, which is not as good, eh Captain Ogilvie? Still, good enough to risk every short cut in the China Sea for. However, gentlemen, I am a merchant and as a merchant I must offer the best at the most competitive price. So I have tried elsewhere for my product. This is from Turkey and this is from Persia. But Malwa remains the best. My problem is to get enough quickly. That is why on this voyage I shall pay Captain Ogilvie a bonus of £5000 in gold.'

Ogilvie didn't thank him.

'My problem is a simple one,' Houqua went on. 'I want more opium more quickly. True, there will be ships which may knock a couple of days off Captain Ogilvie's time, but it will not be significant. They will, of necessity, be smaller ships, and small ships mean small cargoes.'

Ogilvie's head was falling forward. He jerked it up.

'For God's sake, Houqua, come to the point.'

Houqua ignored the outburst. His tired, lidded eyes were on Idrisi.

'You will find that your ancestor Idrisi noted that even in his day the Chinese were trading with Madagascar, Mauritius and the other islands in the Indian Ocean,' he said. 'As a young man I went on a trading voyage. My first. Ten years later I returned from my first voyage. Without fingerprints, without my hands, my face smashed in by little negroes. Emasculated – by the island itself. I spent all that time on Aguada da Boa Paz. I also learned all about opium. You see, gentlemen, they forced me to pick opium – or should one rather say, bleed opium – for ten long years. Let me show you how it is done.'

Barrow and Idrisi went to the desk. Ogilvie's weariness was gone. Houqua took one of the withered capsules. It was egg-shaped. The other was globular. He found a tiny instrument with a concave top. The top was steel with three razor-sharp blades at either point. The shaft itself was bound with twine. He fitted the tiny blades into the lengthwise cuts on the capsule.

'This is an opium-bearing capsule. It is the milky juice which comes from this which brings me my wealth. Eventually, it is made into those.' He nodded at the cannon-ball of opium. He smiled thinly. 'You will see, gentlemen, that it takes a lot of this milky juice to make one of those cannon-balls of pure opium. One gets opium by cutting the fruits of the poppy in a certain way. If you cut too deep, then the juice runs down inside and it is lost. You also destroy the seed, which is good for oil. This little instrument . . .' he held it up . . . 'is a *nushtur*. The drill is to cut the poppy seed and tap off the milky juice—almost like tapping a rubber tree but on a much smaller scale.'

'It seems simple enough,' remarked Barrow.

'Far from it, Captain Barrow,' Houqua answered. 'Millions of poppy fruits have to be expertly incised, tapped and the juice collected. But—and this is the big but—the capsules grow within a very short time to the stage where opium is produced. The capsules only produce the drug after the fruit has turned a sort of light green. It is easy for the expert to tell when they are ready: a bloom, almost like the bloom on a grape, forms. We call it *cougak*. Once we see that, the fruits or capsules must be incised quickly, expertly, by the million. It must be done within a week. Otherwise the opium is lost.'

'A week?' echoed Idrisi.

'Yes, my friend, a week,' said Houqua. 'At the outside about nine days.'

'No wonder it is priceless,' said the Arab.

'It is true,' went on Houqua, 'that there is a subsequent collection when fruits form on the side-shoots of the poppy plant, but the main collection must be within a few days.'

'It must require millions of labourers,' said Barrow.

The scar twitched under Houqua's cheek.

'Yes, but there is another way, when you haven't got millions of labourers to gather it in. You step up—if I may coin a phrase from your country with its machines, Captain Ogilvie—your production rate *per capita*.' He held out the hands without fingers or fingerprints.

'The little men on the Isle of Poppies found that the production rate is stepped up by getting rid of surplus fingers. It helps quite a bit. I know. There is an additional time factor. You see, one has to collect the juice during the heat of the day to get the best results. That means one's working time is confined to incising in the early afternoon—until it is too dark to see any more.'

The hooded eyes rested on the three men.

'Until it is too dark to see any more.'

Not even death would wipe away the torture lines on his eyelids.

'Next morning one collects the juice which has spilled out since the previous day.'

He picked up a tiny knife with a burnished, razor-thin blade.

'This is how it is done.'

It was pure sleight-of-hand. Ogilvie saw the flicker of steel as it slit the round capsule within a minute fraction of an inch from the seeds inside. Houqua raised the blade to his twisted mouth after wiping it with speed and dexterity on a dried leaf. Then it lay across the remaining two fingers of his right hand, with a faint smear of spittle across its surface.

'I fear I have rather lost my touch after all these years,' he said. 'But I am glad to see I can still get exactly the right amount of saliva on the blade.'

'What is the spittle for?' asked Ogilvie.

Houqua smiled. 'It's a sort of built-in lubrication system for the knife. You see, the blade gets sticky from the juice. A sticky blade at that speed would tear the opium capsule. There's no time to dip it in water. So one must dip it in the mouth. The fruit still has to ripen after one has cut it. That's the knack of it.'

The Arab looked at him thoughtfully.

'If the knife blade did all that to your finger-tips over the ten years, it must have done something like the same to your mouth.'

'Yes, it did. Just think, Aguada da Boa Paz was quite merciful really. Imagine a woman having to kiss only scar tissue instead of lips and mouth. Boa Paz took away the desire. Perhaps I should be grateful.'

'In Turkey,' said Idrisi, 'a man who cannot cope . . . ah . . . with a woman . . . he considers himself worse than dead. There is only one thing there – to cut your throat as quickly as possible.'

'Things are different in Turkey,' replied Houqua. 'The flowers of the poppy are white and so are the seeds. On the Isle of Poppies the flowers are red and the seeds are slate-coloured.'

Opium is a branding iron on his brain, thought Ogilvie. On his brain and on his body.

Houqua poked at the cannon-ball opium in front of him.

'You can imagine, Captain Ogilvie, how long it takes a man who collects only a few ounces on the back of a leaf, to get together as much as this.'

'I knew the opium gatherers had it tough, but I didn't know it was as bad as this,' Ogilvie said. 'You were simply a slave?'

Houqua nodded. 'It sounds funny from the richest man in the world, but that is so. Ten years a slave.'

'How did you escape?' Barrow asked.

Houqua shrugged and brought Idrisi in.

'I shall always feel tenderly towards *dhow* captains,' he said. 'One was blown off course and was becalmed for a while off Boa Paz. I swam out to it.'

'I have heard of the sharks at Boa Paz,' said Idrisi. 'You took that risk?'

Houqua shrugged as he answered, 'What had I to lose? It is through my admiration of your fellow-countrymen that I have got you half across the world to be here today.'

Then he went on crisply: 'Gentlemen, I did not ask you to come here today to be witness to a scene of self-revelation, however interesting or repulsive that may have been. I am a dealer in the most valuable commodity in the world. Like Captain Ogilvie, my evils and problems are purely practical. They are, briefly, big supply and rapid transport. Regarding the latter, I have Captain Ogilvie. The former is a little more complicated – that is where Idrisi and Captain Barrow come in. I want opium, plenty of opium, and more quickly than anyone has ever brought opium to Canton.' He addressed Ogilvie. 'Captain Ogilvie, you will agree with the idea that if you carried twice the amount of opium on one voyage, it would save you making two voyages to convey the same overall quantity?'

'That's simple arithmetic.'

'Likewise, if the opium were twice as rich as this Malwa stuff you need only convey the same amount to achieve, in fact, double the quantity?'

'Yes.'

'Then what remains is to translate these abstractions into

reality, not so? To bring to Canton more and richer opium in one cargo, quicker than ever before?'

'It's simple enough as you say it,' answered Ogilvie, 'but how . . . ?'

Houqua tinkled his desk bell.

'Show in Mr Robert Fortune,' he said.

CHAPTER SEVEN

'Opium,' said Houqua, 'you might describe as my whore but tea is my wife.'

Robert Fortune, a man with a heavy, humourless face, looked slightly shocked.

Houqua went on: 'Captain Ogilvie is the keeper of my whore and as such must expect an exciting, dangerous life. Mr Fortune, the guardian of my wife, expects to be patient, virtuous, even dull in the exercise of his talents.'

He let the rhetoric slide.

'Mr Fortune is a noted botanist and collector whom I have brought from England to carry out a full investigation of my tea plantations north of Canton. He is also collecting for the Royal Horticultural Society in London. In China, merchandizing is regarded as somewhat shame-making. You know me as Houqua but my family name is Woo-E. I would never besmirch my ancestors, since I am a merchant, by using their name. For eight hundred years the family has owned large tea plantations in Bohea, the best tea land in China. Mr Fortune is investigating them for me.'

'Is this the captain of the ship?' asked Fortune. Without waiting for confirmation he went on: 'You will take absolute care, Captain, that the tiny plants growing in the glazed boxes are kept in the light on the poop. That means you must have them at least in the main or mizen-top. My principals insist.'

Ogilvie's mouth tightened.

'Who the devil are your principals to tell me where I must put any plants in my ship?'

'My principals,' retorted Fortune, 'are the Royal Horticultural Society of London.' He pulled a paper from his pocket. 'Here is my commission from that society. It says: "You will take care to impress upon the minds of the captains, the indispensable necessity of the glazed boxes being kept in the light, on the poop if possible or on deck, of failing that in the main or mizen-top."'

Ogilvie burst out laughing.

'Christ! Christ, Houqua!'

Fortune ignored the outburst.

'To be conveyed, I have several items which the Royal Horticultural Society commissioned me to obtain on this special mission to China,' he said. He smiled. 'The fingered citron, called *Haong Yune,* and the true Mandarin Orange or *Song-pee-leen,* and lastly, luckily, the Lilies of Fokien, eaten as chestnuts when boiled.'

' " The Lilies of Fokien, eaten as chestnuts when boiled! " ' Ogilvie echoed derisively. 'Next time you'll tell me I must uphelm and run before a squall in order to preserve the Lilies of Fokien or the flaming fingered citron!'

'The Royal Horticultural Society was good enough to advance me £50 in Carolus dollars, to be dispensed at my discretion,' went on Fortune. 'With Houqua's recommendation of you as a captain, I shall offer you ten Carolus dollars for the conveyance of these plants and correspondence to London.'

'Ten Carolus dollars!'

Houqua intervened.

'It is your professional opinion, as one of the finest botanists in the world today, that I want,' he said with a flash of humour. 'I will make a point of adding ten Carolus dollars to your 5000, Captain Ogilvie. Mr Fortune, we were busy on a question of arithmetic before you came in. What is the pure morphia content of Malwa poppy juice?'

'Fifteen per cent, if it's very good.'

'And ordinary good opium – Turkey or Patna, for example?'

'I'd say between eight and thirteen per cent, depending.'

'What is the best you know?'

'I've heard of isolated experiments being made in a laboratory – strictly control conditions which you couldn't reproduce under field conditions of 22.8 per cent.'

'Have you ever heard of the Orange River poppy?' asked Houqua.

'No. Wait a moment though, I have – *Papava Gariepinum.* Not called after the Orange River, but by its Bushman name Gariep, the biggest South African river. The Orange River poppy. Yes, that's it. Something odd about it. It escapes me for the moment.'

'Tell me what it looks like,' said Houqua. His eyes were very bright.

'It has a red flower just like the European poppy . . .'

'Yes?' prompted Houqua.

'But it's tall – about four feet tall. That's its unusual feature.'

'Is that all?' asked Houqua.

'The seeds are slate-coloured.'

A sigh ran through the wizened Chinese.

'Thank you, Mr Fortune,' he said after a pause. 'Please go now. I shall send 1000 dollars to your room with a runner this afternoon. His glance went to Ogilvie. 'Carolus dollars, if you wish.'

Fortune went. Houqua said to Ogilvie, 'He forgot to say that the Orange River poppy is the only poppy natural to the southern hemisphere. Also, its juice yields 35 per cent pure morphia. 35 per cent, Captain Ogilvie!'

Barrow broke in: 'If you know all this – why don't you import the seed and grow it here?'

Houqua spread his hands. 'It grows on the Isle of Poppies.'

'So,' said Idrisi, 'you have solved your arithmetic.'

'In my own mind I had,' he went on. 'But I wanted an expert opinion. It would be worth risking your ship twice through the Paracels for 35 per cent pure morphia, captain.'

Idrisi said, 'I can appreciate that the *Gariep* poppy is an excellent business proposition. Why not simply send to South Africa and get enough seed to grow here? Why bring me and John Barrow half-way across the world to pilot Captain Ogilvie to Boa Paz?'

'The Gariep, or Orange River poppy is wrongly named,' answered Houqua. 'It never came from the Orange River. It came from Boa Paz.'

'But how . . . ?' began Barrow.

'We should have endured Mr Fortune a little longer. A fellow botanist and explorer of his, William Burchell, discovered the poppy on the banks of the Orange River or Gariep River, about twenty years ago. In fact, I wanted Mr Burchell to be here today, but nothing I could offer him would bring him away from Oxford or Cambridge, or wherever he is. Towards the end of the Napoleonic Wars, Mr Burchell made a remarkable exploration of the interior of South Africa. It was during the course of it that he found the Orange River poppy.'

'How do you know about it?' asked Idrisi.

'I have agents throughout the world. Any information on opium or poppies is relayed to me.'

'I don't see where all this is getting us, Houqua,' said Ogilvie.

'Burchell found one isolated specimen,' replied Houqua shortly. 'How it found its way to the banks of the Orange River I don't know. It happened to be called that because by some million-to-one chance Burchell recognized it. Of course it is nothing of the kind. It should have been named the Poppy of Boa Paz. That's where it comes from.'

Ogilvie was slumped in his chair.

'Houqua, how much tireder will you make me with your chatter?'

'You can take a lot more than this.'

'Providing the price is right, yes. But I see no price here.'

'It may be a price even you will be unwilling to accept.' His odd undertone surprised Ogilvie.

Houqua went on: 'The Isle of Poppies is inhabited by a savage race of little black men. The giant poppy of Boa Paz has been cultivated and kept exclusively on the Isle of Poppies for centuries. The tribe is organized as a dictatorship. The penalty for almost every crime is death. They never leave the island except to raid for slave labour for the poppy fields. The mainland and the islands live in terror of the little men. They are fine horticulturists. The poppy was there originally but it has been expertly hybridized and cultivated. Anyone trying to remove any would be exterminated.'

'I think they must have worked on your mind too, Houqua,' said Ogilvie. 'It can't be as bad as you make out or else the Portuguese couldn't have got a foothold.'

Houqua asked Barrow, 'Do you remember the lay-out at Boa Paz?'

'We built a fort called St Gregory on a sandspit on the north-eastern side to guard the anchorage. There was a sea channel between it and the mainland. Its guns guarded the anchorage. It wasn't a success. The strange sickness killed off the garrison. It was abandoned.'

'The strange sickness,' echoed Houqua. 'The natives don't grow the poppy for pleasure but as medicine. On Boa Paz either you smoke opium or you die. Some people use it for malaria, rheumatism, even elephantiasis. On Boa Paz, whatever the malign sickness is, opium counteracts it. I took five to seven grains a day for ten years. I sell opium for men to dope themselves, to create artificial hallucinations, dreams, feelings of peace, ecstasy – all the things opium does. Not so on Boa Paz. The disease . . .'

'Malaria,' interrupted Barrow shortly. 'That's what killed off the garrison at St Gregory.'

'On the contrary,' replied Houqua, 'it is not fever. The patient becomes thinner and paler. He wastes away and his blood is the colour of water when he's dead. The negroes are highly skilled dispensers of the opium, which they all take. They balance it so that between the disease and the drug there is only a slight weakening of their reproductive powers, as well as a stunting of their growth.' He smiled without humour. 'Look at me if you want proof.'

He went on: 'The Portuguese never really got much farther than their fort on the sandspit. They made a few half-hearted expeditions against the natives. The pygmies led them up the garden path far enough for them to get the island sickness and the rest was easy.'

'The place seemed cursed right from the beginning,' said Barrow. 'Da Gama found it when he discovered the sea route to India. I still don't know why he chose Aguada da Boa Paz as a watering-place for his ships. There are plenty of rivers and fresh water elsewhere close by along that coast. It seemed as if something drew him there.'

Idrisi said, 'The Arab sailors have said the same thing in other words for centuries. I never knew why until now. I told you, we never go south of Cape Correntes. And Boa Paz lies a little south of Cape Correntes. I said, Captain Ogilvie, that the sea becomes evil there: it seems as if the land too, is evil.'

'All this gives me the creeps,' said Ogilvie.

Houqua said with an off-beat note in his voice, 'All of us who have to do with opium, believe in something which is not rational, which cannot be explained. You used the word cursed, Captain Barrow. It is almost as if some of the dream-provoking physical quality of opium passes into the fabric of one's thoughts. It is widely held in the East that everyone and everything that has to do with opium is cursed.'

'Nonsense,' said Ogilvie.

'On the contrary, Captain Ogilvie, you might take me as the living symbol of the curse. I have made a fortune out of it, yet it has never brought me anything I really wanted. But I go on in some sort of compulsive fashion. Opium has left me only my mind. Perhaps that is the very measure of its curse. It left me my mind only that I should destroy the remnants of myself with my mind.'

'I can understand if you mean those unfortunate devils who smoke their lives away,' said Ogilvie.

'They are the lucky ones,' Houqua answered. 'What do they suffer? For a few pence they are translated from the realities of the world, from its miseries, from pain, from sex. The future of the smoke in the den is bright and rosy. They lose nothing. No, Captain Ogilvie, it is we who cannot dream because of opium, who are strong enough to resist the blandishments of its sleep, who are cursed. I have over six million pounds in my vaults but what do I want? I want to revenge myself on Boa Paz. I want to take its opium in order to make more money. I shall do so. None of us here can help himself. None of you will withdraw because of the fortune I shall offer each of you and I cannot withdraw because of what Boa Paz did to me. The curse is there, gentlemen, upon everyone who deals in opium.'

'Why try and scare us all with this rubbish?' demanded Ogilvie.

Houqua said crisply. 'There is a great deal to plan. First, a ship . . .'

'Wait a moment, Houqua,' said Barrow. 'How do you intend to get the opium from Boa Paz if the pygmies are as savage as you say? Are you going to trade with them?'

Houqua opened a drawer in reply and brought out a woman's shoe. It was made of pure silver, chased in exquisite filigree work.

'For a very small and lovely woman,' murmured Idrisi.

'Feminine fripperies give me a pain,' said Ogilvie.

'It is not a feminine frippery, Captain Ogilvie. But a sort of currency. It is Sycee silver. A whim of mine, perhaps some compensation for my sexless life. This is specie. I pay in specie for opium. I pay in Sycee silver and every piece that passes my hands is in the shape of these little shoes. Anywhere from Canton to Shanghai you can tell a Houqua deal. You will carry 100,000 dollars in Sycee silver, just in case of trade, to Boa Paz.'

'In case of trade?' echoed Ogilvie. 'You make it sound like a last resort.'

Houqua balanced the shoe in his hand.

'Your mission is very simple, Captain Ogilvie. You will take a fast ship, fully armed, to Boa Paz and raid their accumulated stores of opium. I reckon you should bring back nearly a million dollars' worth of the best opium in the world.'

Ogilvie eyed him. 'A million dollars' worth of opium!'

Barrow gave a long whistle. But Idrisi saw what was behind Houqua's plan.

'When you remove their opium supply the pygmies will die?'

Houqua played with the silver shoe. 'When one robs a hive of its honey, one does not necessarily destroy all the bees. Those that get in the way are blotted out. Captain Ogilvie, you will carry out this raid after they have gathered in the new crop, which will be in a couple of months' time. The Sycee silver is only, as you say, a last resort. I want a clear profit of a million dollars.'

'And for a million dollars, we all get the strange sickness? Impotence as well? No thank you,' answered Ogilvie.

'When you get to Boa Paz you and your crew, Captain Ogilvie, will all take seven grains of opium a day. You will not get the sickness.'

'God's truth!' said Ogilvie, 'now I've heard everything! Raiding crew doped to the eyes! A fortune in silver before I start and a fortune in opium when I return! Aren't you taking a big risk, Houqua? An opium runner like myself, given a fast, well-armed ship and a crack crew, with a fortune under my decks—almost anything could happen.'

'You yourself emphasized the need for insurance, Captain Ogilvie, just as I thought you would. You think a million dollars enough to . . . to . . .' he fumbled for the word.

'Double-cross?'

'That's it.'

'You're asking me for my word of honour?'

'No captain, I am not.' He opened the drawer and took out a bottle containing some white pills. 'The little men of Boa Paz discovered that opium was not the complete answer by itself against the sickness. These pills are a very ordinary substance which every few months the natives of Boa Paz take as an adjunct to opium.' He smiled thinly. 'Insurance, Captain Ogilvie. The harder you drive your ship here from Boa Paz, the quicker you get the rest of the antidote.' He put the pills back into the drawer. 'You'll come back all right, Captain Ogilvie.'

'You scheming, lying little bastard!' Ogilvie exploded.

'It was you who aimed to do the lying and the scheming. I regret having to take such precautions. You haven't asked your fee.'

'The whole scheme can go to hell as far as I am concerned. Get some other captain.'

'50,000 in gold in any bank anywhere in the world?'

Ogilvie nodded.

'25,000 to both the two pilots?'

Idrisi also nodded.

'In what currency?' asked Barrow.

'You can have it in miticals, or cruzados, or reis, or pounds, shillings, pence, or Carolus dollars, or any other currency you can name,' said Houqua.

Ogilvie looked out to his schooner at anchor.

'She's small for all that opium, Houqua,' he said, 'but I can take up some of the 'tween decks . . .'

'You're not taking the *Poppy*,' replied Houqua. 'You're going in my ship.'

'It will be *my* ship. I am the judge of that,' said Ogilvie curtly. 'I'm prepared to inspect your ship but she'll have to be bloody good. Otherwise it's no.'

'*Your* ship is lying in the Creek.' Houqua waved towards a backwater off the main anchorage.

'Hell!' exclaimed Ogilvie. 'You don't have to put her in that sewer. Why not anchor her off Whampoa? If she's as good as you say, I'd like to see her among the cracks.'

Houqua was evasive. 'This is a secret mission, Captain Oglivie, and you will all treat it as such. There are a couple of corvettes hanging about round Hong Kong and I don't want the Royal Navy . . .'

Ogilvie burst out laughing. 'The Royal Navy! Those sea-going tubs! I'd get away from any of them with my hands tied behind my back and conning my ship blindfold through the Paracels!'

After leaving Houqua's office Ogilvie's gig with the four men rounded a bend in the section of sewer-like backwater euphemistically known as the Creek. Ahead, half aground on a mudflat, was a ship, stern towards them, canted over. Her masts were docked. Most of the bowsprit was missing. The standing rigging sagged like an aged breast. Wood showed raw, unpainted. Her copper sheathing was green with verdigris. Houqua waved towards the hulk. Barrow and Idrisi stared at him in astonishment. Ogilvie roared with ironic laughter.

'Now I know you smoke the stuff yourself, Houqua! That for a joke! You take a couple of pipes of dope and presto, you convert the oldest hulk in Canton into the swiftest clipper that ever sailed!' His laughter subsided. 'Good God, Houqua!'

'You are an expert in these matters, Captain Ogilvie,' Houqua said. 'If you don't think the ship is any good we will call the whole thing off.'

Ogilvie's eyes went to the Chinese and then to the hulk.

'I wouldn't sail her from here to the anchorage for fear of drowning myself,' he exclaimed. 'Where did you raise her, Houqua?'

'Perhaps you remember that the British stopped the sale of slavers captured as prizes in 1836. Lloyds was no longer able to auction slavers captured by His Philanthropic Majesty's Royal Navy. There were 24 fine prize ships lying at Sierra Leone in July 1836, Captain Ogilvie. They all had what I want most – speed. This one was among them. It was the last auction Lloyds held. I got her cheap, only £5000.'

Barrow was still nonplussed. 'You didn't get anyone to sail that wreck from Sierra Leone to China?'

'I did, Captain Barrow. All men have their price.'

The boat drew under the stern and Ogilvie looked down the length of the hulk towards the bow.

'Not a bad line at all, Houqua. She must have been a flier – once.'

The boat stopped under the remnants of the after-rigging.

'Quite a line, I'd say,' went on Ogilvie, squinting down her length. He examined the clean line of the bow.

'Houqua, this couldn't be . . . Sam Hall of Boston?'

Houqua shook his head. 'As a matter of fact, not. Have you ever heard of Monsieur Ozanne?'

Barrow started. Ogilvie didn't seem to hear the question: he was staring in controlled excitement at the knife-like bow.

He turned suddenly on Houqua. 'You can't do it to a ship like this! You can't leave her here to rot, Houqua! Look at that wedge-bow! Genius put her together. Look at that flush deck and perfect sheer, the power in that stern! I can't see the midship section from here but I'd guess it's pretty full with a lot of deadrise. No wonder she's lying on her side. She needs a couple of hundred tons of ballast to make her stand upright. But, by God, when she did!' He glanced up at the tatters of rigging above his head.

'How much canvas would she stand, Captain Ogilvie?'

'I'd get 15,000 square feet on her,' he answered. 'Nothing above the royals. Spread, not hoist. No skysails, no moonsails. But stunsails, ring tails, watersails, A Jamie Green and a jib-o'-jib, the lot. She'd take it with a beam like hers. Fitted topgallant masts – we'd be able to get them off her quick in a typhoon. Double topsails on the main and mizen but a single on the foremast. Doubles aren't so good in a light breeze. Can't brace up the yards so well, unless you slack off the lee topmast rigging a bit. That's nothing. I've got a crack crew.'

He took a sailor's knife from his pocket to test the quality of the hull planks.

'Anjer to Mauritius!' he said, holding the knife like a surgeon unwilling to embark on an operation. 'I'd even have savealls and watersails laced outside the lower stunsails. What a sight she'd be!' He ran his hand along the timber. 'You beautiful bitch!'

He tried the hull but the knife-blade broke.

'It's sound!' he said in astonishment. 'No, it can't be. It must be an isolated bit. She must be built of softwood. Lend me your knife,' he asked Barrow, trying again. The blade would not penetrate.

'It just can't be, Houqua! There's no paint to protect it either.'

'I asked you if you had heard of Monsieur Ozanne,' said

Houqua. 'Perhaps Captain Barrow here has.'

Barrow replied: 'Monsieur Ozanne was a Frenchman, and probably one of the finest ship designers known. You saw her similarity to the Baltimore fliers at once, Captain Ogilvie. Ozanne was a genius. The Americans used his ideas for their privateers during the war of 1812. Nothing to touch them.'

'The Americans built theirs of softwood,' Houqua interrupted. 'You know, Captain Ogilvie, with men who carry sail the way you do, how quickly a hull becomes waterlogged. A waterlogged hull – well, you might as well forget about its lines then. Monsieur Ozanne has been well aware of the problem for years.'

'How do you know?' asked Ogilvie.

'I have been in touch with Monsieur Ozanne since I became interested in fast ships,' replied Houqua. 'His problem was that if he used a heavy hardwood like teak or oak, he sacrificed speed. If he used softwood, the hull became strained and waterlogged. But as Captain Barrow rightly says, Monsieur Ozanne is a genius. In time he found the wood which combined lightness with impermeability. He built one ship of it.' He inclined his head slightly. 'This is that ship.'

'What wood, Houqua?' exclaimed Ogilvie.

'You probably know it, since you spent almost a year on the coast of the Cape of Good Hope before you came to China,' he went on. 'They call it sneezewood.'

'I saw some jetty piles at Algoa Bay, which is near the forests,' said Ogilvie. 'The locals said they'd been under seawater for years. They were like new.' He scraped a shaving from the hull.

'I can't smell anything.'

'Sneezewood is perhaps a misnomer, so Monsieur Ozanne tells me,' said Houqua. 'It only smells when newly cut.'

Ogilvie became excited. 'So the whole hull is sound? She's a wreck aloft but Jamie Green and my boatswain and sailmaker will soon put that to rights. We'll re-rig her. I'll want a whole set of new spars, but we can easily get them up from Whampoa. A month or six weeks, Houqua, and she'll be ready.'

He swung himself aboard. They heard him stumping about and then he rejoined them.

'She's all fancy inside,' he said. 'Looks like bird's eye maple panelling to me.'

At the level of his eyes where he stood in the boat he read her name in faded letters on a nameboard.

Waterwitch. Slaver's name. Just the sort of fancy thing they'd choose, when everything below was a stinking hell. His attention was caught by a patch in the planking.

'Shot-hole.'

'Prise that board off,' said Houqua. 'Perhaps her original name is underneath.'

Ogilvie used a belaying pin and the board came away. Underneath letters were sunk into the planking.

He spelled it out.

'I-N-C-R-O-Y-A-B-L-E.'

'*Incroyable*! French!' exclaimed Barrow.

'I don't believe it,' said Ogilvie. 'It can't be the same. Not *Incroyable*!'

'It is, Captain Ogilvie,' said Houqua. '*Incroyable*. Designed by Monsieur Ozanne. Sailed by Captain du Plessis. Raider and privateer – the fastest – ever.'

'Are you sure, Houqua, this is *Incroyable*?' demanded Ogilvie.

Barrow said: 'This ship was a legend before she was a year old. There's never been a ship to touch her. She sailed as a privateer from Boston, after serving in the French fleet before Trafalgar. When Napoleon fell, *Incroyable* disappeared. The French tucked her away in a North African port. Some day the fastest ship afloat might be wanted to sail to St Helena.'

Ogilvie fingered the shot-hole patch. 'I wonder where she picked that up? The Grand Banks? Boulogne? The Channel? The Bight of Guinea?'

'Let's go aboard,' said Houqua.

The four men gathered round the wheel.

'I want a 68-pounder Armstrong amidships,' said Ogilvie. 'Ten guns aside. I've got my gun crews on the *Poppy* and we can train more. The first thing I want is ballast, Houqua. Saltpetre. It's better than sand. At least 100 tons.'

Idrisi said. 'I have a special compass of my own. Perhaps, captain, we can make a separate little platform and put it

here in front of the usual binnacle. Since we are going to
Boa Paz an ordinary compass is – well, not so good in those
parts.'

'Tell the carpenter exactly what you want,' Ogilvie said.
'Get him to fix it your way. Whether we have one or two
compasses makes no odds as far as I am concerned.'

Houqua asked in his quiet voice, 'If the carpenter is available, perhaps I too, might make a request?'

'Go ahead,' said Ogilvie.

'You know we Chinese have a flowery tongue,' he said.
'It is usual to write fulsome inscriptions over shop doors and
warehouses and the like. You are carrying opium, captain.'
His eye wandered towards the bucket-rack immediately
below the quarterdeck rails. 'Here's one for *Incroyable* –
write it over that rack: "The bucket of final peace".'

Ogilvie burst out laughing. 'I like that, Houqua. Yes, whole
buckets of peace. The peace of opium.'

'A ship must have a mascot,' went on Houqua. 'Fortunately,
I managed to save *Incroyable*'s original.'

'Where is it?'

Houqua turned to Idrisi: 'You'll find it in a cabinet in the
big cabin.'

Idrisi returned with a beautiful model fish. It was made
of metal with a dull silver sheen like moonlight on pewter.

Houqua took it from him. 'This is the mascot of the
famous Captain du Plessis himself. It's been in *Incroyable*
right from the beginning. It's not altogether what it seems
though. When the French had Napoleon and *Incroyable* in
mind, they improved on the mascot.' He took the model by
the jaw and felt behind a fin. The jaw swung open revealing
a cavity beneath.

'It's completely watertight. Put it at your masthead, captain.
It brought *Incroyable* luck.'

'No,' said Ogilvie. 'I'll have it specially mounted on a spar
next to the helm.'

Houqua said, 'There was only one ship which *Incroyable*
never outsailed. A British ship, H.M.S. *Plymouth Sound*. A
24-gun corvette. They fought a running action once half-way
across the Atlantic. Ships like men seem to have their natural-
born antagonists. *Incroyable* had H.M.S. *Plymouth Sound*.'
He added, 'You must refit her here out of sight, Captain

Ogilvie. My agents keep me informed of the movements of all Royal Navy ships in Chinese waters.'

'This voyage has nothing to do with the Royal Navy.'

'That's not quite true,' replied Houqua. 'The cut of her jib alone would make her worth investigating. Destination dubious. Mission – more dubious still. Heavy armament.'

'No one will catch this ship by the time I'm finished with her,' retorted Ogilvie.

Houqua said: 'Right now H.M.S. *Plymouth Sound* is lying off Hong Kong.'

CHAPTER EIGHT

'Cape Correntes!'

Ogilvie looked westwards. The day was very bright. The sea hurt his eyes. The coast with its low hills was scarred with white among the its bushes. Here and there a tall tree stood out like a signal beacon. It seemed two, not nine miles away. A wicked shore with what appeared to be a reef running parallel to it as far as the eye could see, loomed under *Incroyable*'s bowsprit. About three or four miles inland was a landmark hill with an odd round top.

Barrow, who was with Ogilvie at the helm, said, 'Bearing north by east, about 20 miles.'

'North by east, 20 miles!' Ogilvie exclaimed.

'Yes,' said Barrow. 'I don't think that's a bad landfall.'

Ogilvie had driven *Incroyable* hard. They'd made Singapore in the record time of a week from Canton and taken every risk racing down the China Sea. In the trades from Anjer to Madagascar, *Incroyable* had reeled off an average of 220 miles a day.

'God's truth!' he exploded. 'Not a bad landfall – only twenty miles out! Is that the sort of pilot you are, Barrow?'

They'd been at one another's throats from the first day out. Barrow had been more or less a passenger until they sighted Cape St Marie, the southern tip of Madagascar, when his pilotage began. Now he was twenty miles wrong in his landfall, off Aguada da Boa Paz.

'Where's the cape?' demanded Ogilvie. 'I can't see anything but a few black rocks where you're pointing.'

Idrisi poured oil on troubled waters.

'Look, the coast is a bit higher on either side of the cape. You can see white water. That is Cape Correntes.'

'What a miserable runt of a thing!' exclaimed Ogilvie. 'I thought Cape Correntes, after all you and Barrow had to say about it, was quite something.'

'Cape Lorrentes is one of the most noted landmarks on the sea-route to India,' Idrisi retorted.

'So you Arab pilots hadn't got the guts to sail south of that merely because of a lot of bedtime stories,' sneered Ogilvie.

'Pilot Barrow has already demonstrated to us the power of the currents,' he answered. 'He was steering to bring us north of Cape Correntes and we've finished up way to the south. To the south, captain – towards Boa Paz.'

Ogilvie scowled. 'This superstitious nonsense is to try and exonerate Barrow. I could have done better myself.'

He walked over to the leeward side of the quarterdeck. Something a little down the coast from Cape Correntes seemed to catch his eye.

'What's that there, Idrisi? Barrow? By heavens, that is Cape Correntes.'

Idrisi shook his head. 'No. That is Cape Correntes's little brother, Ponta Zavora. Like many little brothers, it is worse than the elder.'

'Why do you say that?' demanded Ogilvie.

'It is 30 miles nearer Boa Paz.' He tried to divert Ogilvie's attention. 'The chart Houqua gave me is one of the finest I have seen. The silk is waterproofed.'

'You and Barrow are in a blue funk about something,' snapped Ogilvie.

'Have you seen a sea like this?' replied Idrisi. 'Look at the kind of white bloom on it. Look at the unnatural clearness of the atmosphere.'

'There's nothing wrong with the weather,' retorted Ogilvie. 'Barometer's high and steady. It's just an exceptionally clear day, that's all.'

'Why don't you put a bucket over the side and see what's making the sea white?'

'I did so an hour ago. There's nothing.'

Fatigue in Ogilvie's face accentuated its hard lines.

'Barrow! Idrisi! I want to know exactly where *Incroyable* is. Barrow?'

'About eighteen miles ENE of Ponta Zavora. Say, twelve offshore,' said the Portuguese.

'Idrisi?'

The Arab consulted his curious compass mounted in front of the binnacle. It had a thick crystal covering.

'Ponta Zavora West by South 3/4 South, 15 miles. Nearest

land, 9 miles – NW ½ W.'

Ogilvie rounded on Barrow.

'That's the way I want to hear it. You're finished. Idrisi, you navigate from now onwards. I thought all along you were a chancer, Barrow.'

Barrow's protest was cut short by a hail from the masthead.

'A ship, fine on the port beam, sir! Coming up fast.'

Ogilvie sprang into the mizen shrouds. He was soon back. Idrisi asked. 'H.M.S. *Plymouth Sound*?'

Ogilvie's nod was lost in a rapid fire of orders.

'In all stunsails, watersails, staysails and the Jamie Green. Stand by to go about! Hands to braces!'

He snapped at Barrow: 'This is your fault. Get off my quarterdeck! Look where your navigating has got me – a lee shore and a man-o'-war coming up fast. She's bringing up the wind with her. *Plymouth Sound* on my tail!'

'I'd thought you'd shaken her off,' said Barrow.

'You remember when we saw her in the China Sea shortly after we'd sailed? I said then she wouldn't give up. And there she was in the Banka Strait waiting for us! Why do you think I've driven this ship like I have? That's why.' He jabbed a finger at a pocket-handkerchief of canvas showing up white in the south-east. '*Plymouth Sound*! Now I've got to wait without a wind, for her to get within range. Which is closer, Correntes or Zavora?' He asked Idrisi.

'Zavora.'

'How far?'

'An hour, if *Plymouth Sound* is bringing up the sort of wind I think she is.'

'Give a course.'

'West by South, 3/4 South.'

Ogilvie repeated it to the helmsman. *Incroyable* swung round and headed on a broad reach almost at right angles to her previous course. The pocket handkerchief on the horizon turned to follow.

'Are you going to run or fight?' asked Idrisi.

Ogilvie's shouted orders gave his answer.

'Clear away the long ton amidships. Gun crews to stations!'

'He's got the weather gauge and a ship as fast as yours, captain,' said Idrisi. 'She has all the advantages – wind, position, broadsides. She'll blow you out of the water. She's chased you half-way across the world to do it and she's not going to stop now.'

'Send Jamie Green to me,' replied Ogilvie.

The red-haired sailmaker, who combined the function of chief gunner, came up.

'Jamie,' Ogilvie said. 'There's a lee shore and we're to lee-ward. We can't get away. *Plymouth Sound* will close and squeeze us against the shore. If we go closer we'll run aground. If we turn seawards she'll rake us. See that white splash on the cliff? There's a reef there. I guess there must be a passage through.'

'There's nothing on my chart,' said Idrisi.

'I know that,' answered Ogilvie. 'But Barrow's mess-up has shown me a way.'

'What do you mean?' replied Idrisi.

'It shows that there are two powerful currents running in opposite directions, one offshore, the other inshore. My guess is that they have probably swept a small channel clear inside the reef. I'll be able to see when we get closer . . .'

'It's a desperate gamble, Captain Ogilvie.'

'Will you con her in, Idrisi?'

'Yes. From the foreyard. That will be best.'

'Don't expose yourself. They'll have a sharpshooter to try and pick you off. You know the plan of attack in the Royal Navy. Close the range to half pistol-shot, then broadsides. By God, I'm going to let her come right in to that range! It's your job to keep her off a little, Jamie, with that long sixty-eight. I want some good shooting as she comes in. No broadsides. Just keeping knocking away a spar or two here and there. Fire as soon as you like . . .'

Something in the attitude of the gunner stopped Ogilvie.

'You're not scared, are you Jamie?'

The raw-boned gunner rubbed his hands together.

'Ian,' he said quietly, 'that's a Queen's ship. I've never fired yet on a Queen's ship. You're as good as he is, any day. Maybe better. But she's a Queen's ship, Ian.'

The muscles round Ogilvie's jaw tightened.

'What are you trying to say, Jamie?'

'We ran away from Stornoway together and I've been with

you ever since. I've made your ships sail faster than any others. Each one has had to be faster because you had something bigger to get away from. And now, with the fastest of them all, you are turning every man's hand against you. A Queen's ship, Ian! If you get *Plymouth Sound* they'll hound you to the end of time. I'll not fire on a Queen's ship!'

Ogilvie's voice remained level.

'You remember, Jamie, don't you, you and the others signed the articles – man-o'-war drill, man-o'-war punishment?'

The gunners eyes narrowed.

'I invented the Jamie Green, Ian. I gave you that. And the jib-o'-jib . . .'

'Get on to that 68-pounder and do what I say!'

'Not against a Queen's ship, Ian. Haven't you done enough? You'll be a pariah on the seas for ever. Opium-runner and then pirate! They'll hang you for it, Ian!'

Ogilvie went to the poop rail and looked down on the long deck where the guns had already been run out. Neat triangular piles of shot stood beside them.

He called two men.

'Tie him to the mainmast,' he ordered. 'Fifty lashes. In full view of the crew.'

'Ian . . .' protested Jamie.

Ogilvie was staring to windward.

'No,' he said. 'Belay that. Take a look there, Jamie. See that weather coming up? I'll give you a grandstand view of the weather! Lash him under the bowsprit next to his own sail.'

'But sir,' objected one of them, 'he'll drown as soon as she starts putting her head down.'

'Take your choice,' said Ogilvie. 'Lash him under the bowsprit or you'll be lashed there too.'

The crew stood silent as Jamie Green was led forward. Idrisi's face seemed more aquiline than before.

'Not a good thing when going into action, captain,' he said.

Ogilvie watched the procession along the deck. He signalled to a toughie at one of the guns.

'You there by the port 'midships gun! Come here!'

The man came forward.

'Hayes, isn't it?'

'Aye.'

'American deserter, aren't you?'

'So what? I don't like navy ships. And an opium ship is nothing to boast about.'

'You're a gunner, aren't you?'

'Gun captain, U.S. *Constitution.* Master gunner U.S. Privateer *Sally Jane.*' He grinned. 'We called her Slippery Sue because she was always so wet below the waist. Gun captain, H.M.S. *Arethusa.*' He spat on the deck.

Ogilvie jerked his head at the warship coming into view.

'Would you fire on a Queen's ship, Hayes?'

'Christ, I'd fire on the Queen herself.'

'Then get on that long sixty-eight and open fire as soon as you judge. She's out of range still. I'm going in towards the coast. You've to keep her away from *Incroyable* for a while. That means good shooting. No broadsides – yet.'

The American eyed the big gun.

'I don't like goddam rope rammers. I want a double-ended stave rammer. Can I feel the shot?'

'Do or have any damned thing you wish, Hayes, only keep that ship away from us for a while.'

The American weighed a shot in his hand. 'All British shot is up to maggots. Every one different. How much time we got, captain?'

'Maybe half an hour.'

'See here,' said Hayes speaking rapidly. 'I learned this gimmick in the *Sally Jane.* We had to shoot straight to kill. We fixed a bit of iron round the muzzle so.' He cupped his hands round it. 'A metal strop from a topgallant mast, captain. That'll serve. The blacksmith can fix it inside half an hour. It just needs a shallow rib and the shot spins as it leaves the muzzle. Dead accurate, every time. What's the weight of the charges?'

'Hell, man, I don't know.'

'We'll drop them half a pound,' went on Hayes. 'The spin makes 'em go much farther. But you don't want to overdo it.'

Ogilvie shouted orders. The blacksmith appeared with a small portable forge. Extra men gathered round the long gun. Gunpowder grains stained the deck as they worked to reduce the weight of the charges.

Barrow's face was alive with misery.

'You can't fight a British man-o'-war,' he told Ogilvie. 'You can't, Captain Ogilvie. I forbid you. I'll haul down your colours.'

'You yellow bastard!' repled Ogilvie contemptuously. 'You can either come along with us or jump over the side. You won't have far to swim once we get off Ponta Zavora.'

Idrisi swung himself down from the rigging.

'The reef is in a semi-circle round the point,' he said.

'I'm going right in and then doubling back on my tracks to try and shake her off,' said Ogilvie. 'To do that, I'm taking her inside the reef and turning completely round on our present course. The back double in other words.'

'What is to prevent *Plymouth Sound* doing exactly the same?' asked Barrow. 'She'll still keep you against the shore. She'll still nail you with her guns. You'll only have less room behind a reef to manœuvre in.'

'That,' replied Ogilvie, 'depends purely on Ponta Zavora.'

Incroyable made for the coast. Her towering fabric of sail leaned fitfully. Ogilvie could see now the low ridge of sandhills near Zavora point and the mirror of a long sand-cliff to the north. Inland was one dominant hill. *Incroyable* leaned again as the wind which *Plymouth Sound* was bringing up with her began to reach her. *Plymouth Sound*, out to sea, held course parallel to *Incroyable*, forcing her gradually against the coast. It was only a matter of waiting for the kill.

Suddenly the royals on the British ship vanished. Reefs appeared in her topgallants. She swung sharply towards *Incroyable*.

'She's coming at us!' called Idrisi. 'She's getting down to fighting sails.'

Ogilvie hesitated. It was clear to him what the warship intended. The classic stripping for the kill. Fighting sails. Closing the range. Some sparring with her heavy metal while she worked close in. Then the broadsides with their deadly precision. At half-pistol-shot range. They'd load with double shot for that first punch. Ogilvie felt the first thrust of the new wind. It told him what *Plymouth Sound* was up to.

'Hands to braces!' he shouted. 'Stand by!'

'You're not going to come up with her of your own free will, are you, captain?' asked Idrisi, shaken.

'Hayes!' yelled Ogilvie. 'How much longer? Can you open fire yet?'

'Not yet, sir. Just finishing the spin brake. Ten minutes.'

Ogilvie saw smoke from the warship's side. He didn't see where the one shot fell.

'She's coming at us now because she's afraid of the weather out to sea,' rapped out Ogilvie. 'Look, Idrisi, look out there to port!'

The electro-plated look of the sea had changed to a green-grey. The pellucid clarity too, was gone.

Incroyable swung over two degrees as the strong wind arrived. *Plymouth Sound* came rushing at her. Again the single burst of smoke at her side. The shot was lost in the rising sea.

'Look astern of her!' exclaimed Ogilvie.

'What a squall! You're hanging on to sail very long, captain!'

There was a heavy crash amidships. Hayes's shot fell within feet of the warship's stern. He thrust the new double-ended stave rammer home himself. He talked to the gun.

'My little tart! Steady, you bitch. This is what you want. Hard home. And when you're hot, God, how you'll enjoy it.' He threw the rammer aside and watched the sea, a glowing fuse in his hands. As *Incroyable* rolled, he plunged it into the gun's touch-hole.

'Got her!' he said jubilantly. 'Got her!' He laid his hand on the hot muzzle. 'You lovely, punchy bitch! You little puncher!'

Idrisi glanced anxiously seawards. 'I'd say that if you don't get her off the wind soon she'll go right over when the squall hits her.'

Plymouth Sound was closing the range so fast that she wouldn't have to use her long gun much longer: she'd be ready for a broadside.

The squall hit *Incroyable*. 'Luff!' ordered Ogilvie. 'Bring her head nearer the wind. Luff! Shake the squall out of her! Shake it out of her!'

As if echoing his own shouting, there was a crack in the rigging. The big topsail split right down the centre. Ogilvie himself grabbed the wheel. It was standard practice at that time for a ship when hit by a heavy squall to turn and run before it. Ogilvie was doing the opposite: he was retaining his position by shaking the squall out of the sails, a highly dangerous manœuvre with the clippers' heavy masts and long spars, and he was counting at the same time on *Plymouth Sound* following the stereotyped practice of running before it. Ogilvie's eyes were riveted on *Incroyable*'s tower of canvas. 'Don't let her get aback or the masts will come right out!' he shouted. 'So! So! So!'

The starboard or lee bulwarks disappeared in a welter of water. *Incroyable* responded to Ogilvie's master hand. Hayes, working frantically with a handspike, threw his gun round after the warship.

Plymouth Sound careered off astern. The dangerous but magnificent move had succeeded. *Incroyable* had ducked the punch.

There was admiration in Idrisi's face. 'You've gained a quarter of a mile on her, captain! She's trying the same thing herself now but as gingerly as a bride on her wedding night!'

Zavora Point came closer. *Incroyable* tore at the coast. The long sixty-eight stabbed like a boxer's left jab in the face of the British ship. Not a knock-down punch but a point-scorer. Ogilvie's eyes searched the coast.

'We'll go about and slip round through the reef there.' He pointed to a small indentation on the coast. He called to the leadsman in the chains: 'How much under her?'

'By the mark seven.'

The clipper stormed towards the breakers.

'You're throwing away our lives . . .' Barrow muttered.

'If you don't like it, jump overboard,' replied Ogilvie.

Incroyable jabbed again with Hayes's gun into *Plymouth Sound*'s face. The warship's guns were silent. The two ships raced at the coast.

'Hayes!' said Ogilvie. 'Belay that gun. I want every gun in the starboard battery handspiked round to point five degrees astern.'

'You mean the port batteries,' said Hayes.

'No, I'm going about in a moment. About, do you understand – like a bat out of hell,' answered Ogilvie. 'You will fire the starboard battery on my orders only. Not before, even if the target bears. Right?'

'I don't get it. But after what you done out there just now, I'm not arguing.'

'Five degrees astern,' repeated Ogilvie. 'Feel the current?' he asked Idrisi.

'I see the reef too.' He jerked his head at a channel now visible through the reef.

Ogilvie judged the distance.

'Hands to braces!' he shouted. 'Stand by to go about!' he told the helmsman. 'As she comes round, steer north by west. If she hangs in stays I won't have to worry about your punishment.' He nodded at the approaching warship. Her ports swung open. Gun muzzles with their double-shotted contents came poking through.

Ogilvie took a quick look aloft.

'Get those staysails off her!'

Idrisi asked dumbfoundedly, 'Are you wanting to give her every chance? She'll be alongside if you shorten sail. Keep everything on you possibly can until the last moment.'

'No,' answered Ogilvie. 'As she comes round she'll lie half a point nearer the wind without those sails. That's the way it works. I want every yard of distance I can get. How soon to the reef?'

Idrisi gestured fatalistically.

Incroyable's helm went hard down. Her bow turned into the current racing through the reef channel from the opposite direction. For a moment she hung as she came about. Then she leapt through the gap in the reef. Ogilvie saw the men at the guns of the British ship. An officer raised his hat and the smoking fuses plunged down like a chorus. The concussion was simultaneous but *Plymouth Sound* tore on outside the reef. It was too late for her to follow *Incroyable* into her funk-hole. The blast from her double-shotted broadside rebounded off the cliff overlooking the channel. Splinters of rock and metal churned up the sea in the lagoon. *Incroyable* was untouched.

Ogilvie gestured to Hayes and drew his finger across his throat. Hayes shouted. *Incroyable*'s shot bit into *Plymouth Sound*.

'Five degrees astern,' ordered Ogilvie.

Then Barrow jumped overboard. Ogilvie reached for a pistol and pointed it at the swimmer's head. Then he dropped it and shrugged.

'We'll call that cliff Barrow Point after him,' he said ironically.

Incroyable did an about turn in the lagoon and headed back through the gap in the reef to the open sea. *Plymouth Sound*, away to the south-west, fought the current and wind. Then she started to come again after the clipper.

'Course south-south-west,' Ogilvie ordered.

'You seem determined to commit suicide,' remarked Idrisi.

Ogilvie gestured seawards. The earlier murkiness had turned to black. *Incroyable* lurched through the mounting swell. Her jibs and the mainsail were stowed and topsails double-reefed.

'It's either a gale or a cyclone,' he said. 'By the time *Plymouth Sound* is ready for us the water will be breaking through her gunports.'

Then Ogilvie's expression changed to astonishment.

'Look!'

The warship was standing out to sea, away from *Incroyable*.

'I don't believe it,' exclaimed Ogilvie. 'They don't give up like that in the Royal Navy.'

Idrisi glanced into the binnacle and then into his own strange compass. 'Here's the answer.'

There was a difference of eight degrees between the two instruments. *Plymouth Sound* was following a false course because she had a conventional compass.

'It's the reason why this section of coast is a death trap for ships,' said Idrisi.

'What's inside that thing of yours?' demanded Ogilvie. 'Why doesn't it play false too?'

'There's a sort of secret gyroscopic principle,' he replied. 'The crystal shields the liquid and the crank underneath rotates. We throw in a bit of ballyhoo – if the crystal shines red it's good luck. Yellow is for bad. Green, mediocre.

Suddenly there was a shattering crash astern. The shock threw the helmsman to the deck. The ship's head swung and the foretopmast and main masts broke in a tangle of wires and rope.

Ogilvie and the helmsman threw their combined weight

on the wheel but it remained locked. Then Ogilvie raced to the rail and hung over the side. He tore off his jacket and shirt.

'An axe! An axe! Free Jamie Green,' he told Idrisi, then to the crew, 'Cut away that wreck! Get it over the side! Get it clear or you'll hole her!'

He waited with an axe in his hand until Jamie Green arrived. He had to be supported on to the poop, retching seawater.

'Jamie,' said Ogilvie, 'something bad's happened. I don't know what. Help me save *Incroyable*. I'm going over the side to see.'

'Aye,' replied the sailmaker, 'always Jamie Green in a tight spot! Right. God help us if we don't do something soon.'

Plymouth Sound had recovered from the compass bluff. She was making for *Incroyable* to hand out the knock-out blow.

Ogilvie swung himself overside.

'Get your breath Jamie, and come and help me.'

'Damn my breath!'

They found the snout of a huge sword fish embedded between the sternpost and the blade of the rudder. The sword was twice the width of a man's hand and tapered to a blunt point. Reverse-facing notches prevented it from being withdrawn. It was about fifteen feet long.

Ogilvie hacked at it. The fish wrenched convulsively and the wood in which the sword was buried began to tear.

'For Christ's sake hurry, Jamie, before he tears away the whole sternpost!'

Ogilvie lunged again but at that moment *Incroyable* rolled. The axe missed and buried itself in Jamie Green's shoulder. He gave a scream, a high convulsive sound and Ogilvie pulled the blade free. Blood was everywhere.

Ogilvie chopped away the swordfish and then hauled Jamie back aboard. The crew stood back as he carried the dying man.

'You bastard!' said the American gunner. 'When you can't kill a man one way, you do it another!'

Ogilvie put the sailmaker down, reversed the axe, and

struck Hayes across the head with the shaft.

Jamie Green's screams dwindled as his life ran out, like an exhaust dying in the distance.

Ogilvie asked Idrisi in an unrecognizable voice: 'Is that Boa Paz ahead?'

'Aye, but *Plymouth Sound* is lying across the entrance.'

'Bring me the map,' ordered Ogilvie.

Idrisi steadied it in the wind. There was no escape left.

Ogilvie looked up hopelessly at the wild horizon. He saw something there which galvanized him into action.

'Get those guns over the side! Quick! Storm staysail only!'

A huge wave was rolling in towards the coast behind *Plymouth Sound*. But the warship had spotted it and was coming round to meet it.

'I'm going to ride over the reef on its back,' said Ogilvie.

Idrisi said. 'I only hope it's big enough to do that.'

Incroyable headed for the reef under a fragment of storm canvas. Ogilvie eyed the ruins of the fort of St Gregory on its long sandspit reaching out into the channel which was his salvation but which he dared not use.

'By all that's holy!' he exclaimed. 'There's a ship there!' He indicated the shore, half hidden by murk.

Idrisi also spotted the white cross like a sail above the murk.

'No, captain. It's a *padraoa*.'

'What's that?'

'A cross – Portuguese. White marble. They took them on their explorations and planted them on prominent landmarks as a navigation aid. That hill's Txibange.'

The wall of water raced shorewards towards the crippled clipper.

Ogilvie himself took the wheel. Under the bowsprit the water became white as the wave lifted her. Then she leaped half her length out of the water, lifted, spun and bucked. Finally she plunged deck-deep in a maelstrom of spume and everything went quiet.

She had jumped the reef.

Ogilvie turned to look seawards and terror showed in his eyes.

Plymouth Sound rode in front of a massive backdrop of water. The great wave, successor to the one which had lifted

Incroyable over the reef hung poised. Then the warship heaved up and they saw the masts snap. She rolled completely over.

Idrisi opened the jaw of *Incroyable*'s fish mascot, and put the chart inside. 'We won't have any further use for that.'

Ogilvie stood with the axe as if to fend off the disaster roaring at *Incroyable*. She waited for the great wave.

PART THREE

EAST AFRICA
1960

Boa Paz. 1960.

The old chess carver lay dead on the floor of his small room
behind the bar of the pub A Tendinha. He had fallen from
his chair on to his back, gazing sightlessly at the bridge light
he'd been working by. In fact, he still held his small working
knife in one hand and a half-finished miniature elephant
chessman in the other. I stopped in my tracks at the sight and
then went forward to make sure of him, closing the door
behind me and shutting out the sound of Barrow singing to
an applauding crowd.

I supported myself on a chairback and leaned over the dead
man and as I did so the anti-radiation film badge I wore as
a precaution when handling radio-active isotopes in the lab
at St Gregory slipped out of its clip and fell on to the dead
man's chest. The badge was calibrated according to international standards of radiation emission and the various
danger levels. When the film turned black it meant one was in
the presence of dangerous quantities of radio-activity.

Now the film badge started to turn black.

I simply stood and stared while the party sounds came
through from the main body of the pub. It was one of
Barrow's song nights, the first since my anti-shark barrier
had proved itself about a week before. Shirley was back in
the bar. We'd had dinner together. Dr Pinto was also present
and I guessed that after Barrow's song was over we'd have
the previous routine of the chess game between Pinto and
himself, plus another new set of chessmen. I had decided
to back a hunch and see what the old chess carver was up
to before Barrow's song had ended and the next stage of the
proceedings began. So I'd made an excuse to Shirley and
made my way to the back. The pay-off to my hunch lay on
the floor.

A voice right next to me said. 'Why be scared? He can't
bite.'

My nerves were so shot that I grabbed by reflex and found myself holding Jerry's shirt. I hadn't heard him enter.

'Stand back! He's hot! Stand back!'

'If he isn't cold yet, that's not surprising.'

'Hot – radio-active.'

Something took place behind the man's eyes. They lost their shiftiness and he craned forward to see the strip of film I indicated.

'He can't bite any more, it's true, Jerry, but his body can. He's radio-active. Unaccountably so. How much, I can't tell without lab tests. The film shows whether substances are radio-active or not and turns black when it's dangerous. It's a rough indication only. For closer tests we use a measure of radiation called a rad . . .'

I thought I had misheard his mutter. He must have been greatly agitated to let it slip.

'Rontzen, a millirontzen . . .' He covered up immediately but it was too late. 'We will have to have a priest. The garage man is also the undertaker. I will arrange with them . . .'

Maybe he intended to continue with his dumb innkeeper act because he started to kneel down as if in prayer when I said.

'Jerry – you missed your cue. Men's lives – maybe yours – hang on little words like millirontzen.'

He stopped in mid-bend on his way to his knees and then rose again, with a knife in his hand.

'It would have been more incriminating if I'd said milli-curie, wouldn't it? That's out-of-date now, isn't it? It's hard to keep pace with science, the way they keep changing the terms.'

'It's also hard to keep pace with you. You're no more a Portuguese pub-keeper than I'm . . .'

'No?' His knife hand gave a slight movement.

'Nor is your boat what it seems. A waterproofed, tuned-up engine masquerading under the name of a clapped-out Kelvin!'

'What else did you notice in your sojourn at Boa Paz, Mr Ogilvie?'

The menace in his voice gave me an odd feeling in my throat and I tried to play for time.

'Sojourn! Where would a Portuguese peasant learn a word like that?'

'I repeat, Mr Ogilvie, what else did you notice?'

Any of half a dozen answers might have invited a knife thrust but I was lucky in hitting on one that didn't. 'A channel buoy on a bank out to sea beyond St Gregory for one.'

His garlic breath was close to my face. 'A channel buoy? Where exactly?'

'It wasn't a buoy exactly. More like a caisson. It had a fake tarpaulin over the top . . .'

Shirley came in. She gave an astonished look at the figure on the floor and at the knife in Jerry's hand. Her face blanched. Her paleness ever since we'd located the old sailing ship under the reef had been a source of concern to me but she'd refused to take it seriously. Now that paleness turned to deadly white.

'What . . . ! He's . . . dead . . . !' She recoiled from Jerry's knife.

'Keep away,' I said. 'I'd say he died of radiation poisoning after a long period of sustained exposure.' I explained about the film.

'Can you tell how much radiation he has absorbed?' asked Jerry.

I couldn't accept Jerry playing the chameleon. 'Whose side are you on? What are you?'

'So you've sorted us out into sides, have you?' he asked, his previous oiliness gone. 'I'll answer your questions when you establish how much radiation he died from.'

'We'll have to get him to St Gregory. We can test him with various strengths of film.'

Shirley said, 'There's no mystery. The old man's system simply ran down and he droped dead as he sat carving.'

'Except,' I said, 'that little square of film on his chest.'

'How do you know it's fatal? It might be almost anything.'

'If a man – or a woman – is exposed to a certain amount of radiation, he dies. Like that.'

'Are you sure?'

'A mean lethal dose is about four hundred rads.'

'Over what period?' asked Jerry.

'Four hundred rads in one day and you die in about two

or three weeks,' I said. 'But from the nature of his burns, it is quite clear he has been subjected to a little at a time over a considerable period. Look at his twisted fingers – radiation burns. Now how do we get him to St Gregory?'

'*Txibange,*' said Jerry.

A round of applause came from the bar. 'Dr Barrow and Dr Pinto will want their chessmen. They mustn't be kept waiting.' He picked up the piece from the dead man's hand and put it with the rest of the set. 'Thank you, old man. Perhaps others will say thank you, too.'

He was back quickly and humped the body to the boat using the window instead of the door as an exit. St Gregory was cold under the stars after the long, strained journey across the lagoon.

'The test films are in Barrow's lab,' I told Jerry, who was carrying the body.

When we reached it Jerry glanced curiously round the room and at the metal fish mascot.

He put the old corpse down and I got some film. I didn't switch on the lights but worked by the light of a shooting light. Shirley looked as pale as ever.

'We'll start at the mean lethal dose seeing he's dead.'

I handed Jerry the film and he held it against the old man. As if on cue the corpse started to rise up from the waist, like one of those reducing exercises for middle-aged businessmen. It was only muscular reflex, of course, but it scared the hell out of us. He was still as dead as ever.

Jerry sat back with a thump. Shirley went backwards and cannoned into the mascot. The fish's jaw swung open and a rolled map and a book fell out.

Jerry moved quickly. He scooped them up and shone the lamp on the map.

'Nothing to worry about,' he reassured Shirley, 'This is what's interesting. Looks like Arabic. Here, you're the map expert, Shirley.'

She shone the beam on the oiled silk and then said excitedly, 'Aguada da Boa Paz!'

I leant on Jerry's shoulder to get a closer look. I never saw anything less like Boa Paz.

Shirley stabbed a finger at a corner of the old map.

'St Gregory.'

'Then I'm St Francis.'

Jerry shrugged his agreement.

'The map is orientated east, not north. They often did it that way long ago. Also, this is a Mohammedan map, which used Mecca as its starting point.'

She turned the map round so that north was where we were used to having it and everything dropped into place like a jigsaw.

Jerry studied it and said, 'Here St Gregory is shown on the end of a spit of sand, and there's an island too, there's a channel – by heavens! Cape Correntes! Ponta Zavora! It's been written in Roman lettering and look, Boa Paz is an island, not on the coast as at present.'

It was clear that the topography of the coast had changed radically since the map was drawn.

'This is one of the finds of the century!' exclaimed Shirley. 'It's priceless.' Then she went on. 'After what Barrow did to my own map I became curious. I wrote to my friend Professor Alves at the Castro Museum in Lourenço Marques. He's sent me photostats of the old and new Portuguese maps of the coast. Why was Barrow so angry about the exact position of Boa Paz? Is it 25 degrees south or 24 degrees 53 minutes? What's the significance of it, anyway? What difference can a few minutes out mean in terms of miles?'

'It depends,' said Jerry, 'on what you are looking for, and how exact you want to be.'

'Or,' I added, 'how much you want to cover up.'

'Why did you say that?' he demanded.

I think it must have been Shirley's mention of the Castro Museum that brought into the light of day a fact that had been buried deep in my subconscious until then. The museum is near the hospital where I was treated after the shark attack. I went there on my first venture in public on artificial limbs. As luck would have it, the first gallery I entered was full of stuffed shark exhibits. Upset, I made for an exit but tripped and finished up against a showcase. I was reliving the moment again now. 'What is it?' demanded Jerry, seeing my expression. 'What's eating you?'

I told them about the Castro Museum and how I had fallen.

'In that showcase, Jerry,' I said, 'was a complete set of

elephant embryos. Real ones. Under each one was a card.'

'Yes . . . ?'

'They were scheduled as from two weeks of conception, and then progressively after that each month. Each embryo as it developed straightened up more and more towards the horizontal. You could tell exactly what age an embryo was – you only had to match it to the angle it stood at.'

'What are you saying?' asked Shirley.

'He – Barrow – gave me six weeks. Six weeks! I've got it.'

'I don't get it,' said Jerry.

'Nor me,' she added.

'Six weeks!' I repeated. 'That was the time limit for his anti-shark barrier. The chessmen had nothing to do with chess, or the game they were supposed to be playing. It was a way of signalling time. The development of the elephant embryo read in terms of weeks not months was Barrow's code. Six sets equals six weeks.'

Shirley said. 'I can't believe the old man was engaged in some mysterious time-indicating process.'

'There's a common denominator in all this – radiation,' retorted Jerry.

'Now it's my turn to be dumb,' I replied.

'Barrow went to Pretoria and brought back a load of radio-active isotopes. Life eight weeks. It makes sense to me. Up to now, I've been floundering. This nails him.'

'It may nail him in your mind but it makes you into a bigger mystery man than before. You haven't yet answered my question – who are you? Certainly not Jerry the Portuguese pub-keeper.'

'The information could be dangerous, maybe fatal, to you.'

'Come off it, Jerry!'

He tossed the knife in the air and caught it deftly by the hilt. It reflected a similar weighing-up process going on in his mind.

Then he said, 'I'll have to be a bit autobiographical to start with, if you're to understand.'

'If it's going to take long, let's get clear of this body.'

'It gives me the creeps,' added Shirley.

I found a couple of rubberized aprons in the lab and covered the old man. We withdrew as far as we could.

Jerry indicated his gross body and said, 'In the early days

of our atomic subs they didn't know much about the effects
of prolonged exposure to radiation leaks from the power-
plant . . .'

'*Our* atomic subs!'

'I'm an American. Ex-U.S. Navy. The name doesn't matter.
Hormonal imbalance. Runaway glands, as you can see.'

He wasn't being sorry for himself. He was the sort of man
I'd like to have had around in my dark days after the shark
attack.

'It still doesn't account for the pub-keeper act.'

'Seconded to Naval Intelligence. Hence the front.'

'There's nothing to merit an Intelligence agent at Boa Paz.'

'No? You probably don't know that the submarine cables
which link India, Australia and the Middle East to the rest
of the world via South Africa take the water at Boa Paz. We,
the U.S. Navy, have a vital interest in those cables in case
of a surprise nuclear attack. Having them open to relay an
advance warning could mean the difference between life and
death for half the world.'

'It's only American jitters,' retorted Shirley. 'All this stuff
about cables and radiation time-lapses is just so much nonsense. Boa Paz is a quiet little place whose only interest is
an academic one why there's a discrepancy between its past
and present geographical position. And that's only of interest
to potterers among old maps like myself.'

'Listen!' said Jerry and the way he said it made us listen.
'Russian trawlers have been playing hell with our Atlantic
cables. Off the Canadian coast they've gone so far as to mark
their positions. In the event of a nuclear attack we've got
about fifteen minutes' grace before the thing arrives. The
lines of communication between America and the rest of the
world *must* be secure.'

'How do you know . . . ?'

'One of our destroyers boarded a Russian trawler – the
Novorosisk, off Newfoundland. She'd cut five Atlantic cables
. . . inadvertently, she said. But we know it was a practice
run. The cables are the weakest link in the whole Western
defence scheme. Here at Boa Paz you could black out half
the world. It's my job to see it doesn't happen.'

'Where does radiation come in? And Barrow and Pinto?
Are they spies?'

'What had radiation to do with cutting submarine cables?' asked Shirley.

'The Reds mark the cables with radio-active chemicals,' replied Jerry. 'It's dead easy to pick a cable up once it has been marked.'

'So Barrow and Pinto are Russians?'

Jerry spread his palms and shrugged. 'All the way. Very useful cover, both of them, with their so-called scientific activities.'

Shirley said, 'So two Russian spies, working in close collaboration, speaking and writing Russian, have to have recourse to an elaborate eye-wash of playing a faked game of chess with carved elephant embryos just so they can tell one another the dates of a proposed – what? Cable-cutting? When all they have to do is to meet and tell one another all about it in good, plain Russian! Don't give me that!'

'It was just like that,' replied Jerry, 'and on the surface just as harmless – until Barrow went to Pretoria. Up to that stage Barrow and Pinto used to come to A Tendinha and have a drink, and occasionally Barrow went over to Pinto's place. But when Barrow went to Pretoria I . . . ah . . . availed myself of the opportunity of taking a look at his things and equipment. There was nothing to show he was a Russian spy. There wouldn't be. But I asked myself, what *was* Barrow doing in the line of science? I still can't find the answer to that. There is plenty of elaborate and expensive equipment – for what? There was nothing original in his experiments – I checked through his notes. Can *you* tell me?'

'He told the Director in Pretoria he was experimenting with radio-active isotopes.'

'I also could experiment with radio-active isotopes,' retorted Jerry. 'But what is the purpose of the experiments? Isotopes are not an end in themselves but a means. Somehow Barrow got wind that someone was on his trail. Perhaps I dropped a clue I wasn't aware of. But after his visit to Pretoria, the pattern changed between Pinto and himself.'

'*I* came from Pretoria with Barrow,' I said.

He smiled without warmth. 'I had not overlooked that. I thought you might even have been sent to help me from the British side. A legless shark-barrier expert – talk about perfect cover! Right in the enemy's camp! I've worked out the schedules, taking into account the time factor shown by the embryo's growth and the deterioration rate of the isotopes. It is tonight. If there is a single cable left uncut or working by morning I really am a Portuguese pub-keeper!'

Shirley broke in. 'Before you go any further, I think you should hear this.'

She had opened the little book which had fallen out with the map. She read aloud. 'Log *Incroyable*. Opium clipper. Ian Ogilvie, Master.'

'Go on,' I said hoarsely.

'Cleared Lintin Island, July 19, 1838. Noon, bearing WNW five miles. Set all plain sail. Moderate NE wind. Moved specie chests to trim. Four inches down by the head. Logging nine knots. Moderate sea . . .'

'*Incroyable*,' I said. 'That's the ship's name on Barrow's binnacle which was washed up. If Ian Ogilvie was her captain, it means he was my great-great-grandfather and met his end at Boa Paz. It was known he commanded an opium-runner but his name was a dirty word in the family.'

'Jerry!' exclaimed Shirley: 'We found his ship. She's lying near the reef.' She read again from the old log. ' "War-ship following H.M.S. *Plymouth Sound* at a guess. Shifted ballast to bring her down more by the stern. Making ten knots. Drawing away slightly from warship . . ." '

'It's – it's like opening up a grave and finding yourself looking at yourself.'

Shirley flicked the pages. 'Listen to this . . . "August 21st. Steep head sea. Watch oiling lower stunsail booms. Ordered Barrow off the quarterdeck after dispute with Idrisi about noon position. I have a feeling Barrow is trying to get *Incroyable* off course and making a faked landfall. He is hiding something about Aguada da Boa Paz." '

'Another Barrow and another Ian Ogilvie, 122 years ago!' exclaimed Jerry.

Shirley read on. ' "Cape St Marie, southern tip of Mada-gascar, bearing north-north-east. Pilot Barrow again disputed position. Noted error three degrees between ship's compass and Idrisi's own crystal compass." '

'It's like seeing an old-time film for the first time,' I said. 'There's a pretty girl and suddenly the lights go up and you realize you're leching after what must be an old woman now.'

The thought hit me. 'Crystal compass. That's what is in the chapel.'

Jerry said. 'They've all been dead a long time, Ian.'

'No, Jerry. That's where you're wrong. It's all working out – now, here, living. Something Ian Ogilvie did or Barrow did. Or Ogilvie did to him. Something Boa Paz did. It's been lying in wait all this time. Boa Paz is a wrong 'un, Jerry. It's got in its veins what has been discovered in the blood of alcoholics – tensions and resentment substances, I think they call them. It's part of the make-up and it bloody well comes out whether you like it or not.'

Shirley quoted the end of the log. '"In action against H.M.S. *Plymouth Sound*. 2 p.m. Barometer falling. 29.60. Gale SSE. Heavy sea. 3 p.m. Rudder fouled by swordfish. Carried away foretopmast and main topmast. Cut away wreckage. Cleared rudder. Jettisoned all guns. Isle of Poppies south-west, two miles. That is all." '

'The warship must have got her,' said Jerry.

'No,' I replied. 'She didn't seem smashed up. I must go back and have another look.'

Shirley said, 'I'm going back to A Tendinha to check the old maps Professor Alves sent me.'

'Hold your horses, Shirley,' said Jerry, 'I want to take a look-see first at the crystal compass.'

We went to the chapel. Jerry was enthusiastic.

'The first primitive gyroscope. I wonder who Idrisi was.' Then he said incisively, 'We've got work to do tonight, all of us. Shirley, get back to A Tendinha and bring your maps. Quick. Go to my room. You'll see what looks like a gramophone although it isn't. It's a portable radar. Bring it too. We may need it tonight.'

'Right,' replied Shirley.

He went on: 'I know the cables were O.K. first thing this morning. We test them every day. A Tendinha gets a daily telephone call ostensibly from the wine merchant. A bit of flannel about no broken bottles and the word has been passed about the cables. But we're on to them now. Their ship out there has got just what they need to wreck 'em – mechanical grabs, the lot.'

'Jerry,' I said. 'You should have taken a look out to sea. She's gone.'

'What do you mean, she's gone?'

'*Gripper* sailed two days ago.'

He went across to the window as if to reassure himself. 'Where,' he asked, 'does Barrow keep his radio-active isotopes?'

'Next door.'

'We'll check.'

We did. The orange-painted container which had held a big quantity of isotopes was empty.

Jerry said, 'This thing's growing bigger and bigger. The old man and the amount of radiation he died from isn't the important thing any more. Let's get out there to the shark barrier quick.'

CHAPTER TEN

The bank lay brilliant under the moonlight. The only sound was the breaking of the surf against the reef at our backs. My floating shack was almost as silver as the polished water. The only movement was above the place where I knew the opium clipper lay as the water broke lazily across the reef. We could see St Gregory vaguely outlined and a small silver tongue where the lagoon broke through to the sea. The big Lazy Grey shark which cruised near the drums on which my laboratory floated might have been cut from pale blue nylon mesh. A Diodon coral fish, the size of a football, preened itself near the shark, vaunting its turquoise and porcupine-like quills. A small ray, with twin booms like a Vampire jet fighter, aquaplaned seawards. Boa Paz had never been so peaceful since Vasco da Gama sent his men ashore five centuries previously to fill their water-butts from the lagoon.

Jerry and I had taken up our vigil after Shirley had dropped us off at my floating anti-shark lab and returned with the boat to A Tendinha to collect Jerry's small radar and her own maps. Like all corpses, the dead carver had been an embarrassment. We decided we couldn't leave him at St Gregory for fear of a giveaway if Barrow returned. He was an equal embarrassment to us. Eventually we brought him along to the lab and wrapped him in a tarpaulin and put him as far away from us as possible outside.

'Before you showed me that empty isotope container, Jerry, I was going to suggest we all go back to A Tendinha and break open a case of Campo de Casa and drink this cops-and-robbers stuff out of our systems,' I said. 'It's different now.'

'I wish it was,' exclaimed Jerry. 'Peace, a moonlit sea, not a ship, not even a man! They're up to something here, Ian, but where . . .' He gestured at the quiet sea.

'If it hadn't been for those isotopes . . .' I repeated. 'For want of something better to do, would you like to see how the shark barrier works? I'll fix that brute under there.'

'What's in all these drums – diesel fuel?' he asked.

'No. I've got a single drum for diesel inside. It's something Barrow is doing – he's measuring the lengths of waves. If you look over the side you'll see there's a length of ordinary garden hose trailing from the lab right across the bank. It's about a thousand feet long. He's doing measurements on behalf of the International Geophysical Year. It records on an instrument which works a graph there in the corner.'

'Looks harmless enough,' he observed. 'But it might be good cover.'

'For what?'

'Anything, with a clever bastard like Barrow.'

'He told me the hose records the pressure, frequency and speed of long waves. Eventually they might build up into really big waves, approaching tidal standard, so he said. Apparently there's a world-wide network of recorders and this is part of the chain. He also spoke about pendulum gravity measurements, whatever that might mean. The stuff in the drums has something to do with it all – it's soap dissolved in alcohol. Don't ask me why.'

I switched on an unshaded light. The lab lurched slightly as Jerry moved around. He took the map from St Gregory from his shirt.

'Put it there.' I indicated the oscilloscope. 'It's the only clean spot hereabouts.'

'Shirley would shoot me if I lost it.'

'Like to hear some fish noises first?' I asked.

'Hear fishes?'

'Yes. Fish make panic noises when a shark goes after them. They make different sounds when they are feeding and swimming around. It's rather amusing to listen.'

'With what?'

'I rigged up a sort of hydrophonic fish detector – a piscaphone.' I indicated a set of headphones. 'That's it. A couple of batteries and a few mikes strung around in the water on floats.'

'You're quite an inventor, Ian, one way and another.' He switched on the gadget and grinned. 'Maybe this should be passed back to Washington. You're supposed to soothe your nerves by watching tropical fish in tanks, way to restore jaded

Intelligence men . . .'

Then he stiffened. 'Engine!' he exclaimed. He pushed the headphones tighter against his ears.

'It's only Shirley coming back.'

'She's quite a way away still. This thing is better than I thought.'

'Let's get a few sharks instead,' I replied.

The diesel began its racket and the oscilloscope pattern danced on the screen as the current flowed. In a few minutes the big shark we'd seen earlier was floating belly-up near the raft. Then *Txibange* came in sight and Shirley brought her alongside.

Txibange thumped the floating lab deftly, expertly. Shirley certainly knew her stuff.

'Come on, Ian,' she called. 'Let's take a look at the clipper. I've got new oxygen bottles for our underwater gear.'

The water held her breasts firmly as we manœuvred ourselves on to the quarterdeck of the wreck; she was naked except for her goggles and my scuba gear. I was using an aquathrust, a small powered underwater engine, to help me along rather than my having to swim. Streams of escaping bubbles marked our route like an underwater paper-chase. Shirley gave a flick with her rubber-webbed feet and shone the cyclops light on her forehead on a corroded row of belaying-pins. She was almost horizontal, a couple of feet above the level of the planking, examining the deck, when two large crayfish, one nearly three feet long, reached out claws at us. One was as yellow as silk from old China and the smaller, green, buff and yellow with shocking pink claws. Shirley gestured at what seemed like a rotting box and I ranged up alongside her, but when I reached forward a blur of yellow, blue and grey fish swept across my vision. The box had had an outer wooden shell but the lining inside – like foil inside a tea chest – was still intact. I picked it up carefully. Shirley gave the thumb's-up sign.

Then I gestured towards an open hatchway. Shirley shook her head. I gave a spurt on the Aquathrust throttle, dodged her and went in.

I was surprised to see how relatively untouched everything looked. Shirley followed, obviously disapproving, and tried again to prevent me going through a doorway but I held her firmly by the wrist and gave the Aquathrust more power. The room – it looked like a lazaretto – was stacked with what looked like ammunition boxes. One of them had broken open and I spotted something glinting. I pulled it out.

It was a woman's shoe made of silver.

I pointed upwards and Shirley and I cruised out. We made a circle of the wreck at gunports level but could see no damage. No shot-holes.

We resurfaced and made our way to the mussel-lawn which topped the reef like a coating of sponge rubber. There we shed our scuba gear and relaxed. The fact that she was naked didn't seem to bother her. It bothered me. Before I'd had time to do much about it, she asked, 'How did Ian Ogilvie die? What do you know about him?'

'Not much, except that he was a bastard. I remember my grandmother mouthing "black mud! black mud!" whenever his name was mentioned. I don't know what it means, but I've found out more at Boa Paz than I ever knew before, for instance, that he was an opium-runner.'

'But what was he doing at Boa Paz?' she asked. 'Opium was a trade between India and China as far as I know. What brought him here?'

The present, not the past, was eating into me. I wanted to take her in my arms and make love to her. It showed in my voice when I said, 'What brought us here?'

Our eyes locked. But I fluffed it and the moment was gone because she got up and went to where the boat was tied up to the reef.

'I've got something to show you,' she said. She came back wearing a loose shirt and shorts and carrying a small squash leather bag like a large watch-case.

She took a finely-worked circular object from it. It had a ring like an old-fashioned watch at the top but the dial was marked in Roman and Arabic figures. Inside was a smaller circular dial which was engraved with the signs of the Zodiac. Across the face was a silver pointer, pivoted at its centre.

'Astrolabe?'

'Clever boy. It's a replica Professor Alves has lent me. I want to check the old map against my own.'

'You don't need an old thing like this to check the position of Boa Paz,' I said. 'You could do it with a sextant or find it on any Admiralty chart.'

'It isn't as simple as that, Ian.'

I couldn't get over the fact that I'd missed out with her. It underlay my irritation.

'What the hell's this thing for anyway?' I indicated the pointer.

'That's the sight rule.' There was an odd undertone in her voice. She'd caught the note in mine. 'Alidade,' she went on, 'and this is the rete or star map.' She fiddled with it. 'This plate comes loose and you can read latitude or altitude with it. And here . . .' she unscrewed something else, '. . . this is called a shadow scale for measuring heights and distances, like simple surveying. It was really a primitive sort of theodolite as well as an instrument for reading positions at sea.'

'And the signs of the Zodiac are to tell you that when you sit on a reef in the moonlight with a pretty girl without any clothes on you're in for a lecture,' I retorted.

Then suddenly she was hard against me and her lips were seeking mine. I reached out to take her but she pushed me away and retreated, squatting on her haunches with her eyes going all over my face.

I said roughly, 'We're not platonic nitwits to come and sit naked on a reef together just for the fun of hearing about astrolabes. What's eating you?'

She replied slowly and quietly, 'I want what you want, Ian, don't make any mistake. But one can also be frightened to lose something precious by merely saying it, or saying it wrongly.' Then she said with a rush. 'I've got polycythaemia. Now I've said it.'

'What the hell is that?'

'I expect that is exactly what your tough ancestor would have said.'

'I'd sympathize if I knew what you were talking about.'

'Maybe you've noticed in the past couple of weeks that I've been looking a bit pale. Polycythaemia is a blood disease – one's system manufactures too many red blood corpuscles.'

The night seemed colder. 'Like leukaemia?'

'Oh, no. Nothing as bad as that. It's more a matter of having intermittent treatment, to keep the balance even between red and white. I wanted you to know.'

'Is it – fatal?'

'In time perhaps. Every so often I have my radio-active drink and then I'm like new again.'

Boa Paz's common denominator: radio-activity.

I kept my voice level. 'Radio-active drink?'

'Yes, phosphorous, I think it is. Broadly speaking, it kills off the offending blood corpuscles and restores the balance between the red and white. At the moment I'm a bit overdue for my drink. Of course it's all carefully worked out – just the right amount to blot out the offenders. Otherwise I'd go for a Burton.' Her hazel eyes looked deep into mine. 'I should have gone to the hospital at Quissico – it's about fifty-five miles away – but I just had to hang around somehow.' A great deal was going on in her eyes.

I held up the silver shoe I had taken from the wreck.

'Slipper for Cinderella.'

I crooked her leg across my stump and put the slipper on. It wouldn't go farther than her toes, then her leg went hard against mine and she turned on her side towards me. The water spurted from the mussel-lawn under our weight. Our bodies locked. Then she went dead in my arms and gestured with her head. I saw a torch flashing from the direction of the floating lab. Three dots, three dashes, three dots. SOS. SOS. SOS. Jerry.

'Cinderella goes home from the ball,' she said. She dressed and we headed for the boat. We got her going and made best speed towards the winking light. Jerry was waiting. The diesel was silent.

'Engines!' he called excitedly.

'Where? What sort?'

'Heard 'em on the piscaphone. Clear as day. Ship's engines.'

I was ready to find fault with anything. I wished we'd ignored his signal. We had so nearly arrived . . .

'There isn't a ship for miles. Take a look. It's like a day under the moon.'

'I heard engines, Ian. When it comes to noises in the sea I know what I'm talking about. God knows, I should. I carry my payoff packet around with me all the time. I was a submarine hydrophone expert.'

'Then you should know that you can get all sorts of freak underwater sound effects.'

He listened with an earphone.

'There's not a thing now. But there was. I *know*. I agree you might get a freak sound bouncing off a deep scattering layer, as we call it, but I would have expected it farther out to sea in deeper water. It may have been one of those odd layers that one can't really explain satisfactorily – special conditions of temperature, density and salinity. And deep scattering layers are hell.'

'If the layers scatter sound, how would you have heard engines? It seems to me to work just the other way round.'

'You get a sort of sound-conducting channel between two layers. The sound won't penetrate the layers but it will travel along parallels – for hundreds of miles sometimes. What I heard may have been something like that. But it was damned clear. It seemed to me to be close.'

He fiddled with the mini-radar set and got it operating. 'Not a thing,' he said, 'but its range is not more than a couple of miles and subject to all sorts of humours.' He revolved the screen seawards in a slow arc and finally switched it off.

Then Shirley said in a strained excited voice, 'Look at this!'

She was staring incredulously at the old map lying on the flat shelf of metal where I had rigged the oscilloscope projector. He peered at it too.

She indicated the bottom left-hand corner of the map. 'I said there'd been a rubbing out. Here's what was underneath.'

It was quite readable.

'Perestrello,' she quoted. '*A patraoa dentro as sombras. 1575. 26° Aguada da Boa Paz.*'

'Where did that come from?' asked Jerry.

Comprehension dawned on me. 'The oscilloscope! It did it.'

'An oscilloscope can't make magic,' replied Jerry.

'In this case it can and did. The oscilloscope produces a spectrum. At one end of the spectrum is infra-red light and at the other ultra-violet. The map lay under the ultra-violet spectrum. When experts examine an old painting to see what's underneath, they photograph it under ultra-violet rays. That's what happened here, by a million-to-one chance. Arab cartographers superimposed their map and wording on Perestrello's original vellum. If we had that photographed under ultra-violet the original lettering would probably all show up.'

Shirley was carried away. 'Perestrello was the first man to map this coast. It's quite priceless. King Sebastian sent him specially to chart the coast from the Cape of Good Hope to Cape Correntes.'

I looked at the spidery signature of the long-dead Portuguese. It left me with the same sense of awe as when I saw Ian Ogilvie's clipper first. The past had walked right into the present.

'"*Padraoa dentro as sombras*" – what does that mean?' I asked.

'"The cross in the shadows,"' translated Jerry.

Shirley said. 'I don't know yet. But it does prove me right about the old and the new positions of Boa Paz being different. When Perestrello made his survey in 1575 Boa Paz was about eight miles farther down the coast towards the mouth of the Limpopo River than it is today. It was also an island, not a shore station. That's why the guns of St Gregory apparently face the land – in those days they were in fact guarding a vital channel between Boa Paz and the mainland, where any threat to the watering place would come from. There must have been a major marine eruption.'

'A statement like that is open to all sorts of objections,' I said.

'What I'm trying to say without dramatizing this wonderful discovery, is that the coastline in the sixteenth, seventeenth and eighteenth centuries was radically different from what it is today. From modern Lourenço Marques to Cape Correntes at the mouth of the Mozambique Channel there was a huge bay with arms hundreds of miles long; today it has changed to a relatively straight coastline broken by a chain of lagoons close to the sea. Long ago those didn't exist. Da Gama on his way to discover the sea route to India landed at Boa Paz – an island then – erected his white marble cross and departed. If only we could find that cross!'

'You'll find it here.' I indicated. 'At the old position of Boa Paz, about eight miles from where we are now.'

'You can see now why the Arab pilots had such fear of coming south of Cape Correntes,' Shirley went on ignoring the interruption. 'With the cape at the head of a gigantic bay it would have been the meeting-point of every wind and current at the mouth of the Mozambique Channel.'

'Fine, fine,' said Jerry impatiently. 'It all might be very interesting to your old professor but it's of no interest to me. My job is to keep open vital communications lines.'

Shirley flushed. I rushed to her defence.

'What it shows is that Barrow was either lying or uncommonly stupid about his treasure story. If Boa Paz lay eight miles away then his story about the ship sinking on this bank is rubbish.' I pointed at the old map. 'The position of the ship would have been on dry land on the Isle of Poppies.'

'Thanks,' replied Jerry. 'That is of importance because Boa Paz was situated roughly where you saw the caisson, Ian.' Then he froze, like a pointer stiffening. The loose earphone had begun to crackle.

Carefully almost as if afraid to disturb it, he crossed and put it to his ear. One could sense the electric thrill passing through him.

'Podvodnaya!' he exclaimed triumphantly. 'She's using Podvodnaya automatic guidance control!' Then he went on. 'She's a big sub. Class "W" I'd guess rather than Class "Z". They haven't got many class "Z" ready yet. Here she comes spot on time to cut the cables! Who'd have guessed they'd use a sub? The salvage ship was such an obvious bet.'

He passed me the earphone. There it was – thump, thump – thump, thump.

'Right time, right place, everything.' Jerry said.

'How can a submarine cut a cable when she can't see it?' I asked.

'Barrow and Pinto and his skin-diving boys have marked the cables with isotopes. She'll pick them up with her electronic gear.'

'Would it need all those isotopes merely to mark a couple of cables?'

'No, Gad damn it, it wouldn't! A quarter of what was in the container would have been more than enough. There's something else going on, Ian!' He silenced us both and sat listening, his face tight.

It was minutes before he spoke again.

'She's making in as straight as an arrow. Their Podvodnaya guidance is hot stuff.' He held up his hand for silence. 'She's slowing down. Just for one load of ashcans and a destroyer! She's stopped!'

I went to adjust the accumulator's power load.

'Don't touch a thing,' said Jerry. 'She's bound to be hearing something of those impulses. Leave it.'

The crackle of the earphones cut through the tense silence as the oscilloscope danced its ballet.

'She's completely stopped,' Jerry said. 'Very close. That way. Over towards the lower lagoon.' He glanced at Shirley. 'Just about where you say Boa Paz was before it shifted its position. She's either just inside or outside your shark-barrier, Ian.'

'Where the caisson is,' I added.

'Did you see what it was like inside?' he asked.

'Open at the top. A hatch, maybe. There wasn't time for much more. Jerry, that caisson is a vital link in the whole mysterious set-up.'

'Can you pin-point the spot where the caisson is?'

'No. The lifeboat was swept past too quickly.'

'That compounds our problem because at a guess I'd say she was three or four miles away from it right now. She's also about the same distance from where the cables enter the water. Yet there's no doubt she was guided in by radio-active markers. Barrow used a large quantity of isotopes to put down a series of radio-active markers as a guide and the Podvodnaya picked them up and came in straight as a homing pigeon. And now the sub's come to roost nowhere near the cables. I'd put my head on a block that those cables are not even marked with isotopes.'

He stiffened as the earphone note changed.

'I've never heard anything like this before,' he said puzzled. 'Scraping, grinding, rattling.'

'A hatch . . . ?'

'Yes – it *is* a hatch. She's opening hatches. She must be a "W" class.'

'What are you talking about, Jerry?'

'The "W" class Russian subs fire air-breathing guided missiles called Golems from the deck,' he answered. 'There's a companion class called "Z". They fire their missiles from internal tubes.'

'Then what you're saying is that right now, under our

noses, a Russian submarine is clearing for action – opening up her deck-tubes to fire guided missiles!'

'The caisson must be her launching-point.'

'Why this night or time?' broke in Shirley. 'No one is at war. You don't just launch ballistic missiles!'

'She's going to fire.'

From the earphone came the slow, heavy grinding sound of watertight hatches opening.

'Maybe she's making a practice run or exercising,' I said. 'After all, there's not a damn thing worth firing a Golem at anywhere round here. There's nothing strategic or of military significance.'

Jerry said quietly, 'Golem solid-fuel missiles have a range of about six hundred miles. Very accurate. Africa's two most important targets are within range of Boa Paz. A Golem on each of them would cripple the whole industrial build-up in southern Africa. First, the Kariba Dam, biggest man-made lake south of the equator in Africa. Second, Vaaldam, near Johannesburg, the third biggest lake. It supplies all the water for South Africa's gold mines, many of which are also uranium producers. The world relies heavily on those uranium supplies. The area also happens to be the country's industrial heart. Cut the water supply and South Africa's industrial nerve-centre is destroyed. This is dam-busting on an enormous scale.'

'The South Africans have an early warning radar chain like the Dew Line in Canada,' I retorted.

'Boa Paz is far beyond its range – it's hundreds of miles to the nearest radar from Boa Paz.'

'It might be a practice launch,' I said trying to convince myself.

'It's for real.'

It wasn't Jerry who answered but Barrow. He stood in the doorway balancing himself on the balls of his feet. He was wearing the same scarlet shirt, blue choker and black jeans as on the first night I'd seen him at A Tendinha.

It flashed through my mind that he must have climbed over from the far side because there'd been no tell-tale bump of a boat.

Jerry threw himself at him with a knife. As he began his stroke for the throat, Barrow pulled a trick to divert Jerry's eye at the critical moment – and killed him in that moment.

With incredible rapidity Barrow whipped his own knife to his lips, drawing it across them at lightning speed. Jerry fell for it and his eye strayed. He was a dead man at that moment. Barrow thrust the knife home in the side of his neck. In the same split second he leaned aside without moving his feet, like a boxer dodging a punch. Jerry's knife missed him by a hair's-breadth, and he went on over the side into the sea.

An Astra automatic in Barrow's other hand kept me where I was. He kept the gun on me while he clicked off the shark barrier switch.

'If he is still alive, which I doubt very much, the blood will draw the sharks and they'll finish him off.'

Shirley stood back, shaken and white.

'Rina is patrolling the lagoons,' he went on. 'Given the choice, I am not sure whether I would pick a shark or Rina. Rina was the double precaution against his getting away.'

There was a crowbar on the floor which I had used for winching the barrier cables. It might be used for other purposes . . . but Barrow almost read my mind.

'You're not nearly as quick as your late friend,' he said. 'Stay where you are!'

The sounds from the earpiece were growing fainter but we could still distinguish the grinding-scraping sound. 'She's doing well,' Barrow said. Then he spotted the old map and examined it with the keenest interest.

'So Boa Paz was an island once,' he exclaimed. ' "The cross in the shadows. 25 degrees".'

He drew back and pulled a scrap of paper from his pocket. 'Don't move!'

He then shifted the pistol to his right hand, found a pencil and noted the wording down with his left.

CHAPTER ELEVEN

Then something snapped inside me. I made for the connections from the condenser to try and lure him to the bare charged cable for a moment. He moved quickly and kicked my legs from under me. My head struck the edge of a shell and I fell in a stunned heap.

'A no-legged shark killer!' exclaimed Barrow contemptuously. 'Don't try any games with me, Ogilvie. Time's running out for you too.'

He lit a small cigar whose acrid stench didn't help my nausea.

I sat up. 'Barrow,' I said as collectedly as I could. 'I know about the sub and what she's up to. Think, once those Golems get under way – it means a nuclear war.'

'I knew someone was after us but I must admit I never suspected Jerry until I overheard him here. He was very good indeed. He could have passed for one of us easily.'

'By us, I presume you mean Dr Pinto and Co.?' I asked.

'Yes. You probably suspect if you don't already know, that Pinto's work was a blind.' I nodded. 'What we had to lay our hands on were radio-active isotopes in big quantities. It is really wonderful how easy it is once you've got a good cover.' He burst out laughing. 'Good old United Nations. How did Jerry find out about tonight?'

I told him about the elephants.

'I thought that code unbreakable. You're much too smart to be safe, Ogilvie. A pity, because your anti-shark barrier is a winner.'

'Barrow,' I said. 'Call off that submarine. You can still. For God's sake stop her!'

'And what do you think I would get out of it?'

'Listen. There's an old ship lying there by the reef. My great-great-grandfather's ship. I've had a quick look at her. There's a cabin stacked with silver shoes, which are worth a fortune . . .'

'Do you expect me to fall for that?'

I gestured to where the slipper lay under a bench. 'There are boxes full of them,' I went on. 'It's easy salvage, Barrow. I'll do it for you if you'll call off that sub. A fortune in silver specie.'

His eyes flickered and then he said harshly: 'See here! You're Ian Ogilvie, 1960. I'm John Barrow, 1960. What you don't know is that Ian Ogilvie, 1838 – the captain of that wreck – didn't hesitate to throw an innocent man overboard when he was no more use to him as a pilot. We Barrows know the Ogilvies. We've hated them since that day. You can't get away from it, Ogilvie. The fate of the Barrows, the Ogilvies and their ships is irrevocably tied up with Aguada da Boa Paz. It's in the blood of the Barrows and Ogilvies because of what your ancestor did.'

'Barrow,' I asked. 'What is black mud?'

'Black mud? In what context?'

'In the context of the Barrows and Ogilvies.'

'No idea.'

Shirley began to look dreadful.

I said. 'The Barrows and the Ogilvies can wait. Shirley should be in hospital. She's ill. She needs treatment.'

Barrow looked sceptical.

'She has polycythaemia.'

I saw a flicker in his face. If I hadn't been desperate for her I would have noticed the off-beat note in his voice.

'Polycythaemia?' he echoed. 'Don't they treat it with radio-active phosphorous?'

The common denominator, radio-activity. A warning bell rang at the back of my mind but I ignored it.

'That's right.'

'Unfortunately,' he replied. 'I cannot take the risk of getting you to hospital. That is not to say I will not assist you. I myself will go to Quissico hospital and get your prescription. In the meantime you will stay here. I shall take both boats. I feel sure you won't find one another's company tiresome.' He addressed Shirley: 'You will not go swimming near the reef or the wreck. Is that clear? If you do swim you must confine yourself to this side.'

'Where the caisson is.'

'So you found that too, did you Ogilvie? Yes, you may even use the caisson to dive from provided you don't try and make your way inside. I haven't any objection to your swimming around there.' He gathered up the map and the old log book. 'Who is the doctor at Quissico?'

He seemed to be falling over backwards to be helpful.

'Dr da Sousa,' said Shirley.

I was to know later what the look on his face meant.

The earphone gave a dying whisper as the current ran out.

'Barrow,' I said urgently, 'for God's sake . . .'

'You don't know the firing plan.' Then he laughed, a curious, cynical laugh. 'For God's sake and humanity's sake I'll tell you the kite is not going up tonight.'

I felt suddenly weak. Any reprieve was something.

The light began to fade yellow as the accumulators died.

'Can I use the diesel?' I asked.

'Why not?' he said, making for the door. 'I'm quite sure they . . .' he gestured in the direction of the caisson – 'won't mind.'

He shot a look round the lab and was gone.

I started the diesel, which ruled out conversation. I fed the current direct into the accumulators to charge them up. The shark barrier could wait.

I ran the motor for half an hour and then cut it so that we could talk.

A little more colour had come back into Shirley's face. 'Ian,' she said in a strained voice. 'I'm going to look at that sub. It's desperately important – bigger than the two of us.'

'No! We've got a few minutes' grace and we can use it to get away from here. What purpose will it serve to see what the sub's up to? We know we can't stop them.'

But she was obstinate, obstinate as hell.

'While I've still got the strength I'm going to look. It could be absolutely vital. I'll use the Aquathrust to conserve my energy.'

She started to strip off her cotton dress.

'Shirley, don't! Anything could happen.'

'It won't. I trust your shark barrier and I'll keep well out of the sub's sight.'

So I activated the barrier and she slid over the side.

I switched off the lights and waited. I watched her silver trail as she swam towards the caisson. I turned over every method I could think of to try and escape but came up with nothing constructive. As Barrow had said, the lab was our prison.

Half an hour passed. There was no sign of Shirley. I began to sweat with anxiety. The dead man's head lolled every time the lab lifted.

Nothing stirred in the direction of the caisson. I put the thought of a shark attack from my mind. Nevertheless, I went inside and made sure current was flowing through the barrier. I rechecked all connections. Anything but the waiting.

I spotted the tin I had found in the wreck. For the sake of something to do, I examined it more closely. It weighed about ten pounds and had obviously been made by a skilled tinsmith. The lap seam had been carefully soldered and it had flanged ends. If it hadn't been well made it wouldn't have withstood over a century of immersion in salt water. There was also a small capping-hole about two inches across which was likewise heavily soldered.

It seemed a pity to open it but I couldn't resist the temptation. I tried with my crowbar but I didn't get far. Then I used the blowtorch I had used for welding the barrier, cut open the capping-hole and shook out the contents.

They were ginger nuts.

Despite my growing anxiety, I couldn't help feeling amused. I broke one in half and it was still quite crisp.

By now an hour had passed and I was becoming deeply concerned about Shirley. Had she been spotted by the sub? The more I thought about it the crazier I realized I'd been to let her go. Had Barrow's readiness to allow swimming near the caisson also been a trap of some sort?

I went outside to look for her for the hundredth time and spotted a line of phosphorescence which was the Aquathrust coming towards me. The moment Shirley came alongside I knew there was something wrong. It was an effort for her to lift herself on to the floating platform. I gave her a helping hand inside and she dried and dressed herself.

'What happened . . . ?'

'Nothing. Just tired. The sub's there, all right Ian. I took a careful look. She's big, too.'

I switched on the piscaphone which was now serviceable again, after its batteries had been charged during Shirley's absence. There it was – that scraping, grinding noise again.

'I don't know what a submarine should look like but there were some big things sticking out in front . . .'

'Not upwards?' Missile firing solos are vertical affairs.

'No, in front,' she insisted. 'I did find out how she was guided in though. There's a line of markers each about the size of a portable radio stretching out to sea. She's lying in the middle of the marked channel. The markers converge towards the caisson. I had a look at that too but there's nothing much to be seen except the other end of the hose which begins here in the lab.

'It's odd, Ian, the hose is perforated, not solid. You'd think it would be useless for measuring wave impulses like that. It enters the caisson underneath through a sort of airlock. The caisson itself is about two-thirds submerged.'

I found my attention straying from what she was saying as a new fear – for her – superimposed itself on the other dangers.

'Shirley, did you get close to any of those markers?'

'Of course. I tried to bring one back but it was anchored.'

Her answer gave me a cold contraction in the pit of my stomach. Radio-active markers would be dangerous to ordinary people because of the radiation hazard but to Shirley with her blood imbalance they could be fatal. Normally isotopes are stored in thick lead containers because of the danger. Now she had been exposed directly to radiation and her listlessness was a symptom of its effects. Barrow, I realized, guessed we would investigate the sub – or rather Shirley would, seeing I was immobile. So with devilish opportunism he had given her the go-ahead to swim near the caisson and markers, knowing what would happen to her if she did. And she had. It was a way of doing the dirty work and keeping your hands clean at the same time. His offer about the hospital hadn't meant a thing. If he had meant to dispose of her like that because she knew the secret of the sub, he was obviously going to eliminate me too.

My first concern was for Shirley. She needed skilled attention and quickly. She was sitting now with her eyes closed as if exhausted. Before I'd time to make a plan I heard something on the piscaphone's earphone. When I put it to my ear the thud-thud-thud of the lifeboat's engine was unmistakable. It meant Barrow was coming back for us.

There weren't any weapons handy so I dodged outside to see how close the boat was.

We had our break in the form of a big bank of fog which was moving seawards from the direction of the land, blotting out everything as it came. Shirley had told me previously that an old name for the coast was the Land of Smokes because of this fog phenomenon. And it was a phenomenon, not the normal sort of fog cloud. It advanced, solid as a wall and a quarter of a mile wide, down the channel by St Gregory fort. To my right, upcoast, there were two more towering banks of it, one of which was also travelling seawards as if to outflank Boa Paz from that side. Txibange hill was briefly visible as a landmark in the last moments of moonlight before it vanished: before the fog caught up with it, I had a quick glimpse of Barrow's boat heading towards us towing his smaller outboard-powered dinghy. Then the murk shut down.

Back again inside the lab, I found a weapon in the shape of the speargun we used for underwater fishing. Shirley seemed to be dozing or in a faint because she didn't answer when I spoke to her. I put on my rubberized underwater suit, specially made for me with sponge rubber knee sockets and stiffened legs. Trying to get Shirley into hers was like shepherding a drunk into a taxi, but finally I managed it. Before going over the side I made a final check with the hearing instrument and found Barrow's boat had slowed considerably. My plan was to steal one of the boats from under Barrow's nose in the fog and strike through the lagoons until I was within range of the main road which led to Quissico's hospital and then hitch from there. I had to take the chance that Barrow's wolf would be out patrolling the lagoons; it might equally be with him. Which boat I snatched would depend on the circumstances at the time.

I had the answer to that as I was about to leave. The engine note changed over the piscaphone and I recognized the lighter, more staccato one of the outboard. Barrow had obviously changed over. I had a sufficiently rough sight-and-sound bearing on the boats' position to be able to locate them even in the fog.

I humped Shirley over the side and made her fast to the Aquathrust, the electric-powered craft which I used for underwater work. She murmured when she felt the water but didn't seem coherent. I cast off and the near-silent motor pushed us along. We went on like that for several minutes until I was surprised to hear Barrow's outboard drawing away. If his compass wasn't haywire, either he or I was hopelessly off course. Nevertheless I kept going and then made a time-distance check on my watch and found we only had another three minutes before we'd be beyond the protection of the shark barrier. If my target the lifeboat didn't show up inside that time we'd be as much prisoners as if we'd stayed aboard the floating lab.

We glided on and suddenly the lifeboat loomed up dead ahead. It was so unexpected that I didn't have time to go into reverse. The slight bump as we touched the other craft seemed to bring Shirley round.

'Ian! Where are we? What are we doing? Where's Barrow?'

'Quiet! Here's the lifeboat. Barrow's chasing himself in the fog.'

'I must have passed out for a moment.'

'Quite a moment.'

I was pleased to see her try and lift herself up. I loosened the lashings and explained the plan to her while I trod water alongside.

'The problem is that if I start the engine Barrow is sure to hear it. It makes a noise like a jet.'

'Not when it's silenced – don't you remember?'

I'd overlooked that clever exhaust-silencer system; it now crystallized my getaway idea.

'Fine! Let's get aboard. First priority is to get you to hospital. We can manage it if we don't finish up aground in the fog. It'll be a very tricky ride, though, with all the zig-zags between the lagoons.'

'The road's at the back of Inhagotou marsh,' she replied uneasily. 'Don't go near that marsh, Ian, or we've had it.'

I didn't want to complicate her fears by adding that Rina, the wolf, might also be there. So I merely said, 'Give me some landmarks to steer by – if I can spot 'em. It'll be a hit-and-miss course anyway. More miss than hit, I hope.'

She did as I asked after we had climbed aboard and I'd been below and connected up the hush-exhaust. The warm engine fired on the first kick, mercifully muted. I breathed again and we set off. Shirley's directions were at variance –

degrees out – with what the compass indicated. I didn't know which to trust but for the moment I stuck to hers. When I wanted clarification after a while, I found she had become semi-conscious again.

Then I heard the sound of Barrow's motor coming closer until without warning it cut. I wasn't quick enough to kill the lifeboat's engine simultaneously with the result that he must have heard it before it shut down. The muffled clap of three shots came through the fog. Fog plays games with one's hearing and sense of direction and I couldn't pinpoint him. So I lay doggo, allowing the boat to drift. She began to swing towards the coast, which meant there must be a strong inward set of currents. It was a question of who would crack first at the game of nerves.

It was Barrow. There was the sharp crackle of his outboard as he gunned it hard. It seemed to come from astern and then died away. I sneaked off under slow revs.

The course was a complete poser. What I aimed to do was to make my way through the chain of five or six lagoons of varying size, which stretch parallel to the coast, until I reached one near the road to Quissico. To enter the chain I had first to negotiate the one solitary narrow channel which gave access to them from the sea, namely, that under the walls of St Gregory fort. This was the obvious point for Barrow to intercept us but the way he had gone made me hopeful that he was as lost as we were. The lagoon route itself was winding and difficult because in places the lakes degenerated into marshland while the waterway became very narrow. The biggest marsh, called Inhagotou, lay at the Quissico end of the route and was so big that it stretched right down to the coast itself from several miles inland. The Quissico road skirted it some miles from the sea. If I missed the St Gregory entrance channel I could forget about reaching the hospital.

Now, according to the compass we were heading correctly but not according to Shirley. I couldn't rouse her sufficiently to get any sense out of her to check and none of her landmarks were visible. The fact that she'd been hazy when she'd outlined our route made me decide to rely solely on the compass.

After working up to our best speed and carrying on blindly

for what seemed an age, I knew how wrong my choice had been. One moment the boat was travelling along, the next it gave a violent lurch as a jagged fang of rock tore open the hull and unseated the engine from its mountings. The impetus of her speed carried her on and over the obstacle and then farther on to a reef, on top of which she came to a bone-shaking halt with the engine racing.

But the crash had ripped loose the main fuel line and in 30 seconds *Txibange* was blazing.

I rushed to Shirley. Our rubber suits probably saved us because the flames were everywhere. The shock had jerked her conscious but she seemed incapable of helping herself.

'Get out!' I yelled. 'Get overboard – quick!'

But she remained where she was so I grabbed her and rolled her bodily to the side. Then I remembered my artificial legs in the cockpit. Shielding my face with my rubber-clad arms, I returned and recovered them. The underwater spear was with them so I brought that along, too. I pushed Shirley overside into the shallow water and followed. I was relatively mobile in the water and so half-dragged, half-swam with her through the breakers to the safety of a small beach.

By now *Txibange* was burning like a Viking's funeral pyre and Barrow wouldn't miss seeing the blaze reflected in the fog wherever he was lying in wait.

'Shirley!' I said urgently, trying to rouse her. 'Try and understand! Can you walk? We've got to get to hell out of here!'

She nodded and got to her feet but her movements were as puppet-like as if she'd been on a deep space trip. For my own part I reckoned it was better to have legs than no legs so although the boat might have exploded at any moment I took the risk and put on my artificial limbs. Shirley, mean-while, went stumbling away and I followed as soon as I was ready. There was a hummock nearby and Shirley had dis-appeared over it but when I attempted it I tripped and fell headlong.

Once I hit the soft ground there wasn't any doubt in my mind that we'd finished up in Inhagotou marsh way off course to safety. Its smell was distinctive, a nauseating mixture of sweetness, sourness and decay. I hauled myself out of the muck and joined Shirley, who had come to a halt and stood swaying. It was only will-power which kept her on her feet.

'Shirley! We've landed up in Inhagotou! The marsh!'

'I won't be able to make it, Ian. It's all criss-crossed with streams and channels. It's the marsh of death. You go on alone.'

'Never – that's for the birds. We'll lick it, you and me. We've got to get moving before Barrow comes!'

She linked an arm in mine and we inched forward into the fog curtain. The orange glow of the fire was at our backs but soon the fog soon dampened it. Underfoot the going was soggy and I couldn't sort out the ground from the ooze. So I resorted to the spear as a kind of probe and guide and we moved slowly ahead from one firm hummock to the next.

After a while I was prodding with the spear when it dug into something live which screamed and jerked away with the spike sticking out of its back. It was a small wild pig. The spear couldn't have penetrated very deep but the creature ran off screaming bloody murder like a human infant. The swirling fog seemed to magnify the racket and add to its nightmarish quality. What worried me wasn't its wound but the fact that if Barrow's wolf was loose in the marsh she might hear or smell the pig.

The thought was a sharper goad to me than the spear had been to the pig.

Shirley had sunk to the ground and didn't respond any more, so I fastened my belt around her legs and pulled her along the soft ground until our way ahead was blocked by a waterway. I left her at the water's edge and tested the depth cautiously. The stream was wide but not deep. There seemed to be some movement – live moment – and noise ahead so I went more carefully still. And then there was the sound of mass squawking and squealing.

Ahead of me were two small islands, crowded with little creatures. One was exclusively populated by pygmy wild pigs like the one I'd speared and the other by big rats. In my state of revulsion I couldn't distinguish between them. I just stood in the foul shallow water and stared and they stared back, squeaking and chirruping.

I couldn't take it and went back to Shirley. To my relief I found her sitting up and conscious again. I outlined what I'd seen.

'I've heard of those islands – they're taboo around these parts,' she said. 'One is called the Isle of Rats and the other the Isle of Pigs. They give us a landmark, though – they're in the middle of an area known as the Barren Boggy Waste.'

'That's today's understatement.'

'If we keep straight on, we'll hit the road about three miles ahead.'

Three miles! It might as well have been three hundred, I told myself.

'Fine. Let's go on then.'

We stumbled on into the water, giving the two islets a miss and making for what appeared to be another solid patch to one side of them. Shirley was fine now she was conscious. What I feared, however, was another of her intermittent relapses when her limbs simply ceased to function.

We made progress – generally the ground seemed to be hardening underfoot – and were negotiating a waterlogged stretch when Rina found us.

She stood immobile when she spotted us, simply watching. I stopped too and Shirley leaned against me. I don't know how aware she was of the danger. I realized what was coming and splayed my feet to get a better stance to meet the attack. My feet touched the remains of a skull on the ground, a big bird, from the feathers and bones.

Rina's eyes were luminous through the murk and that gave me an idea for a weapon. She was easily blinded by light, I remembered. And I had a light, the rescue bulb fixed to the shoulder of my Scuba suit-top.

Rina started her attack – a swift, decisive lope towards us.

I waited until she was six feet away and then switched on my shoulder light. Instead of the bright glare I'd reckoned on, it gave off only a pale yellow glow. It didn't stop or even worry the wolf. She leapt, grabbed my shoulder and fell on top of me, growling and worrying. Shirley went spinning.

The animal's fangs didn't penetrate the rubber suit although her jaws were clamped on me. I lay perfectly still, turning my head away from the brute's foul breath. For a weapon . . . !

Something was digging into the small of my back. It felt sharp. I slid my left hand down very slowly and cautiously to discover what it was. The movement brought a growl from Rina and I felt her fangs start to penetrate the rubber and enter my flesh. But I'd grasped the thing under my back and realized immediately what it was: it was the beak, among the other bones of the kill, of one of the giant Jabiru birds which inhabit the marshlands.

It was a first-class weapon, a six-inch, pointed natural stiletto. The problem now was how to use it. If I moved I was afraid she'd switch her grip away from my shoulder to my throat.

Nevertheless, I had to move if I wanted to accomplish anything. I drew up my weapon-hand, a millimetre, I thought, but it was enough for her to dig her teeth in. I broke into a sweat at the stab of agony. I dared not yell for fear of something worse. I needed something to distract her attention for the one brief moment I'd require for the stroke. If I missed her heart the first time, I wouldn't get a second chance.

Then Shirley gave a kind of strangled murmur from nearby. The wolf lifted its head and me with it.

I struck at her rib-cage with all my force.

She let go with a scream of pain, jack-knifing backwards and pulling the weapon clear of her side. It had gone home because I'd felt her pelt against my hand. I couldn't jack-knife but I spun sideways out of reach of her jaws' comeback. I got as far as the water's edge among the mud plants and into a crouch, ready with the stiletto for another attack.

It didn't come.

The brute sank down whimpering, blood gushing from the wound, first down on to her hindquarters and then on to her chest. I knew that I had won when finally her head fell down. When I started up I got another shock – Rina's undertakers were already there in the form of a circle of the revolting rats and pigs.

I threw an oath at them and went to Shirley, still holding the blood-stained weapon. I tried to comfort her but she was incoherent.

'Shirley, we'll be all right! Now – up!'

At first she didn't respond but the urgency of my message finally penetrated because she got to her knees and then to her feet. We pressed on into the marsh.

The next big water barrier proved too much for me, however. It was both wide and deep. We couldn't make it across so I led Shirley back to the bank and went along it searching for a shallower crossing. Some way away through the fog I caught sight for a moment of what I thought—remembering the rats—was the stripped skeleton of an enormous animal. But it wasn't. It was the skeleton of a wooden ship half buried in the soft soil of the marsh. I stood and stared in astonishment but the question how it had got there in the first place took a back seat to the thought of what use it could be in our predicament. As a float one of the beams would be perfect. So I went and swung from one of the beams until it broke. It was too large to carry back to Shirley so I fetched her instead.

Once again the sight of something unusual acted as a mild shock treatment and made her rational.

'What a fool I am!' she exclaimed. 'I don't deserve to be a map-maker!'

'What's on your mind, Shirley?'

But the moment passed as quickly as it had come and she began to look puzzled and vague. Yet still she tried to get over the secret to me.

'That 25 degrees, Ian—it wasn't meant to indicate Boa Paz . . .'

She was drifting away.

'Yes? Try, Shirley!'

'The astrolabe . . . the shadow . . . it's in the astrolabe's shadow . . . not . . .'

But I couldn't get any more out of her and even water didn't revive her. Then I thought of the ginger nuts I'd brought from the tin off the wreck and fed one to her. Afterwards she seemed a little stronger and I dragged the timber to the water's edge and held her on it and we rafted across.

CHAPTER TWELVE

We went on and on through that unending night until the early hours of the morning. The nightmare of stumbling onwards through the marsh was increased by the agony it cost me and by Shirley's off-on fits of consciousness and unconsciousness. There were periods when we simply sat like junkies in a dream, terrified to go on, frightened and unable to go back. When I was beginning to abandon hope I was given a shot in the arm by the distant sight of car headlights moving at speed along the road ahead which was our target. It was the fact that I could see and measure the distance to salvation which made me find the mental and physical reserves to push on. I thought I was suffering from delusions when the lights kept on coming and going. After a while I made out the beams reflected off the dust which hung on the air. The reason that I could see at all was due to the fact that the farther we progressed away from the sea the thinner the fog became.

The lights continued to come and go. At first I merely accepted them and then when I'd had time to think it over, helped to my conviction by the crackle of high-powered exhausts, I realized that we'd been lucky enough to strike a night section of the Total Rally, Africa's equivalent of the famous Monte Carlo event.

Once I'd masticated this fact, new problems arose: first, I had to get to the road before the entire field swept by (the cars had been passing for over an hour since I'd sighted the first) and, second, they were heading down-coast towards the finish at Lourenço Marques, away from Quissico and its hospital. Finally, would a car involved in a cut-and-thrust competition stop at a signal from a couple of hitching scarecrows?

We eventually put the marsh behind us when we hit a concrete highway drain. A gaggle of three cars in tight formation surged past in a shower of dust and noise. They were big and their exhaust notes were heavy. This filled me with disquiet because in this rally the big cars are the back-markers. Maybe they were the last of the field.

I began to be convinced of this when we'd lain on the roadside verge for nearly half an hour and no further traffic had passed. Then I saw and heard another car, probably a straggler because of its lighter exhaust note. It seemed to be upon us before I'd time to get properly organized. I lurched forward into the roadway and switched on my emergency Scuba shoulder light. The car braked, skidded, and missed me by a foot before coming to rest a little farther on.

Three men jumped out and sprinted back.

'Christ!' exploded one. 'What d'ye think you're up to?'

He spread a hand against my chest and the force of it toppled me over.

'Steady, Charlie!' said another. 'No need to be rough.'

'It's my legs,' I said. 'Give me a hand up.'

'Jesus! I must have hit him after all!'

'There's a body here too – a woman,' said the third man.

'See here, you didn't hit me or her. But she's an emergency case and I've got to get her to hospital.'

Charlie the driver gave me a hand up and shone a light. I wouldn't have passed as a male model. I think it was as much relief as anything which made him co-operate.

'I need a doctor and a hospital, quick,' I went on. 'It's a matter of life and death.'

'A moment ago I thought it was death,' he answered. 'Your wife?'

'I'd like her to be.'

'She's bad?'

'Very bad!'

'Then you're lucky twice over. The rest of the field's gone by. We're a radio control car.' He indicated a big antenna fixed on the car's rear. 'I'll call up our control at Quissico and get a message to the hospital and a doctor to stand by. Okay?'

'Thanks.'

'Save it till we get her there. Let's get moving. Mind a little speed?'

'If you take off it can't be fast enough.'

But it was, once he got going. Only later I found out he'd been a racing driver. His track-conditioned reactions were magnificent and he took the car to the limit.

The radio operator started his chant. 'ZS6 AWQ here. Quissico, do you hear me? . . . ZS6 AWQ . . .'

The car had a left-hand drive and I was right behind the driver. The non-standard lay-out was brought to my attention when Charlie lipped the edge of a tight left-hander, swung the back wide and gave the car full lock to correct the slide before accelerating away again. The left-hand set-up brought to mind the odd way Barrow had switched hands over his pistol in order to note down map bearings with his left hand back there at the lab.

If I could have jerked upright in the crowded conditions I would have. Barrow couldn't be a Russian because there's no such thing as a left-handed Russian – the thought swept into the mainstream of my mind from some long-neglected back-eddy that the Kremlin had enforced a regulation that every Soviet child must write with his or her right hand. Since that were so, the submarine in consequence couldn't be Russian either. There *was* a sub all right (Shirley had seen her) but by following Jerry's Intelligence line of thought I'd fallen into the error of assuming she was Red and therefore at Boa Paz on a missile mission.

What was the sub really up to?

What was Barrow up to?

The remainder of the distance – we'd been about 15 miles from Quissico when we emerged from the marsh – evaporated under the heat of my thoughts and the presence of Charlie's throttle foot. Somewhere along the line the radio operator said that the hospital had been alerted.

It was about 3 a.m. when we pulled into the hospital's entrance and loaded Shirley on to a stretcher. She was hurried away and the doctor listened briefly to what I had to tell him. 'Will she live?'

His shoulders moved in a sinuous shrug. 'Who knows? I will do my best.'

'I'll wait here.'

The foyer was about as chilly and unwelcoming as a polar bear's lair.

'There's some coffee in the car,' volunteered Charlie. 'Something to go in it, too.'

'Aren't you pushing on?'

'No. Too far behind now. There was a stand-by car at the next control anyway. He's taken our place.'

'Sorry about this, Charlie.'

'Forget it. Glad to be of help.'

The coffee laced with brandy woke me up. Charlie produced sandwiches as well. I couldn't remember when I'd eaten last. It reminded me that I still had some of the old ginger-nuts in my pocket from the wreck. I thought Dr da Sousa should know I'd fed one to Shirley so I went indoors again and had the night nurse at the desk call him on the intercom.

'I'll come right down,' he said after I'd explained.

I might have been a patient with a high load of infection the way he regarded me when I put him in the picture. I didn't like the glacial look in his eyes or the way he took the remaining two ginger-nuts from me. He clammed up on any further information about Shirley.

'Wait here, please. No, not at the car.'

'Why?'

My question fell like a stone between us.

'Here. It is an instruction.'

I thought it had to do with Shirley, so I hung around, trying not to stare at the night sister because she was a nun and speculate what a pretty face like hers was doing in a dump like Quissico.

Then through the inner glass door of the vestibule I spotted Dr da Sousa approaching again. He wasn't alone. He had with him a rather sleepy-looking gendarme.

The two of them came up to me and da Sousa said, 'In here, please.'

He showed us into a little waiting room which doubled as a first-aid station. There was a couch, glass-fronted cupboards, instruments and dressings.

Da Sousa produced the ginger-nuts. 'You admit having these?'

'Of course. And I don't have to admit it.'

He said something to the heavy-eyed policeman and then spread his hands expressively.

'He says you're under arrest.'

'You're crazy, man!'

Da Sousa went on icily, 'Possession of habit-forming narcotics is an offence.'

'Habit-forming drugs . . . !'

He eyed the ginger-nuts as if they'd bite him.

'Crude opium. Very strong. You will remain here under guard until they send a police van for you. An ordinary man would have to walk.'

'I didn't ask for a wisecrack to be thrown in.'

'I am simply stating a fact.'

Then the full force of what I'd done homed in on me. '*I gave Shirley one of those!*'

'It was obvious when I examined her that she was drugged. Now I know what to apply as an antidote. Meanwhile . . .' he gestured at the policeman '. . . you have a lot of explaining to do.'

'But I volunteered the information about the damn things! I got them . . .'

'You can make a full statement to the police. I must get back to my patient.'

He went, leaving me with the gendarme. I don't think either of us knew how to handle the situation and he was obviously nonplussed. I don't think he was called upon to pick up legless felons every day in Quissico. He said something and motioned me to sit.

If I did, I would sacrifice my mobility. I had to get out, back to Barrow and Boa Paz. I cast myself in the part of an incapacitated drug-runner at the same moment that I noticed that the button of his revolver holster was undone and that the flap was loose. I gave a kind of off-balance lurch and grabbed at him to steady me. Anyone would have reacted to save me. He did. I came hard up against him, grabbed the pistol and wrenched away.

Non-communication in language doesn't mean a thing when you've got six shots and a heavy-calibre police issue to spell out your message.

I spelled out mine. His sense of outrage would have been funny if he hadn't been so angry.

'There!'

I manœuvred him close to the first-aid cupboard, faced him away from me with his hands behind his back and slipped a thick elastic bandage over his wrists. I prodded him with the gun to remind him that he wasn't a patient. I was scared of his legs – a kick could finish me. I kept clear of them while I completed his fetters with surgical bandages. Next I did a mouth job on him with an adhesive strip. There didn't seem any medical corollary to leg-irons in the cupboard so I made him lie on the stretcher-couch while I fastened him down with its straps.

I put out the light, slipped the gun inside my Scuba top, opened the door and went out. I smiled at the nun and continued on out to Charlie's car. He was dozing behind the wheel and the other two were asleep on the lawn next to it.

'Charlie!' I said softly. It was a shame to use the gun on him after what he'd done but I needed him and his car to get me to Boa Paz.

I was already in the seat alongside him before he awoke sufficiently to realize what was happening.

'You shit!'

'Maybe,' I replied. 'But don't broadcast it out loud, will you?' I indicated the gun. 'Quiet!'

'What's your racket?'

'I don't know myself yet. But let's have a Grand Prix start, shall we? And I don't mind how fast you make it to Boa Paz.'

'Stuff you!'

'A man with half a body has only half the patience of a normal one,' I said. 'Mine ran out of my stumps 10 seconds ago.'

He saw I meant it. The engine fired and he left a double rubber spoor on the driveway behind us. His chums hadn't done more than sit up before we were down the road to Boa Paz.

Charlie was either working off his anger on the machine or trying to scare the hell out of me by his driving. If my mind hadn't been so preoccupied he would have succeeded in the latter. We raced along the gravel road flanking the marshes and through patches of fog which came and went like solid barriers across the road. I didn't have time to admire his skill. There was too much to sort out inside myself. If the submarine wasn't Russian – and my conviction was growing that she wasn't, especially when I added to my own discovery the recollection of Barrow's snide grin when he'd remarked that she wouldn't be firing missiles that night – what could she be doing? Cable-cutting was definitely out.

Yet Shirley had seen something unusual projecting from her bow. What? Maybe I'd never learn from Shirley. The thought of her lying between life and death made me feel desperate and angry and inhibited clear thinking about Barrow. All I could find to accuse him of was treasure-hunting. But you don't need a secret submarine, radio-active marker buoys, a caisson and an unexplained gadget like a wave recorder for that. Moreover, the opium clipper was in a different position, miles away from where the sub was operating. She was a piece of cake for salvage: a couple of Scuba divers protected by the shark barrier could comfortably recover her silver and opium. I came to the conclusion that the barrier and the wave recorder were a front. For what, I meant to find out. But I'd have to work fast. The trussed gendarme wouldn't stay that way for long and I'd have every policeman on the coast after me by daylight.

Charlie's chums wouldn't go back to sleeping either. Nor was Charlie himself my ally any longer. If I let him go at Boa Paz once he'd served his purpose I wouldn't get as far as the floating shack before being picked up. I couldn't immobilize him short of shooting him. Yet his silence for a few hours was vital for my investigations. If Barrow didn't get me first.

That thought in itself gave me my line of approach.

'Charlie,' I began, 'I'd like you to drop me at the end of the track among the lagoons once we hit Boa Paz. I'll show you the turn-off from the highway.'

He turned angry eyes from the road for a moment. 'You make it sound like a request.'

'It is.'

'A bastard with a gun! Did you kill the fuzz?'

'No.'

'What's your game, you and the doll?'

'I'll explain the set-up . . .'

'What set-up?'

'I'll tell you. But first, if I don't come back after you drop me and the girl dies, I'd like you to see that she gets a decent burial.'

'With what, may I ask?'

'There's a wreck by the reef. She's carrying a fortune in silver specie and crude opium.'

'And I'm Father Christmas.'

'I'm not trying to shoot a line. I'm telling you, in case.'

It was a good thing Charlie wasn't feeling accident-prone that night the way he took the next bend.

'I don't buy it, that's flat.'

'Don't – now. Later, if I don't make it. Now listen . . .'

I told him about Barrow, the mystery sub, the shark barrier and opium clipper wreck. The fact that it was all known to a third person now was something to nail Barrow if my single-handed sortie misfired.

When I'd finished he said, 'If I couldn't see your eyes and that gun I'd say you were high on the stuff yourself.'

'All I want is a couple of hours to sort it out. You don't have to do anything except keep your mouth shut.'

'And if I don't?'

I shrugged and pointed the gun as convincingly as I could.

'Don't tempt me.'

I indicated the radio speaker microphone fixed into the fascia at mouth-level.

'Silence includes this. I could shoot it away for a start.'

'You bastard! I don't even know your name!'

'Ian Ogilvie, for the record. It may only be for the record.'

'How d'ye intend to make your way out to this lab affair?'

'Canoe. There are plenty of native ones in the lagoons.'

'You really mean it, don't you, Ogilvie?'

'I really mean it.'

'It'd take guts to do what you're thinking of doing, even with legs.'

'Leave my legs out of this, will you?'

'See here,' he went on, sliding into a lower gear to negotiate a water-splash. 'I've often thought when I've been out on the circuit what'd happen if I crashed and they had to take off my legs to get me free . . .'

'You go on feeling your toes for quite a while even though you haven't got any.'

He slowed down. 'Jesus! And you can sit there without 'em and a gun on me and plan what you're planning to do!'

I put the gun on the seat. There wasn't any need for it any longer. I'd won.

'Okay, Charlie?'

'Okay.'

'Don't go soft and slow up just because.'

He grinned and took the car up to maximum revs.

'How much time do you want?'

'Mid-morning should be enough.'

'Not otherwise?'

'If you hear gunfire or explosions you can cut loose.'

'What's the girl's name?'

'Shirley.'

'Doesn't the medic think . . . ?'

'It's an even-steven chance.'

'I'm sorry.'

'No need to cry at this stage.'

'I wouldn't lay money on either of you.'

'I'm not a betting man, Charlie.'

We were coming down the last long straight which leads into the village of Chidenguele and soon the landmark hill would be visible. The night was going and the dawn was showing out to sea. After the village we slowed and picked our way along a rutted track to a point where it finally dead-ended against a lagoon. As I expected, there was a group of native fishing canoes among the waterside sedges.

I got out. 'Thanks for the ride, Charlie.'

'You forgot this.' He passed me the heavy 38 Astra. I checked its six rounds.

'Could you use an escort?' he asked suddenly.

'No, Charlie. This is a one-man mission.'

'Then can't I get closer to the scene of operations?'

'You're at the ringside now. You can keep the floating shack in sight through the channel gap.'

He checked his watch. 'How late is mid-morning?'

'Make it a very late breakfast if you prefer.'

'A late breakfast, then.'

He helped me into the canoe and shoved me into deep water. I paddled past the old fort and made for open water. The surface of the sea was like crumpled foil it was so calm but it was rippled with silver feathers round the reef. There wasn't a ship or a boat in sight.

I went cautiously at first and then more confidently as the growing light revealed nothing. I approached the shack itself from its blind side away from the door but even at a distance it had a nobody-home look. I paddled warily alongside, careful not to bump, and waited with pistol cocked. There was nothing.

It was all so still that after a few minutes I began to feel foolish pointing a gun at emptiness. My explanation and request to Charlie too began to ring mock-heroic. I stood up and made the canoe fast. The tarpaulin covering the old dead carver was still in position and I could see from the hump that the body was underneath. Nothing suspicious there.

But there was something suspicious once I got inside. Barrow had left his visiting card in the form of a lidless case of gelignite. When had he been there? I found the policeman's gun again and felt reassured. My eyes searched every corner but nothing else was out of place. I tested the piscaphone and found signs of life, the first since I'd landed aboard. The scrape-grind, scrape-grind was coming over the instrument from the sub. The sound had me licked. You don't spend your time in a nuclear sub opening and closing the doors of your missile-firing silos like the stops of a trumpet. And if it wasn't that, what sort of sub was it?

I was on edge at nothing and my heart was hammering away like a honky-tonk piano. But my tension was overlaid with a mood of cold deliberation: I was determined that nothing I had built would benefit Barrow if I could help it. That meant the shark barrier.

I found some tools and opened up the big circuit boxes for the barrier cable. To check for faults when the barrier was live, I had stationed half a dozen waverider buoys at intervals along it. Each buoy, painted bright orange, was surmounted by an antenna connected to a small radio transmitter, which automatically relayed any electrical malfunction so that it was possible to isolate the section of the barrier concerned for inspection and repair. Each section between buoys therefore had its own distinctive circuit in the form of brightly-coloured wires in the circuit boxes. When integrated, they functioned as one unit. There hadn't been time to draw detailed wiring and circuit plans and I'd improvised as I went along. The thought slashed through my mind that a jinxed barrier could be a weapon against Barrow.

So I jinxed it.

It didn't take long. When I'd finished with the circuit boxes and control rheostats I wasn't sure whether the thing would blow up in the face of whoever threw the master-switch or electrocute him where he stood. I didn't mind which it was as far as Barrow was concerned.

I went outside to see if I could spot anything in the area of the caisson and where I judged the sub must be. In devising one weapon I'd forgotten another obvious one – the policeman's revolver – inside.

It was too late now, for Barrow's voice cut across the silence.

'Don't move, Ogilvie!'

He was sitting where the dead man should have lain; he had pushed aside the tarpaulin with a stubby-barrelled sub-machine gun, the one now lined up on me.

CHAPTER THIRTEEN

The situation was his. It usually is when you have that sort of artillery.

He got up and came closer. There was no need to really. He could just as well have cut me in half from where he sat.

His slightly muddy eyes were puzzled but if he was tired from a night's vigil this was the only way he showed it. His movements were shark-quick and he had that go-getting air which was characteristic. Only now his prodding was being done by the barrel of as nasty a little automatic as I'd seen.

'You're alone?'

It wasn't a question which was meant to be answered but I did because I wanted to try and get under his hide. I gestured at the empty sea.

'No. The crowds will jump aboard when I blow my whistle.'

'Stow it!' he snapped. 'How'd you get through my cordons?'

'I'm slow on the uptake at this time of morning.'

He regarded me with something approaching respect.

'You're a cool one.'

'That thing in your hands isn't calculated to lowering the temperature.'

'How'd you dodge my men, Ogilvie?' he persisted. 'They were all over after your boat went up.'

'Except in the marsh.'

The beginnings of concern showed in his face. 'Rina was guarding it. You'd never have got past her.'

'Say it again by way of an epitaph.'

His face blurred with hatred as if he had pulled a silk-stocking mask down over it. I thought he was going to kill me when he hefted up the weapon and threw off the lock. His eyes burned. The silence stretched out. The fact that he hadn't killed me and had had men searching for me in the night, meant that I had some importance for him I didn't yet know of. It also blew the cover on the hospital doctor. He was one of Barrow's stooges and the opium cake had given him the excuse to hand me a narcoctics rap with the law while keeping his own hands clean. I wouldn't have remained in police custody long before I'd have been handed over to Barrow. I was pretty sure he had the authorities in his pocket in a small place like Quissico. The whole set-up made me tremble for Shirley.

At length Barrow got a grip on himself.

'*You . . . killed . . . Rina?*'

'With my left hand, Barrow. Note, the left.'

'What's that got to do with it?'

'If I'd been a Russian I couldn't have done it.'

The devils were still in his eyes but there was apprehension now, too.

'Explain, blast you!'

'You know but I'll say it anyway.' I explained about the Kremlin's left-hand ban. 'You're not a Russian. Nor is that sub. Nor is she here to fire missiles. What are you up to, Barrow?'

'You're very observant, Ogilvie. Too observant.' I didn't like the way he said it but I reckoned he'd already written 'expendable' at the end of my contract, so I went on trying to needle him into a mistake or a giveaway.

'It's the treasure ship, isn't it, Barrow? The Portuguese one that sunk hundreds of years ago on the way to India with the expedition's exchequer aboard? The caisson's a marker for it, on 25 degrees exactly. And that's a salvage sub of yours . . .'

'Not up to Ogilvie standards at all,' he retorted. 'No. We've wasted enough time. Get your canoe and we'll pick up my dinghy. I hid her on the reef.'

'Cordons, men searching, a hidden boat – you make me sound important. It's good for my morale right now.'

'The life you save may be your own, if you co-operate.'

'And if I don't choose to?'

He indicated the automatic.

'You'll do as I say.'

'Very old hat.'

He tapped the butt. 'This makes it new.'

Up to that moment I think I'd been a little light-headed because I'd written myself off. But the way he spoke made it apparent that he needed my assistance. In what way I couldn't guess unless it involved my scientific know-how.

And it must be very big if he could shrug off a galleon full of treasure as chickenfeed. And talking of treasure, there was also the opium clipper. Her silver specie alone was enough, apart from enough crude opium to hang on any junkie colony's Christmas tree.

I decided to string along rather than court immediate death.

'Right.' I made it sound as grudging as I could.

'You haven't any choice.'

I hadn't and I knew it.

'How much spare cable have you got inside there?' he asked.

'There's a reel of it – hundreds of feet.'

'Good. Bring it along. Some tools also.'

'What for? The barrier's complete . . .'

'Bring it, I say!'

I fetched the insulated cable which was wound on a size-able wooden drum.

'Now start the generator and make the barrier live.'

I felt a cold tingling where my toes used to be. Maybe that's how it would feel when the 5,000-volt current fed itself back into the metal of the lab when I threw those jinxed switches. There'd be no time to fix them with Barrow looking on. It looked as if my life insurance was about to backfire into death assurance. Barrow's eyes were boring into me with a question starting to form in their odd opaqueness.

'What are you waiting for?'

I indicated the roll of cable. 'Unless I know what that's for I don't know how to regulate the rheostat switch for the barrier. You tell me which: full advance? Retard? Half . . . ?'

My technical bluff worked.

'You're well aware that I haven't a clue about the ins-and-outs of the thing.'

'Well, then?'

'You'll take a lead off the waverider buoy.'

'What for? Where to?'

'Arrange it, damn you! I'll show you later!'

That made it worse from my point of view. Short of admitting what I'd done or spending time restoring the jinxed circuits, there was no help for it.

'Okay. It won't take a minute.'

Then I remembered the case of dynamite inside. If th

circuit blew – and I couldn't see how it couldn't – there'd be sparks enough to satisfy a pyromaniac.

I said as unconcernedly as I could. 'I don't like that dynamite around.'

'It's coming with us anyway.'

He fetched the box and carried it to the canoe. Before he'd finished I got to the diesel and started it. Its racket in the confined space was still not cover enough. I gunned it as hard as I could and it responded with a stammering roar of protest, banging away unevenly. I grabbed the rheostat control and tripped it. The result wasn't spectacular but smelly. A blue flame spurted across the switchboard which dissolved in smoke and a loud plop.

I didn't wait but went outside and started getting into the canoe. It was an occasion when human speech was at a discount. The yammering of the engine made conversation impossible. Barrow hesitated and for a moment I was certain he had heard something but then he followed with the submachine gun still trained on me. I paddled clear of the shack, hoping no shark would show up before we reached Barrow's boat and advertize my sabotage. None did.

There were high streamers of cloud seawards and a breeze was starting up. Barrow was edgy and kept looking across to where the waverider buoy's antenna swung in a lazy arc with the rise and fall of the sea. Out of the tail of my eye I spotted that his face was oiled with a sheen of sweat. But it was I who was putting in the physical effort at the paddle. There was a lot more going on inside him than he might admit. I noted that for future reference. Except there didn't seem any future.

When we'd got beyond the decibel-deafening range of the diesel, I said: 'If it's treasure you're after, Barrow . . .'

'For Chrissake, put a sock in it!' he retorted. 'Is that all your mind can run to? Think, man! Salvage on this bank? There's an underwater race which would knock a diver off his feet before he was 30 feet down. Every season for centuries the rivers have dumped one more layer of silt on top of the treasure ship. It went down in a sudden violent storm. Where in hell would you even start to look? The hulk might be anywhere within a radius of five miles!'

'But the clipper . . .'

'She's not covered in mud because she's up against the reef, and the current through the gap scours it clean. Use your brains, Ogilvie!'

I indicated the cable. '*You* want to use them.'

'You could make it easy for yourself if you wanted.'

Easy as a bullock going to the abattoir, I thought. The result is the same at the end of the road. But a few victims escape or at least they kick up all hell trying to.

I made the best rejection shrug I could, being busy with the paddle.

We reached the reef. Barrow's boat with its outboard motor was parked in one of the tidal pools where a ridge of rock hid it from sight. He dragged it into deep water after we had moored the canoe and transferred the cable, tools and dynamite into it. Then we set off for one waverider buoy which he had obviously selected beforehand. The day was so mild it might have been a holiday tripper jaunt with Barrow standing there on the stern thwart with one foot resting on the outboard steering. The difference was that guides don't cradle automatics on their hips with the barrel pointing into your face.

We reached a distinctive orange-coloured waverider buoy on the barrier limit nearest the caisson. It was anchored to the seabed; a line of smaller bi-coloured marker buoys dotted the water on either side of it for several hundred yards to the next waverider. They were interconnected with rope and fixed by means of shackles to the main buoy itself. This line of surface markers traced the position underwater of the anti-shark barrier. There were about half a dozen waverider buoys altogether and each was surmounted by a transmitting antenna. Their cupola-shaped fibreglass tops were detachable. The object was to break the barrier's lengthy circuit into manageable sections in case of trouble. Inside each waverider was a circuit box. Using this it was possible to isolate any section of the barrier.

'Connect up the cable from the reel,' ordered Barrow.

I stalled: 'Not on your nellie! If you want 5,000 volts to run through you, that's your affair. I know of easier ways to commit suicide.'

I couldn't risk working on the stone-dead barrier with Barrow breathing down my neck. The waverider's automatic transmitter must be bleeping its head off back at the lab. I had to fix that too but out of his sight.

The beginnings of apprehension showed in his eyes. He shifted the gun.

'You mean you won't?'

'Listen,' I said wearily. 'You're keeping the cards so close to your chest that if they were live like the barrier they'd singe you. Before I connect up anything I've got to know what's at the other end.'

'I'm paying you to do a job and not ask questions . . .'

'Payment being in the form of little slugs of round-nosed lead set in brass cases. They call 'em bullets, in case you don't know.'

'Shut up!' he snapped back at my sarcasm. Then he said, half to himself. 'You'll have to know, sooner or later.'

'Surprise parties have always been my special pleasure.'

For the first time that morning he looked uncertain. He considered for a while and then said, 'Leave the cable for the moment. We'll come back to it. Meanwhile attach it loosely round the antenna and we'll pay it out as we go. We'll begin at the caisson end of things.'

But it wasn't a caisson although it looked like one until you came close. It was a bathyscaphe, a self-propelled, steel diving-bell used for sea-bed and underwater exploration work and also for locating objects like wrecks and crashed 'planes. I identified it immediately I spotted the outer hatch which gives access to the entrance chamber. This chamber is also used as a ballast tank during descent. At one stage during my official work on shark control measures it was suggested that a bathyscaphe be acquired to study sharks and their reaction to electric shocks in their natural habitat. The idea had been abandoned on the grounds of expense but it meant that I'd studied and was familiar with bathyscaphe design and lay-out although I didn't know much about their complicated electrics.

Barrow inched the outboard alongside the bathyscaphe and cut the engine. He saw from my face that I knew what it was.

'You're in deep waters, Ogilvie. Literally and figuratively. Unclip the hatch. Get inside. Put on the lights – the switch is by the door. No tricks. I'll be right behind you.'

I did as he said. My mind was racing over the problem

of the sabotaged barrier. The 'scaphe must have its own power supply in the form of accumulators, so what did Barrow want all the extra for? A special deep dive? No, nowhere was the water more than two hundred feet. I'd sounded it myself before laying the barrier. Extra endurance? I couldn't answer that one because I didn't know that the endurance of a bathyscaphe was, I imagined, a couple of hours using all its power-driven equipment.

I had a tough passage down the steel rungs set into the wall of the entrance-cum-flooding chamber which proved small and awkward for my legs. The ladder led to the main cabin which was big by comparison. It was meant to take three men. There was an instrument panel fit to rival a space-ship's with switchboards, breaker circuits, fuse-boxes and dials. The control panel was equally daunting: engine controls, ballast trim and buoyancy, ballast blowing and filling gear. I knew from my studies that a 'scaphe had an ingenious system whereby the compressibility of petrol (stored in external tanks with non-pressure-proof skins) was used in conjunction with seawater pumped in to provide for a descent to the depths; to ascend again the tanks were blown and filled with compressed air. In addition there were several tons of static ballast in the form of iron shot in outside boxes held in position by magnetic circuits, which could be jettisoned in any quantity at the touch of a switch. There was also an impressive array of controls and switches for the craft's quadruple searchlights, which could be operated independently or as a unit.

The control cabin had two windows with jump-stools under them for observation work. All this was standard. What wasn't standard was at my feet. Normally there is a third window situated there to enable the crew to observe the sea-bottom. Barrow's bathyscaphe did indeed have a window but only to serve as a cone-shaped hatch leading to a small lowermost compartment whose floor was constructed entirely of pressure-proof glass. In this chamber as well, was a mechanical arm working off a series of universal joints and gears which was controlled by a 'slave manipulator' from the main gondola above. I knew this gadget well: it was used for handling radio-active isotopes by remote control.

Once you get the hang of it you can work it with the expertise of an extra hand. It was evident that the third compartment could be flooded and the mechanical arm set to work to pick up objects from the seabed.

What were those objects?

Before I'd time to sort that one out, Barrow joined me. He drew my attention to the instrument panel where there was a rheostat control with a notice under it which read, 'flotation filters'. All the other control notices were on embossed metal plates. But this one was different. It was obviously made by a plastic lettering device. It stood out like an afterthought or more likely, something which was deliberately kept secret when the rest of the 'scaphe was fitted out.

'Surprise, surprise,' I murmured.

'Damn your flippancy, Ogilvie!'

'It's my defence mechanism, don't you know?'

His eyes were suffused with anger but he had the sense to set the safety catch of the automatic. Those pressure windows. It's the same danger which enables hijackers to get away with it. Once submerged the gondola was similar to the pressurized cabin of a 'plane. But we hadn't taken off yet.

He said, controlling his voice: 'You will connect the power supply from the shark barrier to this control. There's a water-tight gland on the outside hull ready to take it.'

'Five thousand volts?'

'There's a variable transformer – it can cope with anything up to ten thousand.'

'Does it feed the engines?'

'Yes and no. The accumulators have enough for a three or four-hour dive, provided you don't use the searchlights too much. They eat power – a thousand watts each.'

I wondered how long I could sustain my bluff because I'd nothing left to bluff with. I glanced round. A luminous fathometer, barometer (for regulating pressure in the cabin) and an audience of dials with big and little faces gazed back at me. It was all as clinical as an operating theatre. The oxygen bottles and chemical canisters for scavenging foul air added to that impression.

Barrow handed me a heavy waterproofed plug connection for my cable. It wasn't a big job.

'You could have got any wireman to do this,' I pointed out. 'Get on with it, man!'

I did. First that meant clambering up the rungs again out of the surface hatch. It was as bad, if not worse, going up as coming down. I took my time, hanging like a fly and labouring deliberately for breath. I noticed that the flooding intakes near the ladder were covered in mesh. Maybe that wasn't so unusual. But what was unusual was the fineness of the screen. When I looked closer I saw that the four screens which flanked the chamber were each part of what seemed to be detachable circular metal boxes. They might have been insect-proofed portholes. Except that it would have taken a microscope to see an insect tiny enough to penetrate that mesh.

I re-emerged into daylight and Barrow followed. He indicated the plug-point. Near it was something else. The hose he used for his wave recordings – it took the water back at the shack – was linked to a length of armoured rubber pipe which ran into the 'scaphe's upper flooding compartment. It appeared to lead to those fine-screened boxes. No normal bathyscaphe would have been burdened with so many umbilical cords.

My problem was a simple and apparently insoluble one: how to pretend to Barrow that the cable tapping the shark barrier's power via the waverider to the 'scaphe was live, when a corpse on a mortuary slab couldn't have been deader. There'd have to be some test when finally we linked up. Even Barrow with his elementary knowledge of electrics would require that.

Working from the boat, I did a quick job on the hull connection. I hadn't any option. Then we returned to the waverider to complete the operation. I removed the fibre-glass top and played about with connecting and disconnecting switches and wires. Barrow watched me narrowly but since the design lay-out was my own, even an expert might have hesitated to fault me. I also spent some time fixing the automatic transmitter to stifle its giveaway bleeps for the time when we returned to the shack. *If* I returned.

'Is that all?'

There was worry in Barrow's eyes. He's running against time, I reckoned. That was something to know.

'No problems.'

The problems were in Barrow's next words.

'We'll get back and check it before we dive.'

'Dive?' I made it sound as though I had claustrophobia and it must have seemed convincing because his reply was edged with malice.

'We've got an appointment on the seabed shortly. You're coming.'

'I've never been in one of these things before.'

'Now's your chance to learn.'

My mind raced with the speed of light over that complicated control panel. If I could get Barrow out of the way for a few minutes I might have a chance . . .

But he was right at my back with his gun all the way down through the hatch and iron ladder. Inside the clinical observation chamber my stomach muscles knotted. Once the hatch was clamped shut there'd be no escape. It was worse than planning to take off and fly a 'plane whose engines you knew would go dead. If I kept up the pretext – and I was beginning to get an idea how it could be done, taking into account the circuit boxes behind their transparent covers – perhaps I'd only be digging myself a watery grave. Perhaps the barrier's power was vital to the 'scaphe if it was ever to rise again off the seabed . . .

I stamped on the thought of another Ogilvie skeleton joining that of my ancestor in the depths.

I said, 'Okay. Here it is. Test!'

I tripped the control. Nothing happened of course.

Barrow was fiddling with the sub-machine gun.

'For Chrissake stop it!' I snapped. 'You're making me so bloody nervous I can't tell an amp from an ape.'

'What's wrong?'

'Nothing, probably. Are all the internal circuits in order?'

It was clear he didn't know what I was talking about.

'I guess so. They must be.'

I indicated the dead dial which was intended to monitor the current that never was.

'There's no must be. It's like pregnancy – either you are or you aren't.'

He looked nonplussed and then said thickly, 'We're going down. The 'scaphe has its independent battery supply. The extra power's for . . .'

I kept my hands from trembling by starting in on the circuit boxes. He'd told me part of what I wanted to know and if I was smart I could switch wires and appear to make the dead dial work off the battery supply. I unhesitatingly unscrewed half a dozen leads.

'Lay off! What are you up to?'

I dropped the wires – another point-scorer for me because he'd never know now which was which – and stood back with an air of long-suffering resignation.

'See here, Barrow, either I'm in this or I'm not. I'm merely carrying out a routine check.'

'Why isn't the shark barrier power flowing?'

I gestured at the collection of hanging leads. 'That's just what I'm trying to find out.'

'Don't double-cross me, Ogilvie!' He cradled the automatic menacingly.

'For God's sake!' I turned to the board as if in anger and neatly completed my sabotage under his ignorant eyes.

'One of us will have to go up and check that the socket is properly home in the hull. It may be a bit corroded by sea-water.'

He stood for a moment, angry and undecided. I think toting the weapon up and down the ladder was becoming a bit of a bore, even to him. It was easy to read the reason for his hesitation: if I went alone he was afraid I'd make off in the outboard. We'd moored it to a small buoy which marked the bathyscaphe's position and also served the purpose of a floating platform for the cable from the waverider. We'd arranged it so that we could unwind from the wooden reel during the descent.

'I'll go.'

That was all I wanted. Before he was properly clear of the cabin I'd begun on my second electrical jinx of the day and had the dial working convincingly off battery power. I gave him some elementary directions about the socket to give authenticity to my bluff.

'Good!' I called. 'Everything's fine here now.'

He clumped back and I showed him the indicator needle.

His taut face relaxed. 'Excellent! Now for it!'

On the instrument panel he pressed what appeared to be

an intercom call-up button. I was startled when a voice said through a speaker level with my face.

'Yes, Seahorse? Barracuda here.' I recognized Dr Pinto's voice.

'Seahorse here. Taking her down for a test. I'll keep well clear of you.'

'Do that. Over.'

'Over and out.'

'Phone connection to the sub,' Barrow explained in a more expansive manner than before. 'The cable runs through a gland in the hull. It's spring-loaded. That keeps it from sagging.'

Seahorse was like a puppet strung with wires.

He went on, 'There's no call for you to do anything yet except enjoy the view.' He waved to a porthole. 'I'll give you a searchlight.'

I was relieved he'd offered only one because I'd tapped power from one of the group to activate the dud dial and I didn't know which it was. I kept my fingers crossed it wasn't the one at my window.

Before doing so he went and secured the surface hatch and also made fast the heavy inner door which sealed off the cabin from the top flooding compartment. The only exit below us in the bottom chamber was already closed.

He returned to the control panel, turned on the engine control rheostats and set the ballast pumps in operation. If I'd suffered from claustrophobia I might have missed the moment to begin my attack. It was all so smooth and silent. There was only a faint vibration to show that we were under power. Then the fathometer needle came to life. It was the only way I knew we were going down. We dived.

CHAPTER FOURTEEN

Down, down, down.

It wasn't like a lift because it was too slow and the cushioning effect of the water gave an altogether different ride. But the knots were still tieing and untieing themselves in the place where my stomach should have been. It felt as if it had been blown free of ballast itself and had risen up to where my throat normally was. For at the bottom of this soft descent awaited my moment of truth.

I pretended to peer through the window but in fact I was watching how Barrow worked the controls. It might be useful to know sometime very soon. I noticed he didn't use the engine interlock switch but confined himself to the trim and ballast controls. He pumped in water, thereby compressing the petrol which filled the outer tanks (they provided buoyancy on the surface) and giving us the deadweight required to submerge. He left the rudder and trimming planes alone. It looked fairly easy. I hoped so.

Down, down, down.

I didn't know we'd reached the bottom till the searchlight showed black ooze and some pinnacles of coral. Beyond the cone of light the blackness was like a wall. The patch of seabed became slightly less black and more grey as we eased down lazily. Then there was a slight flurry and a big Lazy Grey shark coasted by with a muscular flick of his strong tail. Above the muted purr of the 'scaphe's motors I was aware of another, familiar sound – scrape, grind, scrape, grind. The sub. She must be close.

I turned back to Barrow who was busy with some fine adjustments to the trim.

'Barrow,' I said more harshly than I had intended: 'You didn't bring me here for the pleasure of an on-site marine display.'

There was an air of controlled anticipation about him and his eyes were bright.

'No, I didn't.'

For an answer he threw a switch and a second searchlight came on directing a vertical beam under the full-width glass floor of the 'scaphe. This searchlight business made me as nervous as Russian roulette. There was one live and one dead one left for him to pick on.

'Look!' he said as lights came on in the lower compartment, showing the mechanical grab. Water poured in as Barrow flooded it and soon the grab was submerged. As pressure built up because of the resulting airlock, Barrow made more adjustments to the trim and we remained hanging a few feet clear of the ooze. Then I spotted something else – an area of seabed pegged out with a number of brightly-coloured, round plastic discs anchored by wires. Someone had staked out a claim on the ocean floor.

Next the floor swung open, straining on its hydraulic securing arms against the water pressure. The action which followed was almost uncannily human. Under Barrow's guidance the remotely-controlled 'hand' reached down on to the ooze and closed on an irregularly-shaped round object. Holding it, the hand brought the ball inboard again and Barrow resealed the compartment and blew out the water.

'Safe now. Open that hatch and get it,' ordered Barrow.

I did so. I was fascinated enough to have put aside any thoughts of jumping Barrow while he was occupied. The gun was on a small shelf beneath the control panel.

I got down on the floor, prised open the cone-shaped hatch and let Barrow drop the rock from the slave manipulator's fingers into mine. It was round and cold and too heavy for an ordinary rock.

I kept up my prisoner-under-duress attitude. 'Fine, fine. You've given me a coral-eye view of the fish but I've seen them all before at the reef. If your mechanical hand is calculated to impress, it doesn't. I've worked a remote-control slave manipulator myself a score of times handling isotopes from an atom-splitter. What's really behind all this, Barrow?'

His answer drew on his reserves of sorely-tried patience.

'That's manganese in your hand.'

'So what?'

'It's called a nodule. It's well known that solid lumps of valuable metals are scattered about the floor of the ocean:

there's a big concentration off the south-eastern coast of the United States and another on the floor of the Pacific between Tahiti and South America. It's been estimated that about a thousand million tons of nodules are lying around simply waiting to be picked up. But how?'

'Try one bathyscaphe, a mechanical grab, and a nut waving a sub-machine gun around.'

He didn't react as I wanted him to but his voice became edged.

'That nodule you're holding contains not only manganese but iron, nickel, copper and cobalt. Briefly, Boa Paz is the richest pocket of seabed minerals known.'

'Says who?'

'Me. I discovered it. It's mine.'

'There's such a thing as state rights over territorial waters.'

'This thing's big, Ogilvie – big, big!'

'I'm all for tweaking the taxman's tail myself but this tail and this tweak look a bit outsize to me.'

He was standing back, profiled against the dials and control lights of the instrument panel. Megalomania has its poses.

'Outsize!' he exclaimed. His breathing quickened in the confined space. 'Outsize is right and also mildly radio-active. Here's the background. In Siberia there's a place they call the Tungus Wonder. I'm quoting the Soviet Academy of Sciences. Early this century there was a gigantic nuclear explosion of extra-terrestrial origin and a massive meteorite slammed into the earth in Siberia immediately afterwards. The Russians found when they made an investigation of the place recently that radio-activity at the centre of the crater which was formed was 50 to 100 per cent higher than on its fringe. Everything was destroyed for a radius of five miles.'

'Go on.'

'Boa Paz was hit by a similar phenomenon at the time your ancestor arrived here in his opium ship. It created a huge tidal wave which sank him and changed the entire aspect of the coast.'

Shirley had maintained that the appearance of the coast, and of Boa Paz, had altered radically since the days of the early Portuguese. What Barrow was saying made sense.

'I too had an ancestor in Ogilvie's ship,' he went on. 'The

legend of a great natural disaster was handed down from him.'

'So were stories of a mysterious wasting sickness at Boa Paz,' I retorted.

'For wasting sickness read mild reaction sickness and you have it in modern terms.'

I weighed the heavy ball in my hand.

'And this?'

'Mildly radio-active – at the moment.'

'What are you implying?'

'Just this. The radio-active minerals of Boa Paz become more activated from time to time.'

'You'll have to add a science fiction chapter to the text-books.'

He'd forgotten all about his gun in his enthusiasm. I hadn't.

'I said it was big, man! The re-activation of the seabed minerals at Boa Paz coincides with the time the five planets are in close configuration. That configuration was present when Boa Paz was destroyed by the giant meteorite which caused the tidal wave. It also recurred at the time of the Tungus Wonder.'

I knew then that he was mad.

'Shall we read my horoscope now or take a collection?'

That got him. He said savagely, 'Hear that noise outside? If we could get close enough in safety I'd show you what the sub's doing. She's fitted with a big mechanical grab in the bow and she's scraping up tons of nodules. Tons, do you hear?'

In quantity, pure minerals like the nodule in my hands would be worth a fortune. Those fissionable materials could make a tiny fish in the nuclear armaments pond into a very big fish in a very short time. The beat-up feeling in my solar plexus region worsened.

Barrow's words anticipated what was in my mind. 'Any individual or group of individuals could hold the world in the palm of his hand with these.'

He took the nodule from me. It left a cold patch on my hand. I jerked my head in the direction of the sub.

'You, Pinto, and who else?'

'A group of idealists. You might as well know.'

I'd heard better exit lines. The look in his eyes made it seem pretty final.

'Meaning?'

'We've work to do, Ogilvie. You and me.'

I looked for something to try and sidetrack him. The only non-functional thing in sight was the box of dynamite.

'With that?'

'Not now. Sometime later the seabed may need loosening up for the sub's grab. It'll need a lot of precautions when we come to do it. That amount of explosive could do as much damage to the sub as a depth-charge.'

His mention of depth-charges made me remember Jerry. He must have found some reference to Russia when he'd ransacked Barrow's papers. Maybe he even regarded the phrase Tungus Wonder as a code, and read into it his whole premise of a spy and missile-firing sub. He couldn't have been more wrong. I was sitting in the hot seat now. My thoughts pulled me along. I still couldn't fathom why Barrow had set up the elaborate front of the shark-barrier or why he wanted its electric power. Maybe that was the work we had to do. I would soon know.

'Come over here, Ogilvie.'

I joined him at the instrument panel and turned my attention to what was immediately in front of my eyes – the check-dial I'd sabotaged. It was anyone's guess how quickly the seconds were running out on that little trick. Barrow pointed to it.

'Everything's fine, I see.'

I wished he'd feed more oxygen into the cabin and set the foul air scavengers to their maximum in order to slow down my heart-beat.

'Everything's fine.'

'Perhaps you're wondering why I should be carrying out wave measurements with the hose connected to the 'scaphe.'

'I've ceased to wonder.'

'It's got a name – the Tsunami or long-wave recorder.'

'I'm slightly stupid this morning. Blame it on lack of sleep.'

'It's an apparatus to record the pressure and frequency of waves. Mine's different. The hose is full of holes. Normally they're solid.'

'Another bluff I suppose like the shark-barrier?'

'Quite a fireball, aren't you, Ogilvie?'

There's no answer to a crack like that. I felt like a man fumbling his way through a minefield, scared that at any moment he might tread on a detonator. His voice rose in intensity as if there were something tearing away inside him.

'Yes. You're right. It was – is – necessary. You see, we are about to do something no one has ever done before. We are going to extract uranium from seawater.'

I needed a cigarette. Better still, a drink. The 'scaphe didn't carry them as part of her cargo. Nor did she carry the sort of vast and expensive apparatus which would be required even to attempt what Barrow was suggesting. Moreover, if such a thing had been a feasible proposition it certainly would have been carried out before now when half the world was crying out for this essential material for nuclear weapons. When Barrow's dream didn't work – and it was doubly stymied without the shark-barrier's power – my world would end in the black ooze under us.

I strung along with his idea. There was nothing else I could do.

'How?'

His words tumbled out. 'With soap and alcohol bubbled through the hose from the lab, when we set the pumps going. The mixture passes into the flooding chamber of the 'scaphe. Uranium oxide is present in solution in the seawater which of course enters the hose through the holes. The pure uranium will be trapped in a series of filters . . .'

'I saw them up above.'

He gave me a suspicious glance but he was too carried away to stop.

'Scientifically it's called the flotation method of collecting minerals. It's not new but its application to the sea is. You could compare it to the way scum collects dirt on the side of a bath. I've tested it under laboratory conditions. It works.'

'That doesn't mean it will under field conditions.'

'True. But I am convinced it will. You will have the privilege of being a witness to a modern miracle of science, Ogilvie.'

And that's something I could do without, I told myself. The whole thing was sick. When I exploded his dream the only thing that would float to the surface would be murder. It might in any event.

'I told you Boa Paz became generally more radio-active when extra-terrestrial magnetic storms rage,' he was saying.

'That's why I've chosen today. Radio-activity is at its maximum. The uranium content of the sea right here is correspondingly at is maximum. Today's the day, Ogilvie!'

I had to keep him talking while I formulated a plan. The face of the gondola was as inhibitive as a straight-jacket.

'Maybe the question's academic, Barrow, but what do you intend doing with the uranium in addition to your nodule minerals once you've got them?'

'Everything has its price. And price is the determining factor for every type of radio-active material,' he replied. 'We have here at Boa Paz the cheapest and largest supply in the world. We can undersell any regular producer. We will corner the market.'

'*We*!' I interrupted. 'Read for that an international pressure group. Power for the few.'

'Could be you're right. The highest bidder gets the product. Perhaps you recall how upset the French were when Gabon wanted to increase the price of crude uranium. I'll be offering refined, ready-to-use uranium at a price which none of the big producers can match. Power, yes, and in my hands, Ogilvie.'

'A moment ago you were saying "we". Now it's "I".'

He was sardonic. 'I repeat what I said before – you are too observant, Ogilvie.'

'In other words, the nodule materials are for your pals but the cream on the coffee – uranium – is for you alone?'

His grin pulled his mouth down and showed his teeth.

'That's why I need you.'

'The big double-cross in the corridors of would-be power.'

His mouth remained ugly and his eyes wary. I had a flash nightmare of urban terrorists using nuclear mini-weapons to bend governments to their will, and even larger weapons spawned by a cynical crackpot. Then Barrow went on: 'You know now. Maybe too much. Get on with it.'

He stood aside for me to manipulate the switch feeding the shark-barrier's power to the 'scaphe.'

I went to it, put my finger on it, and said as steadily as I could keep my voice. 'There isn't going to be any experiment, Barrow.'

His face went inert and blank like a movie frozen into a still. He snapped off the lock of the sub-machine gun; I saw the gleam of the rifling inside the blue mouth of the barrel when he raised it and pointed it at my stomach.

'Throw that switch!'

'It won't help. The power that dial is registering is from the 'scaphe's own batteries. I jinxed the shark barrier. It's burned out. It'd take weeks to fix, if it can be fixed. Today's not your day, Barrow.'

I don't know whether he lost his head and meant to kill or simply gun-whip me because everything went into slow motion and I watched the barrel move at my face in a slow arc and make contact across my left cheekbone and eyebrow. The luminous face of the depth-gauge exploded into a thousand stars. I wasn't conscious of being thrown from the control panel across the gondola but I must have been out for a split-second while my body travelled across it and finished up against an observation window.

Barrow must have missed his footing or overswung because he came crashing down on all fours alongside me, losing the gun with a clatter. His head was within a foot of mine. Either his blow wasn't as bad as I thought or I was working on automatic pilot because I remember selecting the spot where I would hit him just where the nerve to the jaw runs under the ear and wondering whether his skin would be rubbery the way it looked drawn across his bones in a mask of hatred.

I lunged out and struck.

Barrow was on his way up in a half-crouch with one hand on the gun. His impetus plus my chop did the rest. He went over sideways and pitched through the open hatch into the bottom compartment. The gun went with him. If I'd connected where I wanted to I would have had time while he was lying senseless to have got down there and retrieved the weapon and locked him in and the course of events would have been different.

As it was, I'd barely hauled myself to my feet and was hanging sick and nauseated to the control panel when he started to show signs of recovery. My movements were sluggish and I could hardly see for the blood flowing into my left eye and blinding me. But I had enough vision left to note Barrow's stirrings. I could not have hit him as hard as I thought because he had enough sense left to start uncoiling an arm towards the automatic and getting to his knees.

He'd grasped it by the time I realized from the control lever digging into my back that I had a weapon, too, the slave hand. I had to turn much further round to work it than I normally would have because of the blood in my eye. My cheekbone felt as if it were making contact with my spinal column. Then I had the hand operating and came round to confront Barrow. I didn't expect to find him up, but he was. On his haunches. And the gun was coming up, too.

It was a difficult aim through the narrow opening of the hatch and the way the muzzle tracked showed that his vision was still less than 20-20. He got lined up on me just as I got the mechanical hand lined up on him. I was a millisecond faster than him though. I brought the grab down smartly and clamped its talons on to the barrel as he pressed the trigger. It was a single shot – he was not too woozy to realize the danger of a magazine-spray in the confined space – but the acoustics were the same as if he'd loosed off a whole clip. The sound smashed and echoed off the steel walls and deafened me.

I didn't see where the shot went. I was intent on keeping off the receiving end. And I was succeeding, because although Barrow tugged and wrenched he couldn't bring the weapon to bear on me. Then he moved a little to one side to try and get a better purchase and I saw where the bullet had gone. Through the plexiglass bottom of the 'scaphe. Water was spurting in. The glass must only have been starred, not pierced, from the look of the jet but it was only a matter of time before the sea's pressure shattered the whole thing.

'Barrow! Leave it! Look, man! We'll both drown!'

'Sod you, you bastard!'

He seemed to find some extra strength and to my horror he got the barrel almost as high as the hatch. I gave the hand a twist and as he opened up on rapid fire the bullets ricocheted off the steel walls around him.

Then suddenly the firing cut. Barrow toppled over backwards and sideways from his crouch and I was left with his gun in my steel claw.

I was too stunned and deafened to realize for the moment that he'd been hit by one of his own ricochets. I hung there trembling, wanting to gag from the smell of cordite fumes coming up from below.

I didn't give myself long. Barrow was slumped across the hole in the glass bottom but the water was jetting in fast. Already it was washing on either side of him. Priority number one was to get that hatch shut and seal off the lower cabin. But I couldn't leave Barrow in there to drown like a rat in a trap. The water was beginning to lap at his face. So I quickly brought up the hand with the gun, and then lowered it again to help him. It wasn't designed to cope with the weight of a man but at least I'd be able to lift his head clear and then make a race for it to bring him up before the water won.

I might have saved myself the trouble. I manœuvred the slave hand and grasping him by the back of the neck, turned the face out of the water. The ricochet had gone into his right eye and the socket was a wash of red. He was as dead as he could be. I let him go but the head fell staring upwards out of its one dead fish eye.

I abandoned the slave hand for my own to clamp down the hatch. Enough water had come in to raise the air pressure inside the main gondola. I didn't need to consult the barometer to tell me that: my ears were popping. Very soon it would form an airlock and I wouldn't be able to fasten the hatch against its compression. I went into a panic when I couldn't close it first try; finally I sat on it. It was like a bouncy air cushion. I made it.

Reaction hit me so long and so hard that I just sat there gasping on the steel floor with the water a few inches away underneath. It had risen until a pressure lock stopped it. I went on and on gasping like a chain reaction fit until I realized that if I didn't do something about the oxygen and cleaning the carbon-dioxide out with the scavengers I'd be in danger of passing out myself. So I got up shakily and set them going. Immediately I felt better.

I wasn't as good as I thought I was when I came to confront the control panel with the idea of manœuvring the 'scaphe to the surface. I was trembling and not seeing half the switches because of my eye. So I began by finding a first-aid kit and patched myself up. Without a mirror I botched it but at least the blood stopped.

I'm going to black out, I told myself helplessly, facing the array of controls. And if I do while attempting the delicate balance of blowing tanks and adjusting trim I'll make the 'scaphe into my own steel coffin by getting it trapped in the seabottom mud. Then, with the extra weight of water in the bottom compartment I'd never surface again.

At that I plumped for panic tactics. I cut four switches in a row in rapid succession. They were the ones which, when live, held tons of shot ballast in place. When the magnetic fields are broken the ballast is automatically jettisoned.

This lot was dumped in a heap. The fathometer unwound like the floor indicator of a high-speed lift. The barometer needle wasn't as fast but it was too fast. I opened the oxygen taps and fed the gas into the gondola to try and do something about equalizing the pressure. Before I'd finished the depth gauge ceased to register and the 'scaphe took on a rocking motion.

I was on the surface.

I resisted the temptation to go up there where I knew the sunlight must be until I'd adjusted to the outside air pressure. I seated myself on one of the collapsible jump-stools. It was then that the idea came to me that I must destroy the whole evil which Barrow had brought to Boa Paz. That meant the sub. The means was there. Barrow's own words had sunk into my subconscious: 'depth-charge'. The case of gelignite could become just that. The plan dropped into place in my mind.

I opened the hatch into the entrance flooding chamber after I'd got rid of the water. I fumbled my way up the awkward rungs and unclipped the outer hatch leading to the air. Air is as sweet as life when you come upon it like I did then. The sea was sweet, too, and the thin pennants of cloud high above. The only sound was the distant yammer of the diesel. There wasn't a thing in sight. The 'scaphe had come up close to where we'd moored the dinghy – the drag of the cable to the waverider buoy and the hose to the lab had seen to that.

I had no use for them in my plan and cut them adrift. I checked the 'phone cable which led from the 'scaphe to the sub to make sure it was running freely through the hull. Then I went below and fused up the gelignite. I made a quick calculation as to how much fuse would be required – I had a blaster's certificate from the early days when we'd experimented with acoustic repellants against sharks. At no stage did the operation feel like calculated homicide or vengeance. It was a job to do, like destroying a rogue mamba.

I allowed for an extra bit of fuse for the time I'd take to make my way up the rungs out of the 'scaphe and for securing the hatches after lighting it. The inner hatch from the entrance chamber into the main cabin I couldn't secure because the clips were inside but its self-sealing shape would serve.

I tied a length of line to the ballast-flooding switch and ran it to the surface. I laid the case of gelignite against a window to give maximum blast effect. I lit the fuse with unsteady hands, moved to the control panel and turned on the power to operate a small winch on which the intercom cable reeled in and out. This was my means of sending the 'scaphe to its target. I reckoned that since the 'scaphe was now free of its encumbering hose and electric cable it would need only a bare minimum of power to guide it underwater. The other end of the intercom cable was fixed to the sub. Flooding would take the 'scaphe down; the winch would finish the job. That was the plan.

I shut the cabin hatch enough to leave my line running free and scrambled up the iron ladder leading to the air. I tugged the string before clipping the surface hatch fast. It worked and ballast water began to pump in through the inlets where Barrow's filters were in position. I transferred to the dinghy.

The top of the 'scaphe submerged quicker than I'd anticipated, moving away from my boat as the winch began to take up the wire.

I sat waiting in the dinghy and a reaction sweat came over me. The only thing I had to remind me that I hadn't dreamt it all was Barrow's sub-machine gun which I'd brought and put on a thwart. Except memories. At that I went cold and started to shake. It wasn't the chill of the morning; it was warm, clear and peaceful. A perfect day for some quiet fishing. I wondered if Shirley was dead and I began to feel so bad that I half-wished I'd taken the 'scaphe down and blown myself up against the sub's hull as an alternative way of making quite sure of her.

My reassurance that I had done so came in the form of a burp on the sea's surface, a column of water and an

explosive thud which set the echoes going in the hills behind
the lagoons. Then came a second disturbance on the water
- a series of air bubbles bursting, some oil and a few planks
and finally some of the bright plastic markers. The sub.

My reaction wasn't any of the things I might have expected.
I merely felt tired, deadly, deadly tired. I don't know how
long I sat there staring at the growing patch of debris.

It was the continuous hammering of the diesel that made
me decide more mechanically than consciously that I must do
something about it before it tore itself off its mountings. Only
it wasn't the lab engine. It was a police launch.

Charlie must have got off his mark very quickly to have
rounded up the marine posse which was racing towards me.
I'd stood up to start the outboard but my hands didn't go
for the starter cord. They went above my head at the sight
of half a dozen rifles and a pistol in an officer's fist. Charlie
was in the boat too.

The launch went into a turn, holding off and circling warily
about thirty yards off. Police ambush stuff. Maybe they'd
spotted the sub-machine gun. The barrels homed on me were
as thick as a picket fence.

'Charlie! Tell them it's okay!' I called. I kept my hands
up.

He passed it on to the officer who spent a good minute
gesticulating. There was plenty for him to gesticulate at
coming up from the sub. Quite apart from his subordinate
I'd rough-housed the night before.

'You won't try anything?' came back Charlie.

'Humour is out of place. I'm dead on my feet.'

Charlie laughed. The officer was upset. That sort of thing
is hard to translate. But they got my message and came in,
two toughies jumping aboard and grabbing my arms. I was
grateful for the support.

Charlie said, 'The major says he should have shot you.'

'Then he wouldn't have found out what's been happening.'

Charlie eyed my wound. 'It's been happening?'

'It has.'

'He wants to know, quick.'

'Tell him I'll give him the whole story, after I've been
taken to the hospital at Quissico.'

Charlie winced. I thought it had to do with Shirley.

'She's dead?'

'I don't know. I didn't want to risk being picked up. The cops were everywhere. I lay low until I heard your explosion.'

The major interrupted us angrily. There was an exchange between him and Charlie.

Charlie said, 'He says he doesn't bargain with wanted assassins. And there can be no collusion with witnesses.'

'No Quissico, no story. That's flat. He'll never find out unless it's from me. Anyhow, where does he get the idea of an assassin from?'

'You hurt that guy's dignity at the hospital.'

'Get me there, let me see Shirley, and I'll come clean.'

As if to reinforce my point, the sea gave another burp and yielded up some more debris. I had a similar feeling in my insides.

A combination of Latin temperament and outraged author-ity takes some settling down and it was a good five minutes of gestures, oaths and volubility before the major capitulated. I was to go to Shirley under heavy police escort.

Charlie took us in his car. Three gendarmes and their weapons didn't give him scope to exploit his driving skill but nevertheless we made good time to Quissico. I was led into the hospital foyer while Dr da Sousa was summoned.

Charlie said in a low voice, 'I asked the nun at reception about Shirley. Says she doesn't know.'

'Does she?'

He couldn't face my eyes and turned away.

It seemed to take longer for the doctor to walk the few steps from the glass door in the vestibule to me than it had to reach Quissico.

'Shirley . . . ?'

Da Sousa took a good look at my escort. He was correct and strictly professional. He indicated my head.

'The casualty department is next door. I do not treat patients here.'

'For Chrissake – is she alive?'

I felt nothing at shouting him down despite the fact I knew it was his skill on which she had depended.

He replied off-handedly, 'Very weak, but alive. No visitors.'

'Take me to her!'

'I cannot allow . . .'

'Make my point, Charlie. Either, or. It's up to the cops if they want my story.'

For the second time I was treated to Latin temperament. While they wrangled I felt as sick as if Barrow had hit me all over again. Perhaps I owed Charlie more than I knew because finally he said, 'It's okay now.'

Da Sousa kept himself on professional ice. 'This way. Only a short time is permitted.'

I followed him along a concrete corridor and he opened a door to a private ward. Shirley was there and her face was like putty. She looked very tired, like someone who has ridden a long illness. There were blue-black shadows under her eyes.

She opened them at the sound of the door and for a flash the pupils went unnaturally bright. I went to her and kissed her. She kissed me back. It would be a long time before she'd kiss me the way I wanted.

'You're making me cry, darling.'

'I wish male tear-ducts worked the same way.'

'Darling, darling!' Her caressing fingers encountered the caked blood and adhesive patch on my face. 'My poor love! What happened?'

I gave her a quick run-down of the events. I began to think da Sousa was right about no visitors, the way she looked.

When I'd finished I got up to go and said, 'That buttons up the main points. But there are a lot of loose ends still lying around. Like the cross in the shadows.'

She found some strength and sat up and waved me back into my chair.

'I thought I'd told you last night. I remember saying something about it.'

'Only scraps. Nothing, really.'

She managed a faint smile, 'We could be pretty rich when I get out of here. You see, we found the treasure ship; you and I, back in the marsh.'

I couldn't absorb what she was saying in my punch-drunk mental state.

'This is how it was, darling. It all revolves round that mysterious position of 25 degrees. That figure has nothing to do with the geographical location of Boa Paz – it is merely a coincidence that it's similar. Maybe it was fatigue in crossing the marsh which threw up the solution in my mind. It all became clear to me after we'd seen the ship. An astrolabe has what is called a shadow scale and it was used the same way as we use a modern theodolite – to measure angles, not for navigation at all. What the Portuguese did was deliberately hide the position of the treasure ship behind a simple blind which was calculated to mislead. The whole coastline changed, we know, about the time the opium ship arrived and the treasure ship was regurgitated from the sea. The seabed on which it lay became marsh. The marsh has always been taboo – you know the rest.'

'25 degrees – measured from what, Shirley?'

'My guess is Txibange hill. It's the most likely landmark. I'd put my head on a block that if we had an astrolabe and took the angle of the hill from the ship in the marsh it would be 25 degrees.'

'That still doesn't account for the cross.'

'Part of the deception, Ian. I'm sure they had one of their old navigation crosses planted on the hill. A *padraoa*. Maybe it's still there, hidden or lost in the vegetation. For vegetation read, "in the shadows". Maybe another double play on words like the astrolabe shadow scale.'

'What did you say the treasure was worth?'

'Half a million. Could be more, at today's values.'

The effect of telling me exhausted her. I kissed her gently when she had finished. She tried to kiss me back but she wasn't very successful. Then she twined her fingers in mine and closed her eyes and lay back against the pillows. We didn't speak again. The police found us like that when they came to take me away.

Geoffrey Jenkins

Geoffrey Jenkins writes of adventure on land and at sea in some of the most exciting thrillers ever written. 'Geoffrey Jenkins has the touch that creates villains and heroes—and even icy heroines—with a few vivid words.' *Liverpool Post* 'A style which combines the best of Nevil Shute and Ian Fleming.' *Books and Bookmen*

A BRIDGE OF MAGPIES 85p
A CLEFT OF STARS 70p
THE RIVER OF DIAMONDS 85p
THE WATERING PLACE OF
  GOOD PEACE 75p
A TWIST OF SAND 75p
HUNTER-KILLER 85p

Fontana Paperbacks

Alistair MacLean

His first book, *HMS Ulysses*, published in 1955, was outstandingly successful. It led the way to a string of best-selling novels which have established Alistair MacLean as the most popular adventure writer of our time.

SEAWITCH 85p
THE GOLDEN GATE 85p
BEAR ISLAND 95p
BREAKHEART PASS 80p
CARAVAN TO VACCARÈS 80p
CIRCUS 75p
THE DARK CRUSADER 85p
FEAR IS THE KEY 80p
FORCE 10 FROM NAVARONE 85p
THE GOLDEN RENDEZVOUS 85p
THE GUNS OF NAVARONE 85p
HMS *ULYSSES* 85p
ICE STATION ZEBRA 85p
THE LAST FRONTIER 85p
NIGHT WITHOUT END 85p
PUPPET ON A CHAIN 85p
THE SATAN BUG 85p
SOUTH BY JAVA HEAD 85p
THE WAY TO DUSTY DEATH 80p
WHEN EIGHT BELLS TOLL 85p
WHERE EAGLES DARE 85p

Fontana Paperbacks

James Jones

FROM HERE TO ETERNITY £1.75
The world famous novel of the men of the U.S. Army
stationed at Pearl Harbour in the months immediately before
America's entry into World War II. 'One reads every page
persuaded that it is a remarkable, a very remarkable book
indeed.' *Listener*

A TOUCH OF DANGER 95p
A superb first thriller by the author of *From Here to Eternity*
set on an Aegean island where the sun and sex are corrupted by
violence and drugs. 'A believable private eye at last—not too
tough, not too lucky—and a plot built with loving care.'
John Braine, Daily Express

GO TO THE WIDOW-MAKER £1.50
A superb novel about the war between the sexes, set in the
world of rich men and those who cater to them. In Jones's
tale of dangerous living, love is for men and women are for
sex. 'Jones is the Hemingway of our time . . . There is savage
poetry in his descriptions of spear-fishing and treasure-
hunting.' *Spectator*

THE MERRY MONTH OF MAY £1.00
Paris in the spring of 1968: students on the rampage and their
effect on a wealthy American family living in Paris. 'Very
gripping . . . a novel of our time which takes the reader into
the heart of the Revolution. The atmosphere is splendidly
conveyed.' *Financial Times*

Fontana Paperbacks

Fontana Paperbacks

Fontana is a leading paperback publisher of fiction and non-fiction, with authors ranging from Alistair MacLean, Agatha Christie and Desmond Bagley to Solzhenitsyn and Pasternak, from Gerald Durrell and Joy Adamson to the famous Modern Masters series.

In addition to a wide-ranging collection of internationally popular writers of fiction, Fontana also has an outstanding reputation for history, natural history, military history, psychology, psychiatry, politics, economics, religion and the social sciences.

All Fontana books are available at your bookshop or newsagent; or can be ordered direct. Just fill in the form and list the titles you want.
